THE EXILE
OF ELLENDON

THE EXILE
OF ELLENDON

WILLIAM MARDEN

DOUBLEDAY & COMPANY, INC.

GARDEN CITY, NEW YORK

1974

All the characters in this book are fictitious,
and any resemblance to actual persons, living
or dead, is purely coincidental.

Library of Congress Cataloging in Publication Data

Marden, William.
        The exile of Ellendon.

        A novel.
        I. Title.
PZ4.M3254Ex [PS3563.A644]   813'.5'4
ISBN 0-385-01526-7
Library of Congress Catalog Card Number 73–19023

Dedicated to my parents,
without whom the book
would not be

CHAPTER ONE

It was a normal Sunday night until the unicorn report came in.

Sunday nights are generally dead. Sure, there are those nights when a plane will go down or a head-on collision sends four young people on a one-way trip out of this world.

Most reporters will agree, though, that the most exciting news item you'll usually get will be the latest obituary or the arrest of some poor clown for car theft. That kind of thing.

So what you do is bring a good book to the office, which I did that night. *Lord of Light* by Zelazny. It was the only one of his books I hadn't read. I'd missed it when it first came out in paperback more than ten years before, being more interested at that age in super-hero comics.

Now I had it and I intended to finish it before I got off work at midnight. Before going any further, I ought to introduce myself. The name is Horace—as in Greeley—Dell. My friends mercifully call me Hank.

I am employed, not too gainfully, as the police reporter for the Sarasota (Florida) *Herald Tribune*. I was working through midnight because whenever accidents or crimes do happen on a Sunday, they tend to happen late.

It was about 8:30 P.M. I was leaning back in a swivel chair, my feet on my desk, reading the second chapter of *Lord*. Besides myself there were only two editors, state and national, two copy readers and the girls who work on the computers and as proofreaders in their glass booths.

No typing at all. Only the sound of the wire machines—AP, UPI, LA *Times* and New York *Times* wires—clicking behind the glass doors near the proofreaders. Beside me on the desk was the police radio the paper keeps for my use. It was silent. From time to time it would crackle with static followed by the voice of the police dispatcher, but usually with something on the order of looking for a missing cat or a report of a family fight.

I missed the first words of the report. The dispatcher laughed and the patrolman said, "Repeat please. I must have misunderstood."

"No, you heard right," the dispatcher said, in the sexy syllables that could only be uttered by Helen White.

"The lady reports a unicorn. Says she saw it on the beach. The address is 775 Del Mere. Mrs. J. H. Carr."

There was a silence, then "10-4." I 10-4ed it myself and put *Lord* down. For a moment I was torn. *Lord* was a good book, but how often do you get to investigate a report of a unicorn on the beach? Flying saucers, yes. Pink elephants, yes. But unicorns?

I left *Lord* on my desk and approached Dan Lee, the national news editor I work for on the weekend. He's about thirty-five and prematurely bald, a big guy with the most god-awful-smelling black cigar ever present in his mouth.

"What's up, Flash?"

My speed in writing stories is legend, second only to that mythical one-armed newsman with arthritis.

"Report of a unicorn."

He just looked at me for a moment, then switched the cigar over to the other side of his mouth. He stared at me for another long moment.

"I don't know about police reporters, but editors don't have time for damned stupid jokes."

"No joke. A woman just reported a unicorn sighting. Maybe it flew down in a flying saucer."

The saucer craze had died down for a while back in the early seventies after Project Bluebook was throttled. For about five years the "I Flew Beyond Mars with the Blue Spacemen" types had lean times. Then, for some reason no one's ever figured out, people started seeing saucers again. At first the sightings came in slowly, but then the reports began to pile up and the last couple of years from '77 to '79 had been busy.

"Don't tell me. You want to go investigate it."

"Might be a good story there, especially if they find the unicorn."

"You'll do anything to get out of the office, won't you?"

I shrugged off the criticism, although there was a slight element of truth in it. I have been known to grasp at some pretty thin ideas when going slowly stir crazy in our spacious newsroom.

"If they do find it and the St. Pete *Times* beats us to the punch with the story, there are going to be a lot of red faces."

The St. Petersburg *Times* is a monstrously good, and popular, periodical published to the north of us, leading to the nickname of "the Colossos of the North." It fulfills a vital role in the never-ending battle between reporter and editor similar to the role that Russia plays in the annual review of U.S. military appropriations. If there were no *Times*, I probably would have had to invent one.

"I don't think I'll lose too much sleep over the possibility. Why do you really want to go out there?"

"No reason in particular. It's probably just a drunk dream or a pot fantasy, but it might make a nice little bright for tomorrow's paper. Anyway, there's nothing happening here right now."

"Can't argue with that. Okay, take off. Oh . . ."

I picked up my notebook from my desk.

"Watch out for the gremlins."

He grinned. The comment wasn't worthy of a reply so I just left.

It took me only a moment to get my little VW out of the company parking lot. I took off down U.S. 41, the six-lane highway that runs through Sarasota. Traffic, despite the hour, was heavy enough to make me wish that the tourists had never discovered Sarasota.

During the summer months Sarasota's temperature hugs the 100 mark and there's an almost continual horde of sun-'n'-fun seekers who invade the hotels, motels, beaches and shops of what is otherwise still a quiet and beautiful city.

Except for the ever-present outstretched hand that the merchants and city fathers extend to loot-laden Northerners, the city really has little in common with the rest of south Florida.

To explain why it is the city it is, you'd have to know why the city has more millionaires, wealthy oldsters, famous writers, artists and musicians, yachts and concert halls than any other Florida metropolis of any size.

But to really understand what Sarasota is all about, you'd have to stand on Lido Beach or one of the Siesta Key beaches facing the Gulf of Mexico. The address Helen had given was on Siesta Key, one of several islands off the coast of Sarasota and neighboring Manatee County. Homes on the key are reserved for famous artists or wealthy tourists or retirees, the common denominator in all cases being money—lots of it.

It's one of the most beautiful places in Florida and I spend as much time as I can on its beaches. Which was more than a small part of the reason why I was headed out there now.

775 Del Mere was a dead end. There was a lot of brush and palm trees crowding in close to a perfect lawn surrounding the last house on the street. Beyond the house I could see the sparkle of moonlight on water. A full moon floated high above the trees.

The pictures of the dark side didn't destroy the spell it cast. It's still farther away from most people than the hope of heaven.

I saw the patrol car parked near the driveway and pulled in behind it. There was a welcome light shining above the door. The house was something else, as long as two ordinary homes. I could see a very, very expensive red sports job in the garage.

I locked the VW and walked to the door. Even the ding-dong as I rang the bell sounded expensive as hell.

The man who answered the doorbell wore his profession and station in life like a mask. He could only be a doctor. The type of doctor who works out of a private practice for the best people. Good-looking with just the right amount of wrinkles and gray along the temples. Completely unreal.

"Yes?"

"My name's Hank Dell. I'm a reporter for the *Herald Tribune*. I understand a Mrs. Carr reported an . . . an unusual sighting on the beach near here."

"This is none of your business. I don't want to see anything about this in the paper. Good night."

He shut the door in my face. Ordinarily I would have called him a few dirty names quietly and either waited until the police finished their investigation or called the station afterward to get the details.

But he'd rubbed me the wrong way, so I rang the doorbell again.

He opened the door and gave me the kind of look that is usually directed at things that come crawling out from under rocks.

"I thought I made myself—"

"Yes, sir, you did, but I didn't make myself clear. Mrs. Carr made a complaint. That's public record, as well as the report the officers will make on the complaint. It should make a very funny story. You never can tell, it may even be picked up by the AP. If that happens you and your wife will become well known throughout the state. You might even go nationwide."

He looked like he'd swallowed something bitter and was getting ready to spit. Actually, the story would probably be buried among the marriage notices or legals where nobody, including myself, would ever see it.

"You wouldn't."

"I'd like to talk to Mrs. Carr, hear her story. There may not be any real purpose in printing it. Even if we do run something, we won't have to use your wife's name, or any information that would identify her."

He stared at me for a minute as if trying to tell how much truth there was in what I'd said. In a more reasonable tone, he said, "I hope you didn't misunderstand my position. I realize you're only doing a job. It's just that this is the sort of thing that could hurt my wife badly if it gets out, and it wouldn't do my practice any good either."

He hesitated, then made up his mind.

"Come in. You can reach the beach from our backyard. My wife and the officers are out there right now."

I grew more impressed by the foot as we passed through the house. Thick carpet I could have gotten lost in, paintings that looked like the real thing by some early Americans and an out-of-sight bar. As we walked, my guide, who I learned really was a doctor, said, "I only wish I'd been here when my wife saw whatever it was out on the beach. She's not usually excitable. I never would have thought she'd call the police about something like this."

The back door opened onto a patio and a dozen feet away the beach gleamed white in the darkness. It was a silver darkness, the best kind if you're afraid of the dark, which I am. Not that I would admit it under the worst torture. Pull my tongue out by the roots, stick bamboo under my fingernails and I would not reveal it. I do not like the dark, mainly because I can't see what's coming at me.

A woman stood with two officers about fifty feet down the beach. One of the cops was bending over looking at something.

"Hello, Hank," he said as he looked up at Dr. Carr and myself. He was a fifteen-year veteran I'd ridden with a few times when I was trying to work up a feature story on the day-to-day life of a policeman.

The younger cop was Jim Carlin. We'd gotten drunk together and tried to pick up the same girls when I was on a kick of forging closer relations with the police department.

"What have you got?"

The veteran, Bill Johnson, pointed to the sand. Clearly visible was the outline of what must have been an unshod horse's hoof. It was more than a foot wide.

"You're Mrs. Carr?" I asked the woman. She was brunette and as good-looking and well preserved a fifty-year-old woman as I'd ever seen. Fully a match for her husband's distinguished features. Right now she wasn't looking her best.

"Yes."

"I wonder if you could tell me what you saw?"

She looked at her husband and he gave her a nod.

"It . . . I thought it was a horse at first. I had just come to the back door to call Cleo, our cat, inside. Before I could call her I saw it running—galloping—down the beach."

Her voice softened and her eyes took on a dreamy look, as if the phantom animal was running down the beach in the moonlight once more.

"In the moonlight it was like . . . like something out of a dream. As it came closer I saw it was white, white like ivory, and huge. It must have been—I don't know—ten or twelve feet tall. Then I saw it. There was a horn, a huge horn, growing right out of its forehead. I should have been afraid, I guess. It was so big and that horn was as sharp as a knife at its tip. But, somehow, I wasn't."

She looked at me, then at the police, helplessly. Our expressions must have given us away.

"I know it's hard to believe," she burst out, "but I saw it. It wasn't any farther from me than Henry"—pointing to her husband. "I couldn't have imagined it, or that horn. I saw it. I know I did."

Her husband went to her and put his arm around her shoulder. I didn't dislike him as much for that.

"Come on, dear. The officers won't need you any more, will you?" he asked, directing a look plainer than words at them.

"No, sir. You can go on in now. We'll go out through your yard."

When they had gone in Johnson said, "Another page-one story, huh?"

"Not quite. What do you think? She wasn't drunk and if she was flying she was doing it somewhere I've never been."

"Neither one, I think. I'd bet she saw a horse out there. The law says no horses on the beach, but some of the kids do bring them out here to ride at night. The horn? Well, the moonlight can play tricks. It's easy to see something that isn't there. One thing, though. I'd sure as hell like to see the horse that made that print."

"You're not the only one," Carlin said, inspecting more prints farther down the beach. "That's the biggest hoofprint I've ever seen. Whatever made it must be a real monster."

I rubbed my jaw, turning the matter over in my mind.

"There might be a story in that alone."

"You're not going to run a story on this, are you?"

I thought about it. On the surface it would make a nice three paragraphs of light humor and whimsy. On the other hand, one story about a unicorn on the beach would mean twenty calls within the next few days and I'd have enough trouble with the routine silly-season calls.

"No, I don't guess so. Not unless you guys find a twelve-foot unicorn."

I looked up and down the beach for a moment as Johnson and Carlin headed back to their cruiser. Moonlight played on the waves rolling in on the beach. There was darkness out there too, shadows rising up from the sea.

It was almost a shame, I found myself thinking, that there hadn't been a unicorn, that there couldn't be a unicorn. Not in this world, not in a world of freeways, income tax, abortions, H-bombs and the Pill. There was no room for unicorns or witches or princesses calling for help from the barred windows of high castle towers.

When Lee asked me what had happened I answered him fully and concisely:

"Nothing."

And I thought that would be the end of the story, but not quite.

One of the more unpleasant aspects of my job is that the police reporter does not have all his time occupied with car thefts and unicorn reports. There are also the ugly things that if you're lucky you may never see.

Like a drowning victim. Some would say that drowning, as far as the appearance goes, is one of the easiest ways to kick off. If you get the body before the fish get to it there won't be the scars of an auto accident or the ugly hole left after you blow your brains out.

Still, I don't like to look at drowning victims. Sometimes when they're brought out on the beach some clod is unimaginative enough to leave the eyes open, staring out at nothing.

Which is why I was not exactly overjoyed when, two nights later, Helen radioed a report of a "body in the water near the end of Coast Horizon Road."

It was close to 10 P.M. I'd had a busy day, a long feature story, short stories on breaking and entering, obits—the works, in short. A drowning would be just what I needed to close my day out in style.

I gave the word to John Harper, who works city desk during the week, and took off. Coast Horizon Road is also on Siesta Key and the coincidence made me think of the unicorn, already a standard joke around the newsroom.

I had checked half-heartedly around Siesta Key on Monday to see if anyone living on the beach had seen a horse Sunday night. No results at all.

The prints were gone by Monday. It had rained briefly in the early morning Monday and now there was only the unsupported word of Mrs. Carr as to what she had seen. The police had already chalked it up as an early forerunner of the silly season.

Thirty minutes brought me to the end of Coast Horizon Road. The asphalt roadway ran untouched by houses or buildings for several miles before it came to a sudden halt in palmetto roots and knee-high grass. There was a pathway of white sand leading to the open beach.

The water gleamed and I could hear the waves coming in. There was a storm out to sea and the normally placid Gulf looked like some of the wilder beaches on the Atlantic side of the state where I grew up. The incoming waves hit hard, a head of foam on each.

I passed the police cruiser parked near the trees at the edge of the road. The cops were nowhere in sight. I heard voices and walked toward them. The wet, salty smell of the Gulf was strong in the air.

There were two cops and a boy and girl standing only a few yards from where the waves were crashing in. They stood near one of the many groins of irregularly shaped rocks and boulders stretching in both directions as far as the eye could see along the beach. The foam curled up along and over the glistening boulders, then fell back.

It was a wild scene. Only a few miles down the beach were the multistory and multimillion dollar hotel complexes that own the far side of Siesta Key, but here there was no sign of man's presence.

I didn't know the officers very well. The paths of Don Grant and Ken Pendley had never seemed to cross mine. As I got closer I recognized the boy and girl.

He was a New College student named David Hartman. New College is an extremely unconventional, free-wheeling liberal arts college with a student population carefully limited to five hundred. They are the cream of the crop gathered from fifty states and at least ten foreign countries.

In the view of the average Sarasotan who's never been quite sure whether he should be proud or insulted to have the school in this city, they tend to be sort of far-out. David is more or less conservative, with a Fu-Manchu beard and mustache, shaven head and large gold earring dangling from one pierced ear.

I'd met him when I was doing a story on some typical New College students during their first days in Sarasota—how they adjusted to the inhabitants and vice versa. Despite the difference in lifestyles and ideas, we got along fairly well.

The girl was his steady. It's strange to call her that. It reeks of the fifties, but it still fits. She didn't sleep around, so she was his steady. She was a natural blonde with hair down to her waist, fantastic body and as tall as David at five feet eight.

David saw me first and turned Fay, as in the great Dunaway, toward me.

"*Qué pasa*, man?"

That expression had been hot for a while back in the late sixties, died and somehow was resurrected to triumphant life in '77, and was still going strong.

"That's what I was going to ask you."

"Not much, Hank, until a couple of minutes ago," Fay said.

Ken said, "Doesn't look like there's anything out there that I can see. You sure this is where you saw it?"

"Right out there," Fay said, pointing.

Don gave the water a slow sweep with his flashlight, for all the good it did.

"If they were out there when you called in, they're either on shore now or they've been washed out to sea. We'll check to see if the body might have been washed ashore farther down."

They took off in opposite directions along the beach, leaving me with David and Fay. I noticed a white blanket on the sand a few yards away. Fay was dressed only in a thin transparent halter and ultrashort shorts. There was less material there than in a good bikini. It was pretty obvious what my two New College friends had been doing out on the beach.

I tore my eyes away from Fay's titanic bust. It distresses me to lust after the friends of friends.

"Nature studies?" I asked, pointing to the blanket.

"The highest flying there is," David replied, grinning.

"You weren't on . . ."

"No. We were on the oldest and safest high of them all."

Fay didn't blush. I didn't expect her to.

"What exactly did you see?"

"Playing newspaperman again, Hank?"

"It's the way I earn my daily bread."

"Look upon the lilies of the field and the birds of the air. They neither spin nor sow, and yet see how the Lord has provided for them."

"Don't trot the Bible out on me. Anyway, until I sprout roots or grow wings I'll have to stick with my own racket."

Fay said, "Well, we told the bluecoats we saw a girl, or a woman, swimming out there beyond the rocks. It looked like she was having trouble. Then she went under and we didn't see her again."

Something out of kilter in this picture. David was the best swimmer I'd ever known. I couldn't see him letting a girl go down without making even an effort to go out after her.

David must have read it in the look I gave him.

"If you weren't with the yellow press, Hank, I might tell you what we saw out there."

"Okay. For the next five minutes I turn in my press card. I'm just plain Horace Dell, civilian."

"All right, Hank. But I want you to know first, no matter what it sounds like, we weren't on anything."

"I believe you. So tell me what you saw."

"I saw it first," Fay said. "I was standing here, where I am now. I was just looking out at the water, thinking how beautiful it was and about going in when I saw something. I couldn't make out what it was at first.

"It looked like a ball floating in the water covered with weeds. I told David to come over here and look, to see if he could make out what it was."

"Then we saw it was a girl—a woman," David said. "She was close enough and I guess the moon came out from behind a cloud or something. Anyway, it was brighter and we saw it was a girl. Beautiful, and what we thought were weeds was her hair floating in the water around her. It must have been five or six feet long."

Fay took up the story.

"Her hair was green, as green as that painting a guy did a few years back. You remember, a pure green canvas and he called it 'Green.' As she came closer she rose out of the water and we could see she wasn't wearing anything, at least from the waist up."

"And stacked, baby," David added with relish, licking his lips. "Now, a green-haired, nude sex symbol swimming in a heavy surf on a deserted beach is pretty strange, but live and let live. So we called out to her."

"Yeah," Fay said. "We called to her to come in. We thought, you know, she might be somebody we hadn't met at New College. She didn't seem to hear us. That's when she began to sing. I mean, just like that, she began to sing. No words we could make out, just a tune."

"Had a beautiful voice," David said. "You wouldn't believe how beautiful unless you'd heard it. I kept on calling and waded out in the surf to her. She didn't answer and she seemed to be laughing as she sang. Sent ripples up my spine, a real weird feeling. It was the sexiest laughter I've ever heard.

"I began to think she was flying. That would explain the way she was acting and her swimming in a storm. If she was really high there was no way of telling what she might do. She might laugh and dunk her head under water just to see what drowning felt like. It's happened. So I went out after her."

He was silent, staring out at the waves foaming up over the rocks. They were getting higher and harder. I wouldn't have been too happy about going out there even though I'm a fairly good swimmer.

"I got pretty close to her and she started swimming away from me, still singing. There was an undertow pulling me out to her. That hair of hers brushed across my face as I got closer.

"The finest, silkiest hair you could imagine. Like, like the stuff that makes up spider webs, only not sticky. When I got close enough I went under and grabbed for her."

He fell silent again. I was wondering what was going on. Where had the girl gone to? Why hadn't they told the cops the full story?

"The move must have surprised her, because I grabbed her under the water. For a moment she let me hold her, and then, just like that, she slipped out of my grasp. I tried to grab her again, but she was gone.

"I came up and looked around, but she was nowhere. Fay yelled that the girl had dived and hadn't come up. I swam farther out and dived a couple of times, but I still couldn't find her and Fay said she hadn't come up.

"Finally the undertow got so strong I had to come back in. I had a job just saving myself. We kept watching for about five minutes, but she didn't show again."

He gave me a funny look.

"You believe all that, Hank?"

"Sure. Why not?"

"Well, there's something else, Hank. It's what I felt when I had hold of her under the water."

I leered.

"Go on and tell me what you felt."

"When I grabbed her first I got her around the waist with her— lower body—against my chest.

"It was the surprise, I guess, that allowed her to get away from me so easily. It was as if I had hold of a fish, a huge fish. When she broke away I felt the tail of the fish brush my chest. It was one big fin."

I couldn't help smiling.

"Don't tell me. You had hold of a . . ."

"Mermaid, Hank. A damned mermaid with fishy tail and all, like in the old drawings."

Now I was the one who was silent. What could I say?

"I know, Hank. You don't believe it. I don't even think Fay really believes me. She's just going along with me because she doesn't want to believe I've gone off the track.

"That's why we told the bluecoats we saw a girl out there, with none of the other details. I thought if they thought someone had drowned out there they might call in divers. Maybe someone else would see her."

"You sure you weren't on anything at all?"

He turned away from me.

"All right, Hank, forget it. You don't believe it. No one else would. It doesn't matter. I know what I felt and saw, and I know I was all here."

After a moment I said, "I don't know what to say, Dave. Regardless of what you saw out there, or felt, I wouldn't tell the cops that you saw a mermaid. It would only leave you wide open for a lot of bad jokes and hassles. If I was you, I'd just forget it."

"Yeah, Hank. Thanks for listening, anyway."

I left them on the beach, Fay with her arms around David as if to protect him. As I walked back to my car I threw a few glances back at the wild surf. It was a strange story. If David said he wasn't flying, then he wasn't. I didn't think he would lie, and they had both seen the girl.

Still, it was impossible. Mermaids and unicorns, too? What was staid and respectable old Sarasota coming to?

CHAPTER TWO

The mermaid story stayed with me. I tried to talk myself out of it, but it kept creeping back into my thoughts. It began to irritate me, like that spot on your back that you can almost reach—almost. It's always the one that itches like crazy.

Which is why I was staring into space Wednesday night, trying to think of anything except mermaids and unicorns.

My thoughts ranged from the specific to the general, starting with some stories I'd worked on that day. I'd written one on a seventy-eight-year-old man who'd casually stepped out onto the highway and was turned into hash by one of the big super-tanker trucks. Nobody would ever know why.

I'd also whipped out a story on a twenty-one-year-old honey blonde who'd saved the lives of two small children when their parents' boat overturned in Sarasota Bay. Tried to work a date out of the story, but no luck. She was, I learned later, shacking up with one of the junior executives at the paper.

Reflecting on the unfairness of life in general brought me around to my plight. Namely that of a twenty-four-year-old reporter going nowhere on a small paper.

Lightning—the lightning that brings fame, fortune and femmes—does not strike on papers like the *Herald Tribune*. If I had had any ambition I would have moved after my first year on the paper, but two things held me at the *Herald Tribune*. The first was Sarasota itself. After the first six months I was hooked.

And, secondly, I'm one of those people whose lives are controlled by inertia. For better or worse, once I'm set in a certain direction it takes a disagreeable amount of will power to change. Usually what has to happen is that an outside force has to change my mind.

So far nothing had come along to jolt me out of the comfortable rut I was mired in.

The ring of the telephone interrupted my thoughts. I sat my chair back down on four legs, swung my feet down to the floor (I have a bad habit of propping my feet up on my desk which I probably got from watching too many bad movies about seedy newspapermen) and picked it up. Another obit probably.

"*Herald Tribune.* Hank Dell, police reporter."

"You're the police reporter?"

The frightened voice of a young girl.

"Yes. What can I do for you?"

"I—I'd like to report a murder."

"What?"

I snapped to attention in my chair.

"It's Crawford."

"Crawford? Who is he, and who are you?"

"Melanie Harmon. Crawford is . . . was"—a sob?—"my puppy."

Jesus! I let out the breath I'd been holding. A juicy murder can mean bylines and a good deal of exposure. If it's real big and handled right it can lead to a raise, or a better job.

The kid was shook by her puppy's death. When I was that age I would have been too. So I played understanding adult.

"You say he was murdered, Melanie. How?"

Silence and then, "It ate him up," in a fluid rush of sound, like one multisyllabled word.

"I don't think I heard that right."

"It ate him up," and again that sound suspiciously like a sob.

"I don't understand."

"The monster ate him."

Funny thing, I realized I had never thought about the call being a hoax. Some tykes get their kicks utilizing their imaginations over the phone.

"Where do you live, Melanie?" I asked. That's the acid test. The pranksters don't give their addresses. Most of the time. Then again, sometimes they give fictitious addresses and sometimes the people with genuine gripes won't give their addresses. That's what makes the work interesting.

"Why?"

"Well, if I don't know where you live how can I come out to

your house and talk to you and investigate what happened? How can the photographer come out there?"

"Mom and Dad wouldn't want you to come out here. They don't know I'm calling you. They don't believe me."

I should gently have maneuvered the conversation to a close and forgotten it. You get nut calls from time to time. There was something about this one, though.

"You live on Siesta Key, don't you?"

"How did you know?"

"I know, Melanie, and I think I believe you. Tell me what happened."

The reassuring clicking of the wire machines and the typewriter being pounded for all it was worth at the sports desk were unbelievably distant from the cold and lonely place where I sat. Those were the sounds of the real, daily grind world, and I was somewhere else.

What is the magic of three? One report of a unicorn was just an interesting story. A unicorn and a mermaid aroused my curiosity, but it was still just one of those things you swap across a bar after your fourth drink.

Three stories of strange beings on Siesta Key and it stopped being an intellectual stimulant.

"It was today, about noon. Mom and Dad were gone and I was alone in the house. Our house is on the beach. I let Crawford—he's, he was, a German shepherd—out to run around while I watched TV.

"When my program was over I got up and went to the front door to call him. Our house faces the beach. I heard him barking and I opened the door and went out.

"There was no one around on the beach. The nearest house is almost a half mile away. It was so quiet. Then I saw Crawford way down the beach and running fast. I thought he was running toward me."

I listened to her breathing in the silence. I would have bet she was nine or ten years old.

"He wasn't. It was the thing chasing him. When I looked up I saw it."

"What did it look like?"

"It was flying over the beach low, near Crawford. I yelled to Crawford. I told him to run, to run. I was afraid, but I didn't go inside. I yelled and Crawford ran, but . . .

"It came down on him. It held him down with one claw. He was wiggling and barking and I know he must have been looking at me. I know he wanted me to help him."

She was crying now. I don't even think she heard my question. She was living the whole thing over as she told the story.

"And it ate him. It ate him right there. I wanted to help, I did, but I was afraid."

The words were run together and I could barely make them out for the sobbing.

"It tore his head off and blood came out. It was horrible and I couldn't stop looking and nobody will believe me."

"Melanie, if you'll tell me where you live I'll try to see if I can make them believe—"

She hung up on me. I looked at the useless phone for a few seconds, then slammed it back in its cradle. Some kid had given me a fairy tale and gotten hysterical over the phone. Why should I let it bother me? If I didn't watch it I'd soon be at the stage where I couldn't tell the difference between the fantasy in the books and movies I like and the grimy, definitely unfantastic nine-to-five world.

For about five seconds I tried to look at it logically and rationally. Then I rode with my instincts and reached for the phone book.

There was only one Harmon listed in the phone book on Siesta Key. George P. His address was on the beach only a mile from the Carr home. Curiouser and curiouser.

"Mr. Harmon?" I said when a male voice answered the phone.

"Yes. Who is this?"

"Hank Dell. I'm a reporter for the *Herald Tribune*."

"Yes?"

"I received a call from a Melanie Harmon about five minutes ago. I assume she's your daughter."

"Yes, but—she didn't tell you about the dog?"

"I'm afraid so."

"How much—what did she tell you?"

"She told me about the thing that ate her puppy up."

"You didn't believe what she told you, did you? We haven't been able to find out what happened yet. She won't budge from her story. But there's nothing here for your paper."

"Look, Mr. Harmon, I can understand your not wanting to drag the newspapers in on a personal matter like this, and if it was just a little girl's fantasy I wouldn't even ask to come out and talk to her, but apparently something did happen to your dog, didn't it?"

He hesitated a second, then made a decision.

"Yes, something happened. I went out where she said it happened and found blood, a lot of blood, but it couldn't be what she said."

"I'm sure it wasn't, but if any kind of foul play was involved the newspaper might be interested. I'm not saying we would run anything on it and even if we did I'd clear it with you first, but I would like to talk to Melanie and find out what really happened. She did call me and sometimes a child that age can talk more freely with a stranger than her own parents."

While he thought about it I prayed he wouldn't say no. My curiosity would drive me up the wall if I couldn't find out what had happened out on the beach.

"All right," he said finally, "it can't hurt and we can't seem to get anything out of her."

"Be over in ten minutes."

The route to Siesta Key was so familiar by this time it was almost boring. Most of the beach I passed was privately owned and most of that by companies and hotels. The few remaining miles of public beach and the beachfront held by homeowners was saved from the developers only at the last moment, in the early seventies.

Still, there are large stretches of land that are uncleared brush and there's always something lonely and wild about the beach at night. It's as if the strip where land meets water is older than man, and condominiums and beach houses become outposts against the night.

The Harmon house looked naked without a police car in front of it.

I rang the doorbell and a rugged, beefy individual answered it. "Dell?"

He enveloped my hand in something that can only be described as a paw.

"Yes."

"Come in."

Like most houses on the key, it was complete. Rich finish on the walls, ever-present bar, which I guessed to be well stocked, and Japanese figurines ranging from a couple of inches to a couple of feet high on tables and shelves around the living room.

The woman was a startling contrast to her husband. About five four, blond and fragile.

"You're the newspaperman?" she asked.

"Yes."

"What did she tell you? Did she say what really happened?"

"I don't know how much she told you. She told me something ate her puppy."

Swift glances between Mr. and Mrs. carried the unseen message of "I told you so."

Harmon said, "I never expected her to call the newspaper. I expected anything but that. I don't know what she's hiding with this cock-and-bull story about a flying monster, but I'm going to find out."

"Do you have any idea what really happened?"

He shook his head and picked up what looked like a bloody mary off a low, gleaming wooden table.

"When we came home we found her over at a neighbor's house. She was hysterical, kept talking about the 'monster.' The neighbors had already looked, but I went out to see for myself. There was blood, all right, and where she said it happened.

"It was far enough from the water that it wasn't washed away. There was definitely blood spilled and I think it was Crawford's, but whatever happened, it wasn't any damned monster."

"Where is she?"

"In her room," Mrs. Harmon said. "We tried to find out what really happened, tried to make her admit it was only a fib—a lie— she was telling us, but she wouldn't. I've never seen her so stubborn.

"She literally defied us. It's the first time she's ever done anything like that before."

"I don't know why she'd lie about it," Harmon said. "She's never lied to us before and I know she loved the puppy. She wouldn't try to hide whoever or whatever killed it."

He rubbed his chin and drained the glass.

"I don't know, I just don't know. I can't figure this out, and that bothers me."

I refrained from commenting that it didn't bother him half as much as it was beginning to bother me.

"Could I see her now?"

Another silent exchange. Judgment: What can it hurt?

I followed Harmon's broad back through a long hallway. I would have put solid money on his being a housing corporation executive recruited fresh from the ranks of pro or college football.

He opened the door into a pastel wonderland. Wallpaper in pink and green on which Disney-ish creatures cavorted. At one side was a large, fluffy pink bed on which a giant black and white panda with only one eye took a few well-earned winks.

A poster of the Nightcreepers dressed in their spider costumes from their most successful concert tour graced one wall. A wall-to-wall pop art mural of Donald Duck covered the other.

A five-foot-tall doll house stood in another corner. It was one of the new simulations, the ones with at least two dozen rooms and about thirty tiny and primitive robots that can be programed to perform simple actions.

There was a flower-print working telephone on a stand near the doll house.

The only thing in the entire room that jarred the image was the little dark-haired girl lying curled in a ball on the bed near the panda.

"Melanie."

"Go away."

"Melanie," in a firm, no-nonsense voice.

She looked up at him and then at me. Face of innocence, with little rosebud lips that five years from now would be giving some teen-ager fits. She had a little girl's body, with huge dark eyes that stared through me.

"Who are you?"

"This is Mr. Dell, the man you talked to at the paper."

"Mr. Dell?"

"None other. Why did you hang up on me?"

She looked at her father and I began to think I was developing telepathy. Maybe it was the tension in the air that focused it.

Harmon said, "We'll be in the living room."

When he left I sat down on a chair near a white sandlewood typing desk. There was a small, delicate but fully operative typewriter on it.

"Why did you hang up on me? I said I believed you."

She continued to stare through me.

"You didn't believe me. I shouldn't have called you. Nobody believes me."

"Why shouldn't I believe you?"

Contempt dripped from her words.

"There aren't any monsters. I was just making the story up."

"Were you? You shouldn't be mad at your mother and father for not believing you. It's hard to believe in monsters, unless you've seen what some of the people around here have seen."

That caught her.

"What?"

"What what?"

Little girl exasperation at adult stupidity.

"What did they see?"

"Nothing much, only a unicorn and a mermaid."

Her eyes were wide open now, looking to see if I was making fun of her.

"No."

"Yes, and they've all been seen here on Siesta Key. There's something strange happening on this island."

"You mean you really believe me?"

"Yes, sugar, I believe you saw a monster and it came down and ate your puppy."

"I knew it. I knew it."

"You really loved Crawford, didn't you?"

Her eyes gleamed. She nodded her head mutely and then before I knew what was happening her head was pressed against my chest and I could feel her body quivering with each sob.

I never had a sister, but I had a puppy when I was ten years old. A car ran him down one day and crushed his guts out onto the road near our home. I could feel a little of what she was feeling by memory.

"I . . . I'm sorry."

"Don't be. If you loved Crawford you should cry for him."

She shook her head, wiping away the tears with one hand.

"No, I'm not going to cry. I'm going to kill it."

I held her chin gently in my hand.

"Tell me what it looked like."

She looked around the room, then grabbed the panda and pulled it close to her. She began to stroke it while she talked and she never stopped until she'd finished describing the thing.

"It had wings, big wings, like an eagle or something, and hands and claws."

"How big was it?"

"I don't know. Crawford—he was about a foot long, I guess, and it was about ten times bigger than him."

"What else do you remember?"

"It had an ugly face, like a monkey or a gorilla, and horrible teeth. They hung out over its lower lip. It had funny, brittle fur on its face, and feathers."

"This is important, Melanie. How long did you look at it and how far away was it?"

"I looked at it from the time I saw it come down out of the sky. It took a long time to . . . and it wasn't more than fifty or a hundred feet away."

It didn't sound like anything I'd want to meet either in the daytime or, especially, in the dark.

"Look, Melanie, your parents don't believe a monster was here, and they won't believe it, no matter what you say."

"But you believe me."

"I've learned enough to think you're telling the truth, but your parents won't believe you or me. They never will. If I were you, I'd pretend you were making the monster story up."

"But . . ."

"And I'll hunt it down. I promise you I'll do my best to track it down and kill it."

"Promise?"

"Promise."

"All right."

Harmon and his wife threw me questioning looks when I came into the living room with Melanie.

"Momma, Daddy."

"Yes?"

"I . . . I wasn't telling the truth."

I started getting Miracle Worker looks from the Harmons.

"What do you mean, sugar?"

"I really didn't see anything. I mean, I saw some boys walking down the beach before I let Crawford out and when I went looking for him there was only the blood."

"Why the story?" her father asked.

"I . . . I was afraid you'd blame me for letting Crawford out. I know it must have been those boys. They were throwing rocks at the Youngs' dog last week."

"The lousy punks," Harmon said, "killing a little puppy that couldn't fight back. If I could get my hands on them . . ."

He wrung his hands together in a decidedly unpleasant way. It was a good thing there really hadn't been any boys, otherwise I would have been afraid Harmon might get to them.

Mrs. Harmon knelt beside her daughter.

"You should have known we wouldn't be mad at you, honey. You couldn't know what they were going to do."

"I didn't know . . ."

"Well, you know now," her father said.

He looked back at me.

"Thanks, Dell. We appreciate your coming out here, away from your job. You won't put any of this in the paper, will you?"

"No. This will be your own private business."

"Thank you, Mr. Dell," Melanie said. "You showed me what I should have done from the start."

Her eyes were saying something her words weren't. It occurred to me momentarily, walking back to my car, that if there really hadn't been anything out on the beach that ate little puppies I had done Melanie a terrible wrong.

I had encouraged her to continue believing in a fantasy and to lie to her parents. Not a very nice thing to do to a little girl.

So make me the villain of the day. Sometimes you have to do things that may turn out wrong in the long run because you don't have any better alternative. If Melanie had really seen a monster, and I couldn't shake the feeling she had, it would have hurt her worse to be forced to believe she had dreamed the whole thing.

It hit me while I was driving back to the office. Before, when I'd still thought of the whole thing as a tissue of mistaken reports and confused people, it hadn't bothered me to speculate idly about what might really be behind the stories.

But now? Something was happening on Siesta Key. The stories weren't as wild as some I'd heard, but they were too close in time and space and there was something about each one that made it seem more than a trick of moonlight or human fantasy. There was something else I couldn't quite put my finger on, a vague feeling there was something there. Call it a hunch.

That bothered me. When you begin to get the feeling there might really be unicorns and mermaids and monsters popping up in the solid, daylight world, it makes your grip tremble just a little bit.

To put it more simply, I was getting scared.

CHAPTER THREE

It seems incredible now, but two days later unicorns and mermaids were the farthest things from my mind.

The secret behind that marvelous transformation is a piece of mundane, earthbound magic called Helen White. She was a dream of light brown hair worn long and curling around her shoulders like a liquid wave that bobbed with her movements.

She was close to my height of six feet and had a body that went well with the height, but she wasn't ponderous in the way some big girls are.

More than anything else, she moved smoothly. That's the word, smoothly. She never seemed to be rushed, she never made an ungraceful movement, she never tripped.

The closest I can come to describing it would be the feline assurance of a lazy, aristocratic Siamese that doesn't move but conveys the impression of steel under that velvet fur.

She turned me on.

I was trying to fan the flame, get her to reciprocate the feelings, cause some sort of counter-reaction.

However you phrase the effort it was not a huge success. I'd had four dates with her in two months. I kissed her on the first date and things got pretty involved. I congratulated myself as the latter-day inheritor of the mantle of Casanova.

On the second date I tried to go further and got politely slapped down. Still, she was affectionate so I consoled myself that she simply needed more time and attention on my part.

So came the third date and what had first escaped my notice began to dawn on me. She was affectionate, true. She kissed like she really meant it. She wasn't cute in the way some girls are.

But she never lost control of herself. She never seemed to go beyond the point where I was more than just a convenient make-out partner. That bothered me. I realized she was just as affectionate, just as physical, with all her dates, or any of them. If she went out with a guy it was because she liked him enough to kiss him, but nothing more, and I was nothing more to her than another guy.

My pride was hurt more than anything else so I decided Helen White would get the treatment. Friday night opened with dinner

at the Colony Beach Club, which meant I would be eating ham-
burger for a month, but no sacrifice was too great in the cause.

An evening at the Asolo Theater, the best live theater in Florida
and one that would rank along with the best in the country, followed. Then drinks and dancing at the Elbow Room.

I was feeling pretty good about 3 A.M. Saturday morning, lying
on my back on a soft blanket staring at the stars. The wind was just
cool enough and there was the smell of salt in the air. Crickets chirp-
ing in the underbrush and Helen in my arms.

On a beach on Siesta Key. Yeah, I know I should have been filled
with foreboding and dark premonitions but Helen loved this beach,
said it put her in a romantic mood. Who am I to argue with ro-
mance? Besides, two days had made my earlier fears seem slightly
ridiculous.

Helen said something like "Mmmmm" after one long and satisfy-
ing kiss. She was a lot warmer than she'd ever been before and I
was beginning to hope that the prolonged and savage assault on
my bank account might just pay off.

I put out one hand to touch her shoulder, concealed under a
flimsy, see-through blouse. I felt the soft, soft fabric and the softer
skin beneath.

"Un-uh," she murmured, wriggling slightly so my hand slipped
away and turning so there wasn't any room between us to maneuver.

"Un-huh," I responded hopefully, rolling her back over to a more
advantageous position.

Staring up at me with big brown eyes she said quietly, "Is that
why you filled me with liquor at the Elbow Room?"

"Yes."

"Oh."

I put my hand back where it had been and this time she didn't
take evasive action.

Sometime later, when things had gotten very involved, I heard
something. I stopped what I was doing. Then I heard it again, a
twig snapping.

We were lying out on the beach, about ten yards from the trees
and brush. I lifted my head and looked into the darkness toward
the sound. Again and this time a little closer, a very concrete sound
in the darkness and stillness. Something was moving through the
trees.

A soft, strong hand ran across my ear and entwined itself in my hair, pulling my head back down to soft lips. A moment later she said in a soft voice, "If you start stopping, I'm going to yell for help."

I pulled away from her, putting a finger to her lips.

"Sssh. Somebody's out there."

She twisted around to look toward the trees.

"Where?"

"Listen."

Again, even closer, and moving along the edge of the trees. I got to my feet and . . . stopped. The thought of walking among those suddenly dark and menacing shapes wasn't all that attractive. As I mentioned, I'm afraid of the dark, especially when there's something out there.

"Let it, or him, or her come to me," I thought and sat back down beside Helen.

"What do you think it is?" she whispered.

"I don't know. Maybe an animal."

"What kind of animal do they have on Siesta Key?"

"Maybe a Hell's Angel."

She swung and hit me in the shoulder with her fist.

"Ouch. Well, that's the only kind of animal I'd worry about in the dark. It might just be some deviated individual seeking to exercise his perverted desires on a helpless female."

"What are you trying to do?" she asked, painfully raking my shoulder with long fingernails. "Frighten the hell out of me?"

"No, sugar," I answered, not mentioning that I was trying not to let my imagination frighten me.

I remembered Melanie's description of the monster she had seen in the daylight on a stretch of beach where there were houses. What might be walking in the darkest and loneliest hour of the night on a deserted beach? Even thinking about it gave me the creeps. I shudder easily.

Another snap and then another, the sounds paralleling the edge of the trees as our unseen visitor moved toward us.

"I know this is silly," Helen said, squeezing close to me, "but I'm beginning to get very, very frightened. You know, Hank?"

"Yeah," I answered, squeezing her hand, "I know very well, sugar. This isn't doing my cardiac condition any great amount of good."

The sounds stopped. Something was waiting in the darkness almost opposite us. I began to think I could almost hear a faint, rough breathing like that of an animal.

Our eyes were adjusted to the bright moonlight, but there was nothing I could see in among the trees, although it was one of those nights that seem as bright as a sunless day.

With Helen holding onto me tightly, it suddenly seemed ridiculous to be holding our breaths and whispering. A monster wouldn't dare to appear on such a well-lit beach.

"This is 1979," I told myself resolutely, "and there are no such things as monsters. At the worst we've got some peeping tom in there and he'll probably run if he's pushed."

"What . . ." Helen said as I stood up, brushing her hands away. I took a step, but only one very short step, toward the dark trees.

"What the hell do you think you're doing in there?"

I'll admit that even as I said them they didn't seem to be the most impressive frightening-away words I could muster, but I was speaking off the top of my head.

No answer but that heavy breathing, only louder now. Helen could hear it too. She grabbed my arm. Her voice was calm and low, but she was scared.

"Hank, don't you think we should try to get out of here? We don't know who's in there. It could be anybody or anything. Don't play hero for me and get yourself killed, because if you do I'll be out here all alone."

"Your concern for my safety is touching, sugar, but how do you suggest we get out of here? My car is parked beyond the trees. We'll have to go through them somewhere up or down the beach to get out of here, unless you want to swim out in the bay and around to the other side of the island."

"I don't know about you, Hank," she whispered, staring into the woods, "but right now that doesn't seem like such a bad idea."

"Maybe so."

I looked back at the water. The waves showed the surf wasn't heavy and there weren't any dangerous undertows that I knew of along this part of the beach. I wasn't the world's best swimmer but I could make a couple of miles at a fairly good pace without killing myself.

Then I remembered my car. If I went swimming I'd be leaving it to the tender mercies of whatever was out there. By the time we got to solid land and a phone, assuming I could rustle up the moral courage actually to tell a stranger I'd been frightened into swimming a couple of miles by a heavy-breathing phantom, whoever it was could be in Tampa with the car.

Not only did that offend my innate cheapness but it would lend the worst body blow to my finances that I'd ever been dealt. If I had to buy another car it would mean months of scrimping and no social life at all, meaning no Helen at all.

At that moment I understood the motive of the guy who will risk his life grappling with a mugger for his weekly pay check. There may be worse things than living poor, but you'd have to search mighty hard to find them.

"Anyway," I said out loud, my decision already made, "it may be able to swim too."

"Whoever you are," I said loudly, "come out where we can see you."

I was writhing inwardly as I spoke. How could I be coming out with such impossibly tedious dialogue when I usually have a fairly good command of the English language. In the morning I was going to be very glad to forget my masterful handling of the situation.

I felt pretty stupid but I stood facing the breathing, my legs wide apart in the traditional *High Noon* gunfighter stance.

"What do I do if somebody in there decides he doesn't want to come out?" I asked myself.

"Cross that bridge when you come to it," was my advice to myself. I can be pretty practical sometimes.

That particular bridge dissolved as something moved out of the trees into the moonlight. I suppose my jaw dropped as I recognized what it was.

"Jesus Christ!"

It fitted the occasion better than anything else I'd said previously.

If nothing else, he was real. Not a nebulous legend like the unicorn, not a sugar-coated myth like the sweet-singing siren of the sea. This kid was all real, from the shiny cranium surrounding the one huge eye staring down at us from about eight feet above the ground to the two pillars he stood on.

"Hank, I don't believe it. I just don't believe it. It's not real, is it?"

"I don't know," I said, backing away, "and I don't intend to find out."

It was male, no doubt about that, because it was wearing absolutely nothing along the line of clothes. A thick covering of heavy black hair covered its chest and arms.

Helen looked at the water longingly.

"Don't even think about it. There's no way of telling if we could swim faster than that and I don't want to get caught in the water. We'll have to try to make a run for it. He can't be too fast."

We backed away from him, soft white sand scuffing beneath my boots, while waiting for him to make his move. Like a statue, he came alive, moving ponderously toward us. That big eye continued to stare at us and the mouth curled into what would have been a smile except for the discolored and broken stumps of teeth it revealed.

"Run."

I grabbed Helen's hand and though I hadn't done any real running in years I found myself pulling her down the beach.

We ran pretty well in tandem for about a half mile. I turned once and saw the Cyclops just beginning to pick up his stride, not that he'd really have to pour on the steam to catch us. Each of his strides covered more than a yard.

It was like a dream where you run and run and your steps cover less and less ground.

"Break for the trees," I told Helen, pulling her along with me. The Cyclops might have more trouble getting through them than we would, I hoped.

We were almost into them when Helen screamed. Her hand was yanked out of mine. Wheeling around and out of breath, I saw the Cyclops' hand, which must have been a foot wide across the palm, clamped onto Helen's left wrist.

At a time like that it comes down to what is euphemistically called the nitty-gritty. I stood there and looked up and up at that huge eye and those broken stumps of teeth, those arms and shoulders.

He had Helen and I had the funny feeling he wasn't going to let her go. If I let him take her away, wherever he was going, I would be a coward and I would have a very difficult time each morning looking at myself in the mirror. I would also be alive.

If I tried to stop him I would be able to live with myself. On the other hand, I would be dead. And he would still take her wherever he was going to take her.

He pulled Helen to him. She clawed at the massive fist holding her, twisted, but was helpless. She looked at me and cried, "Help me, Hank."

THE EXILE OF ELLENDON 29

It was the look she gave me that did it. Maybe it's an instinctive reaction that doesn't have anything to do with what you know you should do if you want to go on living.

When it comes down to the nitty-gritty you know there's only one person on earth whose safety and well-being really counts, and that's you. Stripped to its ugly essentials, that's the truth of life.

But I couldn't turn my back on her with her looking at me. Not with her looking at me. It's crazy, I know, but if she had been facing the other way somehow I would have found the will power not to tackle the titan.

I stepped toward the Cyclops, making my hands into fists, and the giant grinned. As frightened as I was that made me mad. He was getting a kick out of seeing a pint-sized six-foot runt like me actually make fighting motions.

He swung Helen to the other side out of his way, keeping his hold on her wrist with one hand. The other he held out to his side, waiting. I knew then, if I hadn't been sure before, that he was intelligent. I didn't need an interpreter to know he was telling me to take my best shot because it wouldn't do any good.

I drew my fist back. He still had that damned silly grin on his face like a weight lifter on the beach daring you to hit him in the stomach to show you how much he can take.

"Here goes nothing," I said, making a concise prayer, and kicked him with every ounce of strength I had in what I will delicately refer to as his genital area.

A newly castrated elephant would have been quieter about it. He closed his eyes in pain and doubled over, clutching himself and letting Helen go.

The first thought I had after the immediate relief of still being alive was that I wanted to be dead before he got his hands on me. He wasn't going to forget that kick, even if he ever managed to straighten up again.

I had stepped back but not quite far enough. The giant swung one hand out in a backhanded swipe that caught me on the right side of the face. It didn't connect fully but it sent me backward off my feet.

Into a tree headfirst. The incredible thing is I landed on my feet, took a few steps and wound up lying face-down in the sand, the back of my head tearing itself away from the rest of me.

I pushed myself off the ground on my elbows and looked up. The

Cyclops was stumbling toward me, clutching himself with one hand, and in any other situation he would have looked pretty funny.

I did some staggering of my own away from him but he kept coming. He wasn't grinning now and if looks could kill that would have been it. Unfortunately, in addition to his looks, he had those big paws of his to rely on.

Something hit him from behind. Helen backed away as the tree limb bounced off the Cyclops, but he dismissed her with a glance and kept coming in my direction.

My head was beginning to clear by this time. I tried to get around him to Helen but he cut me off. That's the way it was going to be. He had lost all interest in her for the time being.

I kept backing away from him, trying to avoid being pushed out onto the beach. Once he got me in the open I wouldn't have any chance at all.

Then I was out on the beach, the giant standing in front of me and no way to reach the trees. He lunged at me, hands extended. I dropped to the ground rolling and he overshot me.

I scrambled to my feet and took a step toward the trees, not looking behind me. Something like a vise clamped my shoulder and I went flying backward head over heels into the sand.

When I hit I stayed down. I fell on my stomach hard and had the breath knocked out of me. He was standing over me, one foot lifted up like a man getting ready to stomp a cockroach.

The air caught fire around him, flames of blue and green and red licking at the air, enveloping him. There wasn't any heat. It was like looking at him through a stained-glass fun-house mirror, his body shimmering and distorted, a kaleidoscope of colors dancing over him.

Then he was gone. Zap. Totally and completely gone.

I had seen it happen but my body was still waiting for that size twenty-five foot to come down on my back. Finally I let my breath out and laid my head down in the sand.

I don't know what I thought about. I could never remember. I had known I was going to die then, that fact never really hitting me before in my entire life, and I wasn't dead. It took some getting used to.

"Hank."

Helen touched my shoulder, shaking me gently.

"I'm not dead, damnit," I said, irrationally angry at her for making me act like a hero.

She reached out to touch my face with hands that were trembling.

"You're bleeding, Hank. God, your whole face is bloody."

I hadn't even noticed it before but she was right. Now I was getting the full effect. I could feel a dull throbbing along the right side of my cheekbone and jaw. I put my hand up gingerly and felt the loose flap of skin running from my cheekbone to the edge of my jaw.

I almost screamed when I touched the edge of the cheekbone. It was broken, at least, and from the feel it might be splintered. It felt like I'd been hit with a club.

The back of my head wasn't feeling too good either. I put my hand to it and felt a knot the size of an egg, with a very thin shell.

"What happened, Hank? I saw that thing and I still can't believe it. Did you slip me something tonight? Maybe we were both flying."

I stood up, leaning on Helen to accomplish that feat.

"Not unless a figment of my imagination could slash open my face and give me a good crack across the back of the head."

On my feet the ground seemed a lot farther down than I'd thought it was. I felt something wet on my shirt. It was sand caked with blood.

"We've got to tell someone at the station about this," Helen said. "If that thing was real we can't let it go around on the loose."

"Un-uh," I said, shaking my head.

"What?"

"We don't mention one word about a one-eyed giant. Our story will be that we ran into some Hell's Angels types out there who were out for trouble, and gave it to me."

"But why? Why lie?"

I tried to shake some of the dizziness out of my head and the sick feeling out of my stomach. Suddenly the aftereffects were beginning to hit me. My legs felt like rubber and my heart was racing. I was afraid I was going to throw up.

I said the words carefully, one by one, trying not to throw up all over myself and in general get good and sick.

"Think. What would you say if someone came up and said they'd seen an eight-foot-tall, one-eyed giant that vanished into thin air?"

She thought about it for a moment, then said, "But we saw it, Hank. It was real."

"Everybody who ever saw a flying saucer probably felt the same way. No, sugar, they won't believe you, or me, or us."

We were moving slowly through the trees now and my car was just beyond them. I hoped I was going to make it.

"Hank, we saw it. We know it was there. They'll just have to believe us."

"No."

She turned stubborn then.

"I don't care, Hank. We can't lie about it. That thing might reappear and hurt someone, or kill them. Would you want that on your conscience—that you were responsible because you didn't tell anyone?"

"No, but it wouldn't help. They wouldn't believe us."

"I don't care. I'm going to tell them what we saw."

The conversation had taken us to the car. I handed the keys to Helen and sat down in the passenger side. In the car, stretched out and still, I could talk easier.

"Go ahead, Helen, but if you do I'll say you're making the whole thing up."

"You wouldn't."

"Try me, sugar, and see which one of us they believe."

There was a frosty silence. We were heading down U.S. 41, the highway deserted, before any more words were exchanged. I had been staring out at the glass and metal of the buildings and the streetlights. There wasn't a person on the street now, no cars.

"I didn't really think you could be so callous, Hank. I never thought you were that sort of person, so worried about what people will think of you that you'd take a chance on letting someone get killed."

I shook my head, feeling very sleepy and nervous at the same time.

"Not callous, but we won't do anyone any good by making ourselves laughing stocks. How long do you think my newspaper would need a reporter who saw one-eyed giants on the beach? Just long enough to get a replacement. The police department might wonder about letting a dispatcher who sees giants behind every tree handle calls that may mean life or death to someone. I think they'd find you an immediate risk."

"I still think you're wrong."

"Maybe so, but I'm not going to take the chance that I'm right."

We looked at the lighted storefronts for a little while until she said, "What's our story? If we're going to lie, let's make it convincing."

I found out the cheekbone was cracked, not broken. Two hours after I walked into the hospital emergency room I walked out with a sewed-up face, several bottles of pills and advice from the doctor not to go back to work for at least a couple of days.

The cops swallowed my story fairly easily. They knew Helen and me and our stories dovetailed. It wasn't that strange to have two high fliers roaming the beaches late at night trying to make it with any girl, or in some cases any guy, they find out that late.

I'd fought with them and managed to scare them off, though I got pretty badly cut up in the process. Even to me it sounded convincing. I found myself wishing it had been that way.

The cops gave Helen and me a few moments alone after I left the emergency room where they'd sewed me up. We sat a little apart on a stiff plastic-covered couch. I looked like a reincarnation of the Mummy, with the plaster casing and large adhesive bandage over half my face, just my eye peeping out.

"Did it really happen?"

I understood her question. Every moment that went by made it that much harder to believe.

"I guess so."

"It's so . . . so . . ."

"Unbelievable?"

We laughed together. I don't really know why. Maybe because we were reading each other's minds. It wasn't really funny laughter, it was the breaking of the tension that had gripped us since the Cyclops had appeared.

"Why?"

"Don't hit me with those ambiguous questions," I said, smiling. "Why what?"

She stared at me and through me.

"Why did you risk your life to help me?"

My mind was a big blank. I thought of several very noble-sounding answers, but they didn't sound right.

"And don't tell me it's because I'm something special to you."

I showed my surprise. That was the impression I'd been working hard to give her.

"You don't love me. I'm just a girl with a good body you've got the hots for right now. So I'm curious. Why did you do it?"

I tried to retrieve the situation.

"Well, you've dragged it out of me. I guess I'll have to confess that deep down I'm a hero."

It didn't work. She had a funny expression on her face. An open expression. She looked different in some way than I had ever seen her. I knew in that moment there would be no more nights on the beach. No more nights with her anywhere, anytime. The walls had come crumbling down.

The situation had turned into one of those closed rooms that have only two doors leading out. One led to honesty, or commitment or love. Put your own tag on it. The other door was the one I was going to take.

"Tell me the truth, Hank. I'd like to know."

"It seemed like a good idea at the time."

She kept staring at me and it was as if she was pulling an answer out of me that I hadn't known was there.

"I did it because . . . I would have done it for anyone. A stranger. I just couldn't stand there and do nothing. I just couldn't."

She stood there and looking up at her she seemed to be incredibly far away. I stood also and ran one hand down the curve of her jaw. Touching her, the only thing I wanted was to go back to the hours when we'd been lying to each other and enjoying each other.

"You want to say it's been a lot of fun, and what you mean is good-bye, isn't it, Hank?"

I couldn't answer her.

"Yes, I guess it is," she said finally.

I like to think she said it a little sadly.

When I reached my apartment, which is about a half mile from the hospital in the direction of downtown Sarasota, I flipped back the bed covers, stripped and hit the pillow. I wanted only to sleep, to sleep for a long time, because when I woke up I'd have to go looking for the Cyclops.

CHAPTER FOUR

Eventually I woke up and rested for three days, which stretched into four. I read a lot, saw the movies I hadn't seen, just loafed in general. And thought about what had been happening on Siesta Key.

My experience didn't mean that the stories about the unicorn, the mermaid and the puppy-eating monster were true, but it sure leant more authenticity to them.

Next question. How could they be true? There are no mermaids. There are no unicorns. There might conceivably be an eight-foot-tall hairy giant, but a Cyclops too? It might still be possible, but it was stretching the limits of the word "possible."

Assume they're real. Where could they have come from? The Cyclops might be from a freak show, but a unicorn and the rest? That again was stretching it just a little bit too far.

So what did that leave? The old faithful—invaders, or tourists, from outer space. Even that had its flaws. I just couldn't see the Cyclops as an invader from outer space. I picture invaders from space as pretty sharp types. The Cyclops was, to put it bluntly, a clod.

No class at all. I couldn't see him traveling in a space ship. I'll admit to being slightly prejudiced against big, ugly, one-eyed giants, but then, who's perfect?

Unless Mrs. Carr and David and Fay and Melanie and Helen and I were all hallucinating on the same wavelength, though, these weirdos were popping up from somewhere. The best bet was from outer space.

Where didn't matter that much right at present, I realized. First I had to lay my hands on one of those oddities and keep it around long enough to establish its existence as hard, cold fact. The kind of fact that courts and hard-headed newspaper editors and scientists will accept.

Of course, the minor fact that establishing the identity of one of these creatures and finding out what was going on at Siesta Key would give me a scoop on what could be one of the biggest news stories to come along in a long time, or ever, didn't give me any qualms.

So what if my coverage of the story brought me a Pulitzer, I daydreamed happily. So what if the Pulitzer, plus the stories, brought me a job on a bigger paper at a vastly increased salary? So what if that meant I could live high and wide and go hunting every night in the choicest coops? Was I going to let a few little things like that affect my zeal to run the story down? Damned right I was.

Five days after my welter-weight workout with the world's heaviest heavy weight I began to check to find out who had recently moved onto the key. I narrowed it down to those persons who'd moved out there within the last month.

After I went back to work I did a little interviewing of these newcomers on my own time. I asked each if they had seen anything out of the ordinary since they'd moved out onto the key.

I explained that so far we had only rumors of strange sightings along the beach and that the newspaper was merely following its policy of checking such stories out. I didn't mention I was checking each of them out to see if their arrival on the island might have something to do with our nocturnal visitors.

Nothing. No bells rang at all. Each interview led to the same blind alley. I didn't even know if I'd recognize the right reaction when I found it. Which, when all the new arrivals had been eliminated, left me with the tiresome prospect of haunting the beaches in the hopes that another spook might pop up out of nowhere.

Before I went that far I decided to double-check. I'd already tried most of the logical sources, so now I tried Ben Warbow. Ben is the clerk of the circuit court, which has its headquarters in the Sarasota County building. Officially he's the clerk, or boss of the records section. Unofficially he's Sarasota's one-man intelligence service.

Nothing has happened in Sarasota since 1951, according to Ben, that isn't known in full detail by our clerk. From the official government actions to which county commissioner had trouble holding his liquor to which sheriff's deputy was playing around behind his wife's back, and with whom.

He was in the courthouse snack bar talking to one of the miniskirted lovelies that throng the courthouse, providing fun and games for lawyers, deputies, newspapermen and any civilians lucky enough to wander in by mistake.

"How's crime?" he asked, laughing at his witticism, as he had the last three thousand times he'd made that particular comment.

"Terrible, Ben. I'm wondering if you might be able to help me out."

"Do anything I can, as long as it doesn't involve money."

"No money. I'm just trying to find out something. You wouldn't know of anyone that's moved out onto Siesta Key in the last month or two?"

"You must be a mind reader, or do you already know about it?"

"Know about what?"

"John Smith is back in town."

"Who is John Smith?"

He grinned.

"You're showing your tender age, son. John Smith was big news in this town for a while back in 1954. You mean to say you've never heard of him?"

"I hate to tread on sensitive ground like this, Ben, but anything before 1970 is ancient history as far as I'm concerned."

"Don't be so smug about it, friend. One of these days you'll look around and find out your hair is gone, or gray, your friends are old men and luscious pieces of tail are calling you sir. It'll be quicker than you think, too."

"Not this early in the morning, Ben, I won't be in any mood for lunch. Now, who is John Smith and why was he big news?"

"John Smith was the man with no name and no past. He swam out of the Gulf a few miles off Lido Beach one day in August, I think, dressed in strange clothes and half drowned. He couldn't speak a word of English or any other language. Spoke some kind of gibberish. They thought it was a foreign language at first, but later decided he was just raving.

"He was like some kind of savage. Didn't know anything about machines, couldn't speak in any language. They were thinking of keeping him out at the mental hospital in Arcadia, but the people that found him wouldn't have any part of it.

"Bill Smith and his wife finally talked the law into letting them keep him at their home on Siesta Key. He learned how to read and write English pretty quickly and they tried to find out who he was and where he came from. He couldn't tell them. He said he only remembered finding himself in the water about a mile off the beach and swimming in. Before that, nothing.

"They checked his fingerprints with the FBI and they had his picture run in a lot of different papers and checked by a lot of police departments across the country, but no luck. No one had ever heard, seen or known this guy before he showed up on the beach."

If there is such a thing as an instinctive recognition that something is vitally important, is a key to a puzzle, I felt it then. I could swear the hair on the back of my neck was standing up.

"What happened to him?"

"That's the interesting part. They never could find out who he was and after the publicity died down he stayed on with the Smiths. He worked in their nursery and lived on Siesta Key for two years. The Smiths were in their late fifties and didn't have any kids so they adopted him.

"Then one day he just disappeared. He left the house one morning on his way to the nursery and that's the last anybody ever saw of him. Smith died about ten years ago and Mrs. Smith two years ago. She left the house to a niece, with the provision that if John Smith ever came back the house was to go to him.

"Well, he came back three weeks ago. Found out what had happened to the Smiths and claimed the house. The niece, who was renting it out, put up a little fuss but they checked his fingerprints and they matched. He wouldn't say where he'd been, or why he left."

"Why didn't you tell me about this, Ben, or tell somebody from the paper?"

"I didn't find out about it myself till today and I was busy. You're the first newspaperman I've run into today."

"I must be living right. Thanks, Ben."

"Hey, what's your hurry?" I heard him call out behind me as I went out through the rear glass doors, but I didn't have the time to answer him. I made it back to the paper, only a half mile away, in five minutes and got into the microfilm in the library.

It took more than an hour, but I found the stories. They were substantially what Ben had told me. In addition there was a photo of John Smith. He was a big guy from the description, about six feet four, and fairly good-looking.

John Harper was interested too.

"It's a natural, Hank. Man shows up out of nowhere twenty-five years ago. It's as if he stepped out of thin air. Then, a couple years later, he vanishes as completely, and to make it even better, the old people who'd treated him like a son never lose faith. They leave their home for him if he ever comes back. And when he does come back, it's too late—they've already died. It's perfect, if he'll talk."

"Can I bring along a thumbscrew, just in case?"

"I almost feel like telling you yes. See what you can get through persuasion first."

It didn't take any more than that to send me out of the newsroom faster than a speeding bullet. (Sorry about that, but I grew up on Clark Kent comics.)

It didn't take any journalistic genius to see what John had been excited about. It was a natural, but it was a lot more than just a humdinger of a human interest story. It didn't require any great brain to see also that Smith's reappearance in Sarasota coincided almost exactly with the rash of strange happenings.

The home was, for Siesta Key, old fashioned and slightly run down. I parked in the dirt driveway and walked to the front door. Behind the house was beach and the nearest home was almost a mile away. It was probably as isolated as anybody could get on this increasingly tight little island.

I knocked and waited. I couldn't quite laugh when I found that my heart was pounding faster than it had any right to. I remembered the Cyclops, but that had been on a dark beach and it was a sunny 2 P.M. now.

The door opened wide enough to reveal only a pair of eyes and a strong nose staring down at me.

"Yes?"

"Mr. Smith, my name is Hank Dell. I'm a reporter for the *Herald Tribune*. I'd like to talk to you, if I could."

"Why?"

I wanted to hear him talk some more. In just those first two words I'd caught something strange. There was an accent, I was sure, but I couldn't identify it.

"I'd like to talk to you about where you've been for the last twenty-five years, Mr. Smith. You must have seen the stories our paper ran when you first appeared in this area. There was a good deal of interest in you. Then you vanished and you reappear here. You've got to admit that's enough to make anyone curious."

He opened the door wide enough for me to see his face. Even though I knew the picture I'd seen was twenty-five years old, it was a shock. He'd lost most of his hair for one thing and there were a lot of wrinkles in the well-tanned face. There was a three-inch scar running from under his right eye down to his chin.

"I'm not going to talk to you," he said calmly. "Why I left is a private matter. I don't have to talk to you about it, or anything else. I'd appreciate it if you don't come out here again."

It wasn't my month. I never could figure out why reporters are not beloved of the many.

"I can't force you to talk to me, Mr. Smith, you know that, but I feel it's only fair to tell you that my editor is interested in this story"—the old editor is an ogre but I'm a nice guy technique—"and we'll print something, if only the fact that you have returned.

"This is such a great story that I'm sure it will be picked up by the wire services. They'll be sending their people down to talk to you and so will the TV people, not to mention a lot of other newspapers.

"Now, I hate to admit this, but there are a lot of pushy, bad-mannered newspaper people. They won't take no for an answer. They'll hang around and bug you until you either go up a wall or give in and give them the story. Why not tell me the story and keep them off your back? It'll have to come out sooner or later, believe me."

He'd looked puzzled for a moment and I could almost see his lips making the words "up a wall." Which brought the interesting thought that he wasn't familiar with the phrase.

"I don't believe that so many people would be interested in my actions, Mr. Dell. I think you are exaggerating to get a story. There's nothing I can tell you."

He was closing the door when I remembered what I was really interested in.

"Mr. Smith, wait."

To help him make his decision I stuck my foot in the door. He pulled it open again.

"What is it now?"

"I'd like to ask you a question about something that has no connection with you personally. It's something you may have seen around here since you came back."

"What?"

"Our newspaper has been receiving reports of strange sightings out here on the key for the last few weeks. I was wondering if you might have noticed anything like that."

"No."

"I'm glad to hear that. I never believed in the rumors. Talk about unicorns and mermaids and flying monsters. It's ridiculous."

He laughed, a second too late. His reactions betrayed him. For just that fraction of a moment he reacted the way a man does when he hears something he didn't expect, but is aware of.

"I don't drink," he said, laughing unconvincingly. "Good-bye," and he closed the door on me.

Harper was disappointed that I hadn't gotten a story, but he said we would do as I'd warned Smith and go with a story on his return. I tried to act disappointed, but my true feelings came out as I hummed at my typewriter.

"What the hell are you so happy about, Dell?" he asked.

"It's just that this is a good story, anyway," I lied. I found it hard to sit still and type out the story knowing what I knew. Of course, the only thing I really knew was that Smith was connected in some way with the strange happenings on Siesta Key.

And the only thing I had to go on for that was what I believed I had read into an expression on his face during a few minutes of conversation. As any defense lawyer could have pointed out, I'm not an expert in expressions.

Still, it gave me a place to start, and that place was named Smith.

To make things even better, as I was typing my phone rang. It was Ben.

"Hank, I thought you'd like to know. A couple of hours ago John Smith called a realtor I know and said he wants to sell the house, quick."

"You're not bucking for my job, are you?"

"I wouldn't have it."

"I'll sleep better tonight knowing that. Thanks."

A few hours after I'd talked to him Smith was trying to sell his house and, I would guess, leave town. The possibility of having his picture run in a lot of papers must really have scared him.

That night I got off at 11 P.M. as usual and drove out to Siesta Key once more. This time I didn't go empty-handed. In the glove compartment was a .38 caliber snub-nosed Police Special I'd picked up a year before when my coverage of a Negro militant's trial for the murder of a policeman in Sarasota had made me temporarily unpopular.

His friends hadn't liked the stories that appeared in the paper, although I thought they were impartial, and when he was sentenced to life imprisonment in the state prison at Raiford his buddies in a para-military group, whose members had their own firing range and practiced karate, had included me on their must-kill list.

I'd picked up the gun and gotten a license, meaning to hold onto it only until the heat died down, but I'd just neglected to get rid of it and I still had the license.

I drove the car to a parking lot of a public beach nearly two miles from Smith's home, parked it and got out. I stopped walking when

I'd gotten within a hundred yards of Smith's house and squatted down. If some late-night lovers or the cops happened to stumble over me I'd have an excuse for being out there.

I had brought a camera and flash attachment with me. If I was discovered I'd simply say I was trying to get some mood shots for the paper. I doubted the cops would check with the paper, but I'd gone out on assignments without the prior knowledge or approval of my editors before and they would back me up if I said I was on legitimate newspaper business.

I squatted on the sand and began to play with the camera. If anyone should come by I might as well pretend to be working.

An hour passed. Nothing. The bay was lovely and—to appropriate an apt phrase—dark and deep, silent except for the rustle of waves hitting the shore and rolling back. There was enough wind to take the sting of the heat off the beach.

I stood up and rotated my head around, back and forth, trying to exercise the stiffness out.

The flames appeared a dozen feet away, dazzling me. My eyes had become accustomed to the darkness. They were multicolored like the ones that had sprung up around the Cyclops. Red and green, blue and yellow and unbelievably beautiful. Again it seemed it was flame crystallized into transparent glass, glowing without heat.

Two figures appeared in the flames. The glow made them dark, manlike shapes. I rubbed my eyes to wipe away the tears, then pulled my .38 out from under my shirt. I centered on the figures, the camera held loosely in my left hand.

As abruptly as they'd appeared, the flames vanished. The switch to a dark beach left me blinded. I stepped back, holding the gun where I thought they'd be and hoping they were at as much of a disadvantage as I was.

My returning vision revealed the two metallic creatures, both standing about my height or a little less. The moonlight glinted off their bodies and off the swords they carried.

The two figures had appeared facing away from me and I'd made no sound. One said something to the other in a language I'd never heard before. The second one, half a head taller, nodded at whatever was said.

The shorter one lifted its sword, gleaming very sharp and dangerous in the moonlight, and pointed at the Smith house. Again the tall one nodded and said something. They started toward the house.

"Hold it right there."

I said the words in a normal tone of voice, but it sounded like they were loud enough to rouse the entire island. There was no immediate hue and cry, though, so I suppose no one heard it—except my two visitors.

They whirled, bringing the three-foot-long swords very quickly and efficiently into what must have been fighting stance.

I saw they were men. The metallic skin was some kind of light armor covering their chests and groins, arms and legs. A helmet covered everything but eyes and nose.

The impressions came quickly because the taller one lunged at me with the sword held high and aimed straight at my chest a second later.

I brought my pistol to the same level instinctively, holding it at arm's length, and pulled back the hammer.

In the last instant before I pulled the trigger and the tip of his sword touched my chest he saw the gun barrel reflecting the moonlight. Somehow he stopped himself, holding the sword in the same position but standing very, very still.

There was no doubt in my mind that he knew what a pistol was and what it could do to a suit of light armor. I let out the breath I'd been holding and backed away, easing up on the trigger.

"Be very careful what you do with that thing," I said softly, gesturing with the gun toward his sword, which was less than two feet away from me. I didn't expect him to understand the language but I thought he got the message.

The short one said something to the guy who'd planned to puncture me. Without replying, my friend with the long reach stepped back to the other, whose sword was held down by his side.

He started to say something, his voice soft and high-pitched. It had a nice ring to it but the words were nonsense.

I examined my two captives in the darkness, suddenly feeling pretty helpless. I mean, I had the gun and the upper hand, but . . .

I was in the same bind I'd been in before they appeared. Unless these specimens had three eyes or some kind of outer-space gimmickry scientists would accept as proof of their extraterrestrial origin, I'd be back where I started.

The police and courts would say I'd nabbed two nuts wandering around in Halloween costumes and speaking gibberish. While they were checking into the incident the cops would get around to asking me what I'd been doing with a .38 caliber pistol on the beach near midnight. My head began to swim with the possibilities. Undoubtedly some of our finer new residents of Siesta Key would come forward to report I'd been quizzing them about unicorns and mermaids and such.

That, with my story of the knights from outer space, would give me a front place in the unemployment line for a long, long time.

I felt like the man who'd grabbed the tiger's tail. I couldn't let go and I sure couldn't hang on much longer.

The short one came closer, gesturing with an empty hand. I moved the gun barrel toward him. I yelled and grabbed my hand as the big one caught it with the flat of his sword, knocking the gun loose. It felt like that blade had broken some fingers.

I tried not to swallow. Because if my adam's apple had done any moving around at all I'd have cut my throat on the finely honed edge of the sword the big man held.

The edge of the blade pressed harder against my throat and I wanted to scream that this was absurd, absurd to die by the sword in the year 1979. It just wasn't done any more.

One word by the short one saved my adam's apple and my head. The pressure of the blade eased and I took in some badly needed oxygen. The one who'd saved my life looked me over like a cattleman inspecting stock before an auction.

He motioned toward the house and the big man stepped behind me, prodding me with the tip of the blade. The bite of steel into my spine made an unanswerable argument for going their way, at least temporarily.

There were no lights in the Smith home. No one had seen or heard anything. If I was going to get myself out of this mess, I'd have to do it with whatever resources I had at my own command. Which, outside of incredible stupidity, didn't seem to be too great.

I stopped and winced as the sword was pushed into my back.

"Now hold it a minute," I said, turning to them and hoping they wouldn't decide to kill me on the spot and leave me out on the sand. I was hoping they had some reason for keeping me more or less healthy. I had the feeling that if they got me into Smith's house I wouldn't be coming out again, so I had to move now.

Since no inspired plan of escape leapt into my mind I settled for what must be the oldest routine in the world.

"Hey, am I glad to see you," I said loudly, gesturing to someone a little to the left and behind the big man. It worked like a charm. He turned to see who I was talking to, swinging the sword away slightly at the same time.

I pushed the sword to one side with my left hand and swung at his unprotected jaw with my right. He went down hard but I felt like I'd hit a brick wall.

The short one, who seemed to be running things, had not yet drawn his sword. When I'd turned and swung he'd hastily moved away and reached for his equalizer. I hit him hard in a modified football tackle—modified to avoid cracking my head on his armor.

He went down under me fighting. As I fell on top of him he gave me two good shots to the ribs with his metal gauntlets. I grunted and tried to pin his arms but he kept pounding me around the back with those gloves.

He tried to pin my arms but I managed to break free and slugged him. With my right hand, naturally. Tears ran down my cheek as I nursed it. Every knuckle must have been broken.

His head lay back on the sand, eyes closed. He was out of it, but his friend was shaking his head and making fighting noises as he got to his feet. I made it back to my pistol, which they'd left where it dropped.

I centered it between the tall one's eyes using my left hand. My ribs hurt where they'd been pounded and all of a sudden I had to go to the men's room very badly. I assumed the short fellow had given my kidneys a good workout while he was pounding my back.

I'd been so scared before that I was seriously afraid I'd make a very messy situation of my underclothes. Now I was mad. My back hurt, my ribs hurt, my hand hurt, my cheekbone—which had largely healed—was throbbing and the scar where the doctors had sewn up the gash burned.

I hurt just about all over and it had been these weirdos, and their friends, who'd been giving me lumps for more than a week. I seriously considered taking the time to repay them, with interest.

I changed my mind. All I wanted to do was get them away from Smith's house and into the clutches of the law before anything else happened. I made myself believe there were enough witnesses to the strange goings-on around here to convince the law I hadn't gone around the bend, and I did have two prisoners.

I motioned to the tall man, who'd been rubbing the back of his neck, to pick up his friend. He took one look at the still form of the second man, then grabbed his sword off the sand and came at me.

I pulled the hammer back again but I could see in his eyes that he didn't care if I killed him or not, as long as he took me with him, and I couldn't speak to him to tell him his friend was alive.

"Rellim."

The word was so faint I wasn't sure I'd really heard it, but it stopped him in his tracks, and for the second time in those few minutes I pulled a trembling finger away from the trigger. (The most excitement I usually get is dodging elderly motorists on the Sarasota streets.)

Rellim, if that was his name, ran to the fallen man's side, kneeling down beside him. He placed one hand under the other's head and helped him to a sitting position. They talked quickly. The big one was angry and glared at me, but the other shook his head at his words.

I motioned for them both to get to their feet. After a moment they did, Rellim helping his friend to his feet.

"Come on, move," I said, gesturing.

They started walking in front of me down the beach. They hadn't taken a dozen steps when they lit up.

Blue and green and orange licked and twisted, curled in the air like cigarette fumes, a rainbow flaring in the night. The short one laughed, musical triumphant laughter. That did it.

After handing me those lumps they weren't going to get away scot-free. I dived through the flames, freezing and burning at the same time, and hit him high, taking him down outside the flames.

He fought like a wild man underneath me, managing to knock me off him and reach his knees, but it was too late. Even as he did the flames blinked out and his companion was gone.

He turned toward me and met another fist and down he went. Undoubtedly had a glass jaw. I expected the police at any minute because the roar I let out as I connected with my right hand should have smashed windows miles away in Sarasota.

After I'd moaned a little bit I took a look at my piece of proof. I lifted his head and pulled the helmet off.

And felt very proud of my courage and skill in putting her down.

Long blond hair that had been concealed by the helmet cascaded out. The mouth, bleeding as it was, was made more for good times than giving orders or fighting.

Still no lights in the Smith home. I was certain now he wasn't in. I doubted that any of his neighbors, as far away as they were, had reported anything to the police, but there was no point in hanging around.

Even with the armor, which was surprisingly light, she didn't weigh that much. I hoisted her over my shoulder, retrieved my gun and put it into my belt. I picked up the camera and headed back to my VW.

I put her in my car, armor and all. Before I turned the ignition on I put my hand on her cheek, her head lying on my shoulder.

I shook her gently, hoping I'd get some reaction. She hadn't moved in a long time and she was beginning to worry me. The skin was very, very soft and I found myself tracing the line of her lower lip. It was a necessary task all right, taking in an alien invader, but there was no reason why I shouldn't enjoy my work.

She opened her eyes, looked at me, and said weakly but clearly, "Keep your grubby hands to yourself."

CHAPTER FIVE

My jaw dropped about a foot.

"You speak . . ."

She looked around wildly at me and the interior of the bug, then grabbed at the door handle. If she hadn't tried to pull the lever up instead of out she might have gotten out of the car, she moved that fast.

I got my arms around her and she commenced pounding on me again.

"Stop it," I yelled into her ear, "or I'll let you have it again."

I was almost ready to swing on her when she calmed down and said, "Get your hands off me, you dirty s.o.b."

Somehow, that just didn't seem right coming from her. I let her go, warily.

"Don't try that again. I don't want to have to knock you unconscious, but if you even look the wrong way I will."

She didn't say anything to that, only moving as far away from me as it was possible to sit and still be in the car. I have seen looks of contempt and looks of contempt, but this female had the original patent. I felt like crawling under a rock.

"Now, who are you?"

I was still going to take her to the police station, but since she spoke English there was no reason why I shouldn't satisfy my own curiosity first. There was no answer to my question. She rubbed her jaw and then her eyes widened. She looked around at the interior of the bug.

"Is this an automobile?"

"None other. Haven't you ever seen one before?"

"No, in Ellendon . . ."

Then she gave me a look that for hostility far outclassed any previous and said, "No more. I'll save my words for the animal whose boots you lick, that traitor Krell. Take me to him and I'll spit in his face. Dalien will never surrender to him, though I be tortured in a thousand ways."

I had gotten lost on the roller coaster of curves she had just thrown me. Krell? Dalien? Torture? Somewhere along the way I'd missed a turn in the tunnel.

"Krell?"

"Yes, that damned scheming, two-timing, double-crossing, black-hearted monster. Your master. Dear old uncle Krell."

"I think you've got me mixed up with somebody else, lady. I don't know what you're talking about."

"You don't know?"

It had started out as a contemptuous comment on my lack of talent for lying and ended up a question.

"No."

"You don't serve Krell?"

"I've never heard of anybody named Krell."

"And you weren't out there to protect him?"

I just shook my head, not bothering to explain that I would hardly be protecting somebody I didn't know existed.

"Then why were you out there, where I sensed the presence of the Ring, and why did you threaten us with your weapon?"

"Look, I don't have to explain what I was doing out there. You have to explain to me, and the cops, what *you* were doing out there."

She looked really frightened for the first time.

"No, you mustn't. I can't be questioned by your police."

"I'm afraid you're going to be. I can't just let you walk away, not now."

She looked at me differently now.

"You don't serve Krell? Then let me talk to you first. That's all I ask. Later, if you want, you can take me to the police."

I had to think about that one. I couldn't trust her. What good was a promise from her if she really was an invader? She would lie and escape the first chance she had. On the other hand, where could she escape wearing a suit of armor?

In addition, I had begun to feel sorry for her. Part of it, of course, was the fact that she was a good-looking girl. She was that special kind you want to protect from all the bad things that could possibly hurt her.

She must have been pretty frightened when she found herself alone, captured on a strange planet. Yet she hadn't shown it. She had courage.

Besides, if I took her with me I'd have to keep an eye on her continuously, which wouldn't be too hard to take.

So instead of saving the world, I took her home.

My lodgings consist of a bedroom, kitchenette and bathroom—together about the size of a living room, one of seven in a little motel. I parked the car outside my door and got out, avoiding using my right hand.

I opened the car door for my alien, who seemed to expect it, and unlocked the apartment door. I hoped no one was up to see me bringing a girl in armor into my room. Ordinary amorous adventures don't ruffle the feathers of the management, but a girl in armor? They might begin to wonder what kind of kinky tenant they had.

Inside I locked the door behind me and went into the bathroom to run some water over my right hand. I let out a yelp as the cold water hit the skin. I held my wrist gently and managed to stagger away from the sink. I bumped into the girl in the metal Maidenform.

She looked at my hand and said, "Let me have it."

"No, I need a doctor. I probably won't be able to use it for a week."

"Perhaps, but let me see it for a moment anyway."

She held it lightly on her upturned palm, then she brushed the knuckles with her fingers, so lightly I almost couldn't feel them.

She closed her eyes and began to hum a wordless tune. She swayed slowly back and forth, never losing her light but effective hold on my hand. Then she opened her eyes and looked down.

"Flex your fingers."

The first time tears came into my eyes. The second time it hurt less and a half-dozen tries later there wasn't any pain.

I looked at my hand as if I'd never seen it before.

"How did you do that?"

"It's a gift. It is a small one, but sometimes it can be useful."

I examined her while I rubbed the knuckles that now might never have felt pain. Beautiful face only one step away from plainness. Change some small something and she wouldn't have been the beauty she was, but for the life of me, I couldn't have told you what to change.

It was the kind of face that two men can look at and one will see only a plain girl. Another person might look at her and see beauty. I saw beauty.

So it was even stranger what she had done. I wondered what kind of technology she had used, could have used, to perform that little trick. As advanced as we are, a little stunt like that just isn't in the cards, not without drugs and equipment, and she had done it with a song.

If she could do something like that, what was there to stop her from zapping me with the latest model death ray? Suddenly it seemed like the odds were absurdly against one of us—me.

"You're probably hot in that armor," I said, the perfect host always. I was wondering what was under the armor, and hoping.

"Yes," she said and proceeded to strip the armor off. It came off easily, with enough economy of movement to indicate she had done it many times before.

Underneath she wore only a green pant-suit arrangement. No zipper, only a knot at the middle of a belt. Untie that and there would be no more mystery about my alien at all.

She was no sex symbol. There was nothing jutting out of the green costume to indicate a really stacked body, but the way it clung to her indicated that what she had was nice.

"What is it?" she asked curiously and I realized I'd been staring. It came to me this wasn't simply a good-looking girl in my apartment in the early morning hours for a good time, and I just wasn't as gung ho to save the world as I had been.

"Nothing. Have a seat and tell me who and what you are."

She sat down and took a deep breath.

"I thought at first this might be some plan of Krell's to worm information out of me, but he would not be so elaborate. It's—all this is exactly as Iverson said it was. The cars and the buildings. Before I tell you who I am, please tell me who you are."

I hadn't followed any of that but I didn't resent her turning the tables on me, mainly because I wasn't frightened any more. Appearing in a circle of rainbow flames, wearing armor and carrying a sword, she was an alien. Now she was just a girl.

"I'm a reporter. I work for the *Herald Tribune*."

She nodded in recognition of the word, saying, "Iverson spoke of you."

She thought for a moment, then said, "You are like heralds, right?"

Right about then everything seemed to come apart. What was a space traveler doing wearing armor, carrying a sword and talking about heralds?

"Now I understand what you are, but I still don't know what you were doing out on the beach with a weapon near Krell's house."

I was beginning to get a headache from the conversational runaround so I got up and asked her, "Would you like something to drink? I know I would."

"Such as what?"

"How does scotch on the rocks sound?"

"Scotch? Iverson spoke of it warmly. Yes, I'd like some."

I was getting very curious about who Iverson was. I poured her a fairly tall glass of scotch over some ice, poured one for myself and sat back down.

"To answer your question—and what's your name, anyway?—I was sitting out on the beach waiting for you."

"I am Syana, Princess of Ellendon."

She had put the scotch away in two gulps, now wiped her lips daintily and said, "It's good, but a trifle weak. Have you anything stronger?"

"I'm afraid not."

"Oh well, I'll have another, then."

While I refilled her glass she said, "How did you know I was going to arrive? Your people do not even know that Ellendon exists, from what Iverson says."

"Look, sugar, let me answer this last question and then you give me your story, right? Otherwise we may be here all night and I still won't know what's going on."

I explained for about a half hour how I'd been sucked into the strange happenings on the beach. She listened carefully, nodding her head slowly when I finished.

"Yes, it fits. The unicorn and mermaid must have been brought through by accident. Perhaps the Chorbal and the giant were, too, though I think they may have been agents of the Hann, searching for Krell also."

She saw the expression on my face and said, "I know this will be difficult for you to believe, because all this is new to you and Iverson said our land was strange beyond belief to your people, but I will try to explain.

"The man you know as John Smith is named Krell, and my uncle. He is an exile from my land, which lies behind a magical veil from your own."

"A magical veil?" I couldn't keep quiet any longer. "Come on, lady, give us stupid earthlings credit for a few brains."

"I know of no other way to describe it. One minute I was in Ellendon and the next the rainbow flames surrounded me and I was in your land. Our two lands must be very close, but there is something that prevents them from meeting."

Dimensional travel. An old concept. One world is separated from another by a turn in the stairway of infinity. Find a way to punch a hole through the veil and you reach the other side. It had been old in science fiction long before I was born, but this girl was saying it was real.

"My land is a simple one, and beautiful. We have nothing such as I saw traveling here, the buildings and the strange lights without any fire to cast them or your automobiles. My home is so large a man on horseback could ride ten days without crossing from one end to the other.

"There are other lands outside Ellendon, but I know little of them, for they are blocked by fire from the ground and high mountains, and on the north by an ocean that has no end. So we have only Ellendon, but it is enough.

"My uncle Krell was the Chancellor. My father, King Bytus VII, died when my brother and I were scarcely into our teens and it was decided Ellendon needed an older man to guide the affairs of state, so the Council chose Krell.

"He was invested with the two symbols of authority of Ellendon, the Wanderer's Ring and the Sword of the Gates, given to our ancestors by the Lords of Ellendon at the Beginning. Krell ruled for five years. In that time he lived well and he ruled harshly, but he was the Chancellor and he did not rule harshly enough to raise the people against him."

I was shooting suspicious glances at the bottle of scotch. Was the world getting drunk, or was it just me?

"Then, no more than a year ago, the troubles began. There have always been bands of robbers in the western part of Ellendon, where few people and many strange things live, but they began to range out of the west in greater and greater numbers until finally the King's army had to be called up.

"The bandits were beaten and forced to flee back into the wilderness, but we learned there was a reason for their sudden restlessness. They had been whipped into a rag-tag army by Suldurus, a wanderer from the Hann.

"There are legends that thousands of years ago the two lands were one and that they were split by the First Great King of Ellendon, Dorian, wielding the Wanderer's Ring and the Sword of the Gates. Legend says that for a short time every five hundred years afterward the two worlds draw close together again.

"Each time a King of Ellendon has wielded the Ring and the Sword, which must be used to re-create the wall between Hann and Ellendon. The Hann, larger and fiercer than any man, have fought every time to conquer Ellendon, but they have always been beaten back."

I sat there knocking away the scotch while she matched me two for one and hadn't begun to show the slightest effects yet. I had the strangest feeling I'd wandered into the *Lord of the Rings* and that at any minute a tall, elderly man with a flowing white beard would open the door and ask, "Pardon me, but has anyone around here seen Frodo?"

I couldn't really buy what I was hearing, not yet, and yet I knew that what I'd experienced the last couple of weeks was real. And that meant that all my ideas of what was real were cockeyed, that there were princesses in high castles, mermaids, monsters, ogres and heroes.

"We believed Krell would lead our people into battle against the Hann, but he hesitated and made excuses for not calling the soldiers up, not planning for the battle that would come.

was really no room left in this world for heroes. So, who could say that I didn't have the qualities of hero-dom.

I asked the inevitable question heroes always ask in such situations.

"And if the Hann overrun your world?"

She stared moodily into her half-empty glass and said, "I don't know. They will grind us into the dirt and then cast their eyes on other worlds, but they will not cast their eyes on your earth."

That threw me momentarily. I couldn't think why they wouldn't want to invade rich, opulent, fat earth—the lean and hungry savage syndrome. It was beloved of conservative politicians two decades ago when you couldn't open a magazine without finding an article comparing the West to a rich, fat and decadent Rome and the Russians with the lean and hungry barbarians who overran it.

"Why not, aren't we good enough for them?"

"They wouldn't be so foolish as to try to attack your earth. Even the Hann would be no match for the savage inhabitants of your world."

"The savage inhabitants?"

"The name of earth is known on Ellendon, and from the few travelers we have received from other worlds, there, too. On every world the warriors of earth are known and feared.

"We have legends of the warriors who came across five hundred years ago, short stunted men who rode ponies and swept across the land like fire, destroying what they did not rape. Five hundred years before devils in armor, from whom we designed ours, nearly defeated the armies of Ellendon, though the earthmen were few in number.

"There are other legends of the men who came before them. Then Iverson told us of your guns and planes and things so horrible it is difficult to think of them. There is no world that would dare to molest your earth."

Thinking nonheroically for a moment, I realized the truth of her statements. The Roman legions, the Greek mercenaries, medieval knights or Huns would have been mean and tough bastards no matter what kind of enemies they went up against, human or not.

What kind of magic could Ellendon, or Hann, wield that could match the bomb, or germ warfare, or poison gas, or the machine gun, or the intercontinental ballistic missile?

How would the Hann do if they ran up against the Russian Army, or the Chinese, or, for that matter, the North Koreans?

"That's why I didn't speak English when I was first surprised by you out on the beach," she said. "If you had been someone of authority it would have been better to pretend to be insane than to let your world know of Ellendon's existence. Iverson has told us of what happened to the people of your own world who were not as advanced in warfare."

Iverson was smart, and he had the right idea. With the utmost confidence in my government and people, I wouldn't like to witness what would happen if we ran into a primitive culture. There are too many examples already on record.

"But your world will get racked, huh?"

She nodded. I thought about what she had told me and I remembered growing up during the Tolkien craze. I had read *Lord of the Rings* when I was just coming into my teens and it had left an indelible mark on me.

Life would be better in Middle Earth. It would be better where there were monsters to be racked up, princesses to be fought for and where a man's friends would stand by him to the pit of hell.

I was drunk. When I get very drunk I get depressed at the meaninglessness of life, followed shortly thereafter by unconsciousness. Before I get to that state I get the Godlike feeling I can do anything, I can break the chains that life and the past have forged around me.

The only thing is that I always wake up with a miserable head and the knowledge that the chains are still there, as strong and unbroken as ever. But now, now there was a way to break them. There was a way to really break the hell out of them. I looked at the pretty girl dressed in green and I could have cried with happiness.

"Princess, would one slightly hung-over knight come in handy right now?"

There was a new expression on her face as she said, "Do you mean . . ."

"I sure do, sugar. Lead on and we'll catch Krell by surprise, snatch back your Ring and Sword, go back to Ellendon, save the kingdom and live happily ever after."

She stood up slowly as I approached her.

"Why? You have no ties to Ellendon. It will be dangerous and I have no right to ask you."

"Oh, I'm not doing it for free," I said and pulled her toward me. She might have fought back but a moment's hesitation cost her the impetus and by then it was too late. I let her go a little bit later and idly wondered if I was going to get my face slapped.

"I owe you now," I said, grinning foolishly.

"No one has ever done that before," she said slowly and neutrally, rubbing her lower lip with one slim finger.

"Kissed you? Come on, Princess, Ellendon can't be that different."

"No, I have been kissed but never by a commoner and never without my permission."

"There's always a first time, Your Highness, and besides, I'm a perfect beast when I'm drunk."

She didn't say anything to that and I didn't waste any time worrying about it. Instead I walked to my drawer, pulled out six bullets and dropped them in my pocket.

"You can take your sword along," I told her, "but leave the armor here. With me holding this," I said, flourishing the .38, "I doubt Krell will put up too much of a fight anyway."

I was feeling very Errol Flynn-ish at the moment. The Princess gave me a funny look as I swayed, ever so slightly, walking to the door.

"Are you sure we should start out now?" she asked, looking at me more than a little critically.

"Yes, sugar. If I stop to think about this quest logically and wait until I sober up we may never go anywhere except to a police station."

That decided her. She picked up her sword and followed me out the door. As I was locking the door the thought occurred to me that maybe I should be taking some underwear or clean socks with me.

"Can't go off to the wars without clean socks," I murmured to myself. My joke was so funny it broke me up completely and I bent over laughing until I gasped for breath.

Syana was waiting for me at the door of my Volks, a lady in Sherwood Green carrying a King Arthur-ish sword, getting ready to go off in a green bug to combat the villain. That sent me into another paroxysm of laughter.

I finally got myself under control and we took off for Krell's place.

I had a spell of comparative lucidity as we drove over the bridge to Siesta Key. It was as common and prosaic by night as it had ever been. In the distance I could see the lights of Sarasota, like the decorations on a huge Christmas tree, gleaming across the water.

The thought that stopped my reverie was the question of whether they had electric lights in Ellendon. Of course not, I answered myself. That made me sad.

There is something incredibly beautiful about city lights at night, about any kind of electric lights. A line of poetry from a song popular late in the sixties came to my mind:

"The city lights, the pretty lights, they can warm the coldest nights . . ."

Would Ellendon have TV or space probes or newspaper comics or paperbacks or instant coffee? Would it have discotheques or nude go-go girls, pop music, Novocaine or dentists?

The answer to all the questions would be no. Most of all, they wouldn't have any room for a guy who gets his kicks writing about events, not living them. There was plenty of room in Ellendon for heroes, none for newspapermen.

It even occurred to me, thinking harder about it, that at its best I would get tired of being a hero all the time. I mean, once a month or every other year, that would be all right, but all the time? It could very easily get to be a grind.

I had gone too far to back out, though. I was driving a good-looking princess to whom I was already one kiss in debt. I had a .38 in my pocket and I was prepared to join this girl in green in her crazy dream about some mythical world beyond the "veil."

The thing that kept me from dismissing the whole ridiculous nonsense as ridiculous nonsense was the fact that there was no other halfway decent explanation for the strange things that had happened.

Maybe, just maybe, when I got her and Krell back to their own world I could forget about Ellendon. I could go back to brooding behind the safety of my typewriter about the condition of the world and life and get drunk regularly.

Suddenly I didn't feel too heroic.

CHAPTER SIX

There were no lights in the Smith-Krell home when I pulled up off the road a short distance away. No sense in driving right into his driveway and letting him know he had visitors.

"Think he's barhopping?" I asked, as much to relieve my own mood of gloom as anything else.

"He is inside," she said, in a tone that indicated she wasn't guessing.

"How—"

"I just know. I can feel it."

"If you say so."

I got out of the car swaying pretty badly. The drive had sobered up my thinking, but my body was beginning to play tricks on me.

A thought stopped me for a moment. What if something went wrong, for example Krell calling the police if we woke him up entering, and we needed to get out of there quickly? Knowing myself, I knew it would be safer to leave my keys in the car, so if we had to make a run for it all I'd have to do would be switch on the ignition. At this time of night no one was going to come along and steal it. I opened the car door and put the keys inside.

"Should we knock?"

"No," she said, either not getting or appreciating the humor. "He will awake and become aware of us. There is no telling what he may do. Look for another way in—possibly through a window."

"Jesus, and me a crime reporter."

The house didn't have one of the newer automatic alarms, I hoped. I found a rear bathroom window, the bottom of the pane at bellybutton level. I took the .38 out and, wrapping it in my shirt, which I'd taken off, gently smashed in the bottom pane of the window. When the hole was large enough I reached in carefully, not wanting to sever any important, or even unimportant, veins on the broken glass, and turned the latch on the old-fashioned window.

The window opened inward. I put my shirt back on, grasped the window sill and pulled myself in. I hoped Krell was a sound sleeper —the window maneuver was a little louder than I'd anticipated and I didn't show any great promise in the burglary profession.

When I helped Syana in she moved to the middle of the bathroom.

"This way," she said, pointing at the closed door. I bit back with great effort the comment that this must be some wonderful sixth sense she had that told her we had to get out of the bathroom to get at Krell.

She opened the door carefully, tiptoed out into a hallway and followed it to the left. She stopped in front of another closed door.

"In here," she whispered.

I found the time to wonder why Krell had been so negligent about alarms or traps to keep intruders out, since he'd been here long enough to set up something like that. For a traitor who was sure to know that two very hostile groups were looking for him, he was playing it very cool and careless.

I held the gun in my right hand and gingerly opened the door with my left. The creak it made was as loud as a block of granite hitting the floor in the dead silence, but there were no sounds of reaction to it from inside the room.

I held my breath as I pushed the door in, hoping against hope it wouldn't make any more noise. Sure enough, the miserable door squeaked very, very audibly as it swung inward.

There was almost no moonlight in the room. Curtains blocked the light from the big windows beside the bed, where something lay, but I couldn't quite make out what. My imagination was getting very hairy about then. I stepped into the room, staying very close to the wall, and found the light switch with my left hand.

Syana stepped into the room behind me, holding the sword out. It seemed to gleam faintly, which was a little unnerving, as there wasn't anything in the room to cast the light it reflected.

"Here goes nothing," I said softly into Syana's ear, breathing in the sweet smell of her hair, and switched on the light.

Smith was sitting up in bed looking at us.

He recognized Syana first, glancing at the slim sword pointed in his direction. Then he glanced at me and a second later he had tabbed me.

I had the .38 pointed straight at him, trigger pulled back. I don't know why, but he looked menacing lying in bed, naked to the waist. Without his clothes you could see a lot of impressive muscles. His hands, above the blanket, were lying empty at his sides.

"Don't make any sudden moves, Krell," I said, marveling that my voice was as steady as it was. "I assume you recognize what I've got in my hand and you know what it can do."

"Oh, I know very well," he said calmly, "and I shall be very careful not to make any sudden moves."

The three of us stood there for a moment, looking at each other. I began to wonder, what now?

"I've come to take you back," Syana said. "For what you've done they will execute you in public . . . slowly, Uncle."

Krell almost smiled at that and there was a twinkle in his eye when he answered her. "You'd let them kill your poor old uncle? You're a very disappointing niece, Syana."

"Because of what you've done many men have already died. And many more will."

Krell didn't answer that. Instead, he said to me, "I knew you were not what you seemed, but I couldn't figure out what could tie you to Ellendon. Why are you with her?"

Syana spoke before I could answer.

"He is a newspaperman, as he told you, but now he knows who and what you are. And he will help me take you back to Ellendon."

"You will?" he asked me. "Why? Ellendon is nothing to you, and you cannot know the true story of why I am here in exile from my home. Perhaps she has told you that I am some sort of villain, but how can you be sure? For all you know, she may be the traitor to Ellendon, her and her brother and Iverson, trying to steal the throne from the rightful ruler, myself. You are a stranger, an outsider, and you have no part in this."

"Lying won't help you, Uncle," Syana said. "He knows the truth, as I do."

I was beginning to feel queasy at a particularly inappropriate time. When saving worlds you do not throw up all over yourself. It just isn't done. Not in your better circles anyway. I put one hand out to the wall to steady myself.

Even more disturbing, Krell's words made sense. I had no way to check Syana's story. What if she was the villain of the story and Krell the good guy in exile?

The only things I had to go on were her words, the fact that she was a good-looking girl and that I was pleasantly drunk while she gave me her story.

I began to see why hero-ing is such a difficult business.

"Why?"

There was a new tone in her voice as she asked the simple question, and I remembered that she must have grown up with this man lying in bed. He must have tossed her on his knee, or whatever they do in Ellendon, when she was a child. He was her uncle, and she would have to take him back for execution.

The smile vanished from Krell's face and I almost pulled the trigger, feeling that I'd gotten locked into a cage with an animal poised to spring.

"You wouldn't understand, girl. You wouldn't know what it's like to go through life wiping the nose of your dear brother, who sat on the throne only by an accident of fate. Or finally to grab what you've wanted all your life only to see some young idiot casually take it away from you without trying. To know you'd spend the rest of your life as you had the first, as a servant, a work horse with a title and nothing else.

"No, I deserved to be King. And if I can't be, I'll be just as happy to see no one sitting on the throne."

There was no expression on Syana's face now, and her words were steel.

"Where are the Ring and Sword?"

He smiled and said, "Do you really think I would give them to you?"

"If you don't give them to us willingly, we will kill you and find them ourselves."

This didn't seem to shake him up too badly.

"You might have a problem finding the Sword. Along the way it got misplaced and I really don't know where it is myself. That's a pity, because if I had it we wouldn't have had all the visitors from Ellendon that aroused Mr. Dell's curiosity. But the Ring—that is easy enough to find."

He turned over his left hand, which had been palm down on the bed, and I saw the Ring for the first time. My first impression was that it was a loop, a figure eight formed of some glowing silver metal about two inches long and an inch wide. As I looked at it closer, it seemed to be twisting, moving, almost flowing.

The longer I stared at it the more I got the impression that it was alive in some strange way, like living quicksilver; it was more than a simple three-dimensional ring. The flow of the metal seemed to be going somewhere, but it hurt my eyes to try to follow it.

The more I looked, the dizzier I got. I tore my eyes away from it with an effort and looked back at Krell.

Suddenly Syana was on fire, weird blue-green-yellow-red flames licking at her skin, up her back, along the long blond hair hanging down over her shoulders. I looked out through a maze of colors I couldn't touch as the flames raged around me.

"Tell Iverson when you see him that I am enjoying the earth, and that I will think of you all often as I live out my life here and you writhe under the heel of the Hann," Krell said with a big smile.

"Shoot him," Syana said, pointing at Krell.

My mind seemed to be rolling along in slow motion, and I couldn't figure why she wanted me to kill her uncle. I had never killed a man in my life, and I wasn't going to start. Guns make ugly holes in the human body. Even in pictures, I don't like the results.

"No need to get violent," I said. "He can't put up too much of a struggle with his bare hands."

"You fool," she said, and lunged toward the bed faster than I would have believed possible.

She vanished and I knew I had blown it. I had had one big chance to be a world saver, a world shaker, to be a subject for statues and for children to try to emulate, and I had thrown it away because I didn't like to see human bodies punctured by sharp and fast-moving objects.

As I raised the gun in my hand, the unfairness of it all hit me. This really wasn't my fight. This was for the storybooks, for writers of epic fantasy. What the hell was I doing in the middle?

My stomach flip-flopped and I hit the grass rolling. When I stopped rolling I lifted myself up onto one elbow and looked up at the world. It was raining, a soft summer rain. Cool drops pelted down on me. The grass was wet and my clothes were damp where I had rolled in it.

It must have been early morning, about 7 A.M. That kind of daylight. The air was fresh, clean and had the smell of something sweet like apples or oranges, only neither was it.

It was the kind of impossibly beautiful day that frustrated city dwellers dream about having when they become gentlemen farmers and move to the country.

Raindrops trickled down my hair, over my cheekbones, down over my lips and chin, running down my neck. I licked my lips, tasting the cool, clean water.

"No, man, no way. No way. No way."

If I said it long enough I'd begin to believe it. I was still in Sarasota. Undoubtedly I was asleep now, in my bed, covers down around my toes, twisting and tossing and turning. It was probably early morning.

Outside my room, down the block, the cars were racing down U.S. 41. The coffee shop down the street was open, the waitresses bringing steaming hot cups of coffee to the workers out for an early morning break. The tourists were already out on Siesta Key and the Lido beaches, broiling their flesh.

I closed my eyes tightly. Any moment now, any second, something would wake me up and I'd find myself in bed. I'd yawn and stretch and yawn again, rub my eyes and stumble to the bathroom and dowse my face with cold water.

Then I'd remember the strange dream I'd had, and I'd smile. I'd smile and say to myself, "You should have stayed there, Hank. You always wanted to be a hero." But I'd know there was really no way to make it to that land of dreams.

I sank my fingers deep into the ground, feeling the dirt beneath the grass. Then I snapped my eyes open, water running in them as I staggered to my feet. I was wet, sick to my stomach, and definitely awake.

Syana sat slumped against a tree trunk a dozen yards away. Her head lay in her arms, her sword lying on the ground beside her. When she looked up there were tears in her eyes but there was no softness in her voice.

"You've killed Ellendon, you know that? There's no way, now."

The hell of it was, she was right. I tried to meet her level, unflinching gaze for a moment, then dropped my eyes. There's nothing in the world more terrible than being despised by somebody, and knowing they have every right to feel that way.

"I'm sorry, Princess. It's just—I've never really hurt anybody, much less killed someone. I just couldn't."

There was more silence, until I thought about something she'd said before.

"Princess. You told me that the first time Krell came to earth your —your Talented Ones, or something, found him and brought him back. Couldn't they do that again?"

She answered without looking up.

"That was different. When a person is caught and sent to another world by accident there is a—a wrongness. It is fairly easy to bring them back because that is the way things should be. But Krell left using the power of the Ring and the Sword.

"Besides, the countryside is full of roaming bandits, looters. They are aware that the army is being brought together and so they strike wherever the army has been removed. We don't have the time, or the men, to launch an expedition of the size that would be needed to find Krell again."

"What was that?"

She didn't answer. There was a faraway look in her eyes. She shook herself and gave a little shudder.

"A Chorbal."

The name didn't ring a bell for a fraction of a second and then I remembered Melanie. How had she described it? A monkey's face with fangs and ten feet tall.

The pistol suddenly felt light as a summer breeze in my hand as I swung it up toward the treetops. In my innermost depths, I'd been a skeptic before, telling myself there had to be a rational explanation for all this. But that growl had made me a believer.

Syana laid a soft hand on my wrist and tugged the pistol downward.

"No. The Chorbal is probably scouting for a bandit troop. One shot and we would have no chance of escaping from here."

I looked up at the leafy canopy over our heads, thankful for the first time for the cover it provided.

"It can't fly in here, can it? The branches, and all, I mean?"

She nodded.

"Right. It is too big to maneuver in here, but it is patrolling the sky over this area. There are several open spaces we will have to cross before we leave the mountains."

Though the air was warm, I suddenly felt cold all over, and the familiar cramps began to knot my intestines. This was no game, no game at all.

"Let's go," I said without thinking. Syana looked at me strangely, then took off ahead of me. She didn't chop as freely at the vines and creepers now. Instead, she tried to push them to one side to avoid making as much noise. Behind her I pushed the thorn-studded creepers to one side with my hands and cussed a lot under my breath.

From time to time I'd hear the weird, guttural growls coming from above the treetops. There was nothing to see, only the dim sunlight filtering through the treetops.

With no advance warning I found myself standing almost on top of Syana at the edge of another clearing. To one side of us the trees grew so thickly together and the vines formed such a formidable mesh that there was no way we could have cut our way through them. To the other side was a rocky wall.

I realized then we must have landed on the side of a mountain.

A mountain with a very gradual incline, but a mountain neverthe-
less. We must have been climbing down gradually.

There was an open meadow a hundred yards across. On the other
side were more of the sparsely spaced-out trees. The meadow
looked like a lithograph of a pastoral American setting, with wild
flowers below and lazy summer sun overhead. Things that looked
like bees were buzzing among the yellow, blue and red flowers.

"Through?"

"Through."

I made a feeble joke.

"After you."

She didn't laugh.

"We go together, and try not to trip on the way over."

We came bounding out of the semi-lit forest primeval into the
bright, sunny day. Despite my hunger and exhaustion, I almost felt
good. I've always liked running and it was like being a school kid
again, out for a summer vacation, racing through a lazy day that
would never end.

Two thirds of the way across I heard that ungodly growl and
turned my head to look back, tripped and fell.

To this day I'll swear there was a stick or stone or something there,
but basically my feet are my worst enemies.

I was lying on my elbow looking up at a nightmare, maybe fifty
feet above me, coming down like a bullet. Huge, impossibly long
wings, great gnarled talons and fangs. And that face. God, what
Hollywood would have given for a plaster mold of that.

Cross the worst features of an eagle and a Hollywood version of
a killer ape, beady eyes and all, and you've got the Chorbal. You
can keep it.

Syana was bending down beside me, grabbing my arm and pulling me up.

"Come on, run."

Even as I jumped to my feet I knew it was too late. We'd never
make it. I shook her arm off and raised the pistol in the direction
of the Chorbal.

She hit my arm, knocking it wide, and shoved me. Off balance,
I went down again. I looked up to see her swing the sword in an
arc over her head at the Chorbal's talons.

It moved so fast I couldn't follow it with my eyes. It swooped over Syana and behind her, skimming above the ground and coming back for a second try.

I was up on my feet but not fast enough. She swung the sword at it again and got nothing but a few feathers. The impact of one of those ten-foot-long wings, however, sent her to the ground, still clutching her sword.

It came back at her as she sat up. She raised the sword but it was knocked from her grasp by a furious heave of another wing. The Chorbal pinned her wrist to the ground with a talon that was easily a foot wide. I lost sight of her as the Chorbal's body blocked my view.

I fired three shots into the creature's back from ten feet away. It screamed so loud it could have been heard ten miles away, and fell away from her. It turned and I saw the blood on its furred chest.

It made two staggering steps toward me and I fired in the direction of its face, without aiming especially.

The bullet turned the face to a bloody mess. The Chorbal fell backward and lay on the ground twitching.

Syana was on her knees and gave me a murderous look. Her wrist was bloody. I reached for it, but she pulled away from me.

"Hank Dell, I think you are working for Krell. Now we have to get out of here. The others will be coming."

I picked up her sword and handed it back to her. Not a word about my saving her life, but I didn't expect thanks at this point. I was beginning to think that Jonah was a good luck charm compared to me.

I gave the Chorbal one last glance before following Syana into the forest. Its great talons were still twitching spasmodically. I wondered if this was the one that had eaten Crawford. Probably not. It would have been too much of a coincidence.

Still, this was the area where the barrier had been breaking down, and it might have been the same one. I hoped it was, for a little girl I'd made a promise to.

Now it was a frantic, almost comic race as I tried to dodge through the underbrush and stay close to Syana, who was traveling like she was on skates. Even so, from the way she would stop and look back at me, I knew I was slowing her down.

If I'd been a real gentleman I would have told her to take off. She would undoubtedly have a better chance on her own than with me tagging along. But that much of a gentleman, I'm not.

Twenty minutes more and I was bushed. I leaned back against a tree trunk, gasping for breath.

"How much farther?" I said between wheezing.

"Miles, many miles."

The kind of broken field running we were doing would wear me out a long, long time before we got to safety, I could see that. I clutched the pistol in my hand, rubbing its barrel lovingly. It was the only thing I had to remind me of home, and the only chance I had of surviving to get back home.

A mosquito brushed my cheek and I heard a soft thud next to my ear. I cocked my head and found myself staring at the plain wooden shaft of a three-foot-long arrow from one inch away.

Syana had heard it too and jerked. Then she said, "Down," and took her own advice.

I was some immeasurable fraction of a second slower than she in dropping, but I hit the ground before she did.

I could see nothing through the tangle of trees.

"You see anything?"

She shook her head silently and gripped my arm, pulling me toward her. As I bent my head toward her, she whispered, "No noise. No talking. We have to get out of here, now."

"I'm all for the idea."

Still on her knees, we scrambled around to the other side of the tree we'd been leaning against and started an awkward stumbling. I could feel the pressure of the unknown archer's gaze as he sighted in on the middle of my back, but there was no sound.

Not that there would be any. There would only be the sudden gasp as the narrow piece of wood was forced through my back and stomach and vital organs and then out through my abdomen.

Sometimes I wish I didn't have such a vivid imagination.

I stumbled again and stopped my fall by putting one hand down against the soft, leaf-covered ground. A sudden flame burned along my back as I jerked and then stifled a groan. An arrow quivered in the side of a tree a half-dozen feet away.

I reached around to my back and came away with a red stickiness on my fingers. I let out the breath I'd been holding without knowing it. There is no feeling in the world, none, that even compares with finding out there isn't an arrow in your back.

Glancing back through the trees, patterns of blinding spears of light against deep shadows, I thought I saw a manlike figure. There

was no way I could hit him at that distance, but I fired at him anyway. And felt a hundred per cent better.

The .38 made a sound like a cannon in the silence of the forest.
I thought I saw the figure drop out of sight. The echoes of the shot
rang what seemed like minutes afterward.

Even if it didn't do any good, and if these guys had never seen a
gun, it might make them take a second glance at the situation. The
sound of the pistol in the forest gave me back a little courage.
There was something dreamlike and blood-chilling in running for
my life in complete silence.

Syana had stopped, waiting for me. I motioned with the pistol.

"I'm right behind you," I said, and we were off again.

We came to another clearing about five minutes later. There had
been no more arrows and no way of telling if we were still being
followed.

"Now what?"

"We circle around."

We started around the outside of the clearing, staying low.

We hadn't gotten a hundred feet when an arrow buried itself in
a tree next to my head. I turned and saw the archer who'd fired the
arrow. I aimed at him, then pulled my finger away from the trigger.
I had seen the archer standing a dozen feet away from him, and
then another standing a little farther away.

Looking around slowly, I saw a line of men dressed in ragged
green and gray clothing, all carrying what looked to me like long-
bows. All had arrows in their bows, ready to let fly. If I pulled the
trigger of my .38 I'd kill Syana and myself.

The world froze around me. Syana stood beside me, her sword
raised halfway up as if she hadn't made up her mind whether or not
to die right now.

A guttural voice rang out behind me. I turned and got my first
look at the Hann.

He was easily seven feet tall, as broad as a tree across his chest
and resembling one in a lot of other ways too. Grayish skin, more
like hide, covered everything that a close-fitting suit of light mail,
similar to what Syana had worn, did not.

There was no hair but a spiny ridge like the crest of a rooster atop
its head.

The face, though, was the thing. None of the silent line of archers would have won any prizes in a beauty contest, but the Hann made them look homey and friendly by comparison.

Eyes like torches set deep under horned brows glared at us above two small holes where a nose should have been, and out of a lipless mouth two large, yellowish fangs easily two inches long jutted.

It wouldn't be fair to say I was frightened at that point. I'd been afraid from the moment I found myself in Ellendon, and the little chase I'd undergone hadn't done wonders for my peace of mind.

But, staring at the Hann, looking into those two inhuman eyes, I stopped being afraid because I knew that if I stayed afraid I couldn't move, and if I didn't move, I was dead. Just that simple. I got so busy thinking I didn't have the time any more to be afraid.

Syana, sounding like somebody who'd already lost all hope of living, said, "I'm sorry, Hank. I shouldn't have said the things to you I said. There was no excuse for the way I acted."

"That's all right, I don't blame you. Why apologize now, for God's sake?"

"Because they are going to kill us. In a second I am going to try to reach Suldurus and kill him. I don't think I'll make it, but I don't want to be taken alive."

She looked up then, and I didn't know whether it was to take a last look at the sky or offer a silent prayer to her Lords of Ellendon.

My .38 was held in my hand, waist-high. I had turned and hadn't lowered it.

"Nobody lives forever," I said to no one in particular and snapped the gun up, holding it out in front of me, barrel centered where the Hann's heart should be.

I pulled the hammer back and waited for the shock of the first arrow.

CHAPTER SEVEN

It was the longest five seconds of my life. I heard movement behind me, men shifting position, and I could imagine them drawing back their bowstrings.

The Hann didn't move, just flicked his gaze away from me at them and the sounds ceased.

He opened his mouth and I listened with half my mind on the

growling sounds coming out. All I could think of was what those thin, needle-point teeth could do to a man.

"He says to drop your weapon or his men will kill us both," Syana said.

I could only glance at her out of the corner of my eye, but I tried to put as much meaning into that glance as I could. I wanted her to have some idea of the bluff I was preparing to run.

I spoke loudly for the benefit of our new companions. It sounded like somebody else speaking.

"You tell him I come from earth, if he's ever heard of that place, and I don't throw my weapons away for anyone. You tell him that what I've got in my hand will tear his heart out of his body before any of those arrows reach me. That if I'm going to die I want the satisfaction of seeing him die first."

I saw she understood.

"If—if it happens," she said softly, "try to kill him before you fall."

"It'll be a pleasure."

She translated and I watched Suldurus' face. When she'd finished he stared unblinkingly at me. He raised a mammoth hand to his chin and began to stroke his face like a man thinking real hard. I hoped it wasn't a signal for his men to cut me down.

He barked something at Syana that I recognized as a question.

She answered quickly, without bothering to translate for me.

He waited another aching few seconds, then made a wave of his hand. I could feel Syana relaxing.

"You've won, for right now."

I kept the pistol where it had been. She looked down at her sword and then at the Hann.

"He'll still kill us, Hank. He's not afraid of you or your gun, the Hann aren't that way. He's heard legends of earth and the men from earth and he's curious. I ought to try to kill him anyway. I wish I had the courage."

"If we could bottle what you've got the world would be a better place, sugar. I don't know if I could have gone up against those arrows with just a sword."

"I ought to be willing to die before letting them take me. I ought to, but I want to live, and I'm ashamed."

"Well, I won't spread around the scandalous news that you want to go on living. It'd be terrible for your reputation."

Suldurus gestured to the left. I took a chance and let the hammer ease back down, keeping the gun pointed in the general direction of Suldurus, who walked ahead of us. We followed him, surrounded by archers.

I felt light-headed as we marched through the trees. I've been in danger before. Once I overturned a car going down a mountainside and rolled a few times. But I'd never had the experience of being surrounded by men who wanted to kill me.

We came out of the trees into a mini-valley through which a stream ran. We splashed through the stream, which was about a foot deep. I found the time to get irritated because the water was going to be hell on my shoes and socks.

The clearing beyond the stream was cool and dappled with shadows thrown by surrounding trees. In another situation it would have made an ideal camping spot.

There were tents drawn up at the edge of the clearing. The Hann motioned us to one. Holding the gun carefully at my side, I walked to it with Syana.

My earlier elation at having death postponed for a short time was disappearing. That's the way of it. People are never satisfied. Now I wanted to go on living for, who knows, maybe another hour or two.

I sat down awkwardly, feeling the water slosh around inside my shoes, and told the Hann what he could do to himself in English. Syana almost grinned, indicating that old Iverson had taught her more than textbook English.

Suldurus stood looking us over curiously, seeming to stand so tall his head scraped the sky. On closer inspection he was even uglier than he first appeared. There was no emotion, none at all, that I could read in those burning eyes.

He pointed to my gun and said something.

Syana translated, "He wants to see you use your gun."

My stomach rumbled, but not from hunger. The moment I had most feared was at hand. I had only one bullet left in the gun, not having the time to reload, and only six more after that. That was the only edge I had. Once I'd fired those seven bullets I was unarmed, and I had the shaky feeling that meant dead.

Besides, I wasn't that good a shot and I didn't want them to know it. I've practiced every once in a while at the police pistol range, but I never was more than mediocre, at best.

Looking at the Hann, though, I realized there was no choice in the matter. If I fired my last bullet I might be dead in the long run, but if I didn't use the gun, I was dead in the short run.

I looked around the camp, avoiding the bored, unfriendly eyes of two dozen men. I finally picked a tree branch a dozen feet away as the best bet and pointed to it.

It was close enough that I was sure I could hit it and thin enough that it would probably be shot away from the tree. The sound of the shot alone in these close quarters would be impressive.

"All right, friend, here goes."

I sighted along the barrel. My hand took a long time getting steady but finally I was satisfied. I tried to ignore the pressure of the eyes upon me and squeezed the trigger.

I jumped as the gun jerked in my grasp. There wasn't a man in the camp sitting down as the branch hit the ground. Quite a few were a little white, with one major exception.

Suldurus sat where he had before the shot was fired. I could have fired a cap gun for the effect it had on him. I blew the smoke away from the barrel and opened the cartridge chamber. I reached into my pocket and began sliding my last bullets into it very casually.

If they had wanted to jump me right then, that would have been it. Unfortunately, they could jump me at any stage along the way, and that would also be it.

"Do you think he's impressed?" I asked Syana. She didn't respond. She didn't think we had any chance of getting out of there and, it came to me, she must be thinking of what was going to happen to her after these animals got tired of playing with us.

I clicked the cartridge case home and walked back to Syana. "Tell him I'm a dead shot with this thing. Tell him that one of the blasts from this thing could kill him, or any man in any armor on this world."

She translated while the great, gray statue sat immobile. He said something in the barking sounds that were his language.

"He wants to know what you are doing in Ellendon."

I thought about that one. I wished I could answer the same question, which I'd put to myself several million times in the last few hours. I could tell him it was because I grow very stupid when drunk, or because I'm very stupid generally. But that would do neither Syana nor myself any good.

"This lady," I said, pointing to Syana, "was transported to earth accidentally. She was captured by men under my command. This world sounded like a plum ripe for the taking, so my men and I decided to take it for ourselves."

He barked another question and Syana said, "He wants to know if you are going to take Ellendon by yourself."

"My men are coming after me. There are more than a thousand of them, armed with weapons that make this"—gesturing with my pistol—"look like a toy. I came first to look this world over."

I didn't have to be psychic to read his mind at this point. No matter how many men I claimed, I was alone now. I had to drive that dangerous thought out of his head.

"I am battle commander of a legion of men who are going to be looking for me. You might be able to take me, although I would kill you first, but eventually my men would find you and hunt you all down like animals."

I thought I was doing very well on the spur of the moment. The story sounded impressive to me. Now all I could do was hope that the reputation of earth's ferocity was all that Syana had said it was.

He showed the first facial expression I'd seen—a blood-chilling smile—and said something.

Syana looked as if our death sentence had just been pronounced, and in a way it had.

"He says," she whispered, "that you lie very badly."

I didn't have time to think about that because in the next second Syana screamed a warning and I whirled, trying to bring the gun up to cover the three men who leapt from the trees at my back.

The gun thundered and rang in my ears as I saw one of the three, a big, dirty-haired man, put his hand over his chest and stumble in full charge. Time slowed down, or maybe it was just that I was standing somewhere outside my body watching the fun and games.

A big, smelly body hurtled at me, driving itself into my gun. My hand was shoved back as I squeezed the trigger twice. But the man came on like a robot and I was carried with him off my feet.

I was down, with his hot body on top of me and his blood pouring out over me. I was blinded for a second as I tried to push him off me and then I screamed, or anyway I think I did.

The world exploded in the area of my kidneys and it felt like somebody had kicked my ribs through my heart. I heaved the body off me and was turning when I was kicked again—this time in the groin.

I've never really believed that old saying about seeing red, but it's true, as I know from personal experience. There was a red haze in front of me and a roaring like a diesel in my ears. For a second I hurt so bad I couldn't really pin down where the hurt came from. It seemed that my whole body had been mangled by one of those earth-crushing machines. I heaved and threw up all over myself.

A moment later I realized I didn't have the gun in my hand any more. Somebody had kicked it out of my hand and then stepped on my fingers for good measure.

As I struggled, only dimly aware of what was happening, somebody kicked me a couple of times in the stomach. Or they might have hit me with lead pipes, I really couldn't say for sure.

They topped it off by beginning to kick me below the belt again. At least they did once. The last thing I remember was thinking how weird your own screaming sounds.

I woke up a few months later as somebody was trying to drown me. I coughed and spit and then tried to throw up again as the pain in my crotch hit me again. There wasn't anything left in me but slime by this time and I spit it out as somebody jerked my head up by the hair.

They splashed some water in my face and the world slowly stopped its wild spinning. Someone jerked my hair again and I found it less painful to stagger to my feet.

I opened my eyes and coughed painfully as I stood up, stooped over, holding myself with one hand. Later I was to remember and for the first time feel a little sorry for the Cyclops.

The big man I'd shot first lay at my feet. Somebody had turned him over from where he'd fallen on his stomach. There was a big red stain in the area of his heart and blood had gushed out of his mouth and nose onto the ground. It was still dribbling out of the side of his mouth.

The other man I'd shot was curled up on his side a few feet away. I could tell he'd lost control of his bodily functions as he'd died. He stunk like hell.

Tucked in among the crazy confusion in my head was joy at killing those two animals and the fervent wish that I'd been able to kill every man there the same way, only in a longer and more painful fashion.

They yanked me around and I saw the third body. For a moment it didn't register because I had never seen this body before. Take a beautiful young girl with fire and courage and strip her.

Throw her to a pack of human wolves to tear and snap at. Let them use their hands and nails on her body, and this was what you would have.

Even the face didn't look like the Syana I had known. One eye was swollen shut, the skin around it already turning black and blue. Her lips were swollen and there was a cut over her other eye.

They had taken away much more than her clothes and her days as a maiden. They had taken a princess and turned her into a mass of bloody flesh. They had taken Syana away from her.

There was a line of men waiting their turn, laughing and joking. I tried to pull away from the two men holding me but I was weak as a baby. They laughed and one struck me across the face again.

Even as I staggered I spit at him through teeth that were throbbing now and loose in my mouth. It must have made him mad. I didn't see the punch, but it sent me out of Ellendon.

The guys in the dungeon really loved their work. The big ugly man in black caressed his rack lovingly, oiling all the critical junctures, stroking the screw that would stretch my ligaments.

The whipmaster, dressed only in shorts, cracked his twenty-foot-long whip in the air, playing with it. He kept snapping out the candles until the guy with the red-hot spikes told him to stop messing with the goddamned lights, he needed them for his work.

The spikeman, who I noticed resembled a crabby third grade teacher I'd had, kept blowing softly on his spikes until they glowed white like hot diamonds.

Then they each rubbed their hands together in gleeful anticipation of the fun and said, "It's time, Dell. Let's go."

Not wanting to appear chicken, I hopped onto the rack, lying down on my back.

"No, damnit, not on your back. What kind of outfit do you think this is?" grumbled the whipmaster, turning me over onto my stomach.

The spikeman grabbed my hands and tied them to the crosslike rails out on each side of the rack while the rackman got me settled onto his machine.

"Boy," chortled the rackman, "you're going to get it, Dell, if you don't tell us what we want to know."

Nary a word I spoke. That is, until the rack began to tighten. At first it merely felt uncomfortable, then my neck began to hurt. There was a loud cra-a-k and I nearly jumped out of my skin.

"Jesus," I screamed, "that hurt."

At that moment the spikeman gently hammered the first spike home with one solid blow. Around the smell of burning flesh, my own, I screamed, "All right, I'll talk. What do you want to know?"

They began to laugh then, in time with the creaking of the rack and the popping of my joints, the crack of the whip on my back and the hammering of the remaining spikes into my hands and feet.

"Jesus, what do you crazy idiots want to know? You must want to know something. You must . . ."

I opened my eyes to darkness and spit out blood. I closed them again for a moment and felt the ground beneath my head, the leaves and grass masking the harsh earth beneath.

My neck hurt as if I had been on that rack and my right hand felt like somebody had hammered a spike through it and my back hurt as if somebody had laid a whip on it.

Breathing slowly, I ran my tongue carefully over my lips and teeth. The teeth were all there, although a couple were loose. The lips were cracked and split in three or four places.

I tried to reach up with my left hand to feel my mouth, but found that my hands were tied in front of me. Exploring with my fingers, I found a band of some kind of hide tying them together at the wrists. Not too tightly tied, but tightly enough, as I discovered when I tried to wriggle free of them.

Unfortunately, my wriggling moved my body just a little bit and that was enough to make me gasp. The pain in my crotch hadn't gone away. Breathing in slowly did some good. After a while the pain was reduced to a throbbing comparable with, say, having a hernia operation without anesthesia.

They had really worked me over. Taking a mental inventory, I could feel bruises over my back and stomach and chest and arms and face and hands and . . . I spent a good deal of time just cataloging where they had hurt me.

Come to think of it, the old torture chamber wasn't really that bad. I wouldn't have minded going back to it. At least I could escape from that by waking up. Here, I couldn't.

A low moaning drew my attention away from my own troubles and I managed to turn my head and saw another body lying next to me. I propped myself up on one elbow and saw long, golden hair.

They had covered her with a rough blanket and put her torn tunic back over her, but they couldn't hide what they had done. Suddenly I felt very petty for being upset by what they had done to me.

Now I almost wished I'd used the gun on her when I'd had the chance. Because they weren't going to let her die easily. They were going to use her as hard as they could, and if she was unlucky, she'd live for a while.

To keep my mind off my own pain, I tried to think. I could see why they'd kept Syana alive, but why hadn't they killed me? I didn't like the answer that popped into my head at all.

There are many, many ways of killing a man slowly. Virtually every culture you could ever think of has come up with its own variations. I had read enough to know that the number of ways of hurting a man is limited only by your imagination. They could work on the groin, or the eyes, or the ears, or the tongue, or the chest, or . . .

As I said before, I hate my imagination because it's so vivid.

They weren't going to let me slip quickly away with an arrow in the guts. They were going to make me pay for killing two of their men. And even if I hadn't killed them, they probably still would have tortured me. Because, without ever having any experience in this kind of situation, I knew instinctively that they were the kind of animals who would enjoy it.

If I could ever pin down the one moment in my life when I was most scared, that would probably be it. Not only did I know they were capable of hurting me and enjoying it, I was helpless to stop them.

But, as with the first moment I spotted Suldurus, I stopped being afraid, or at least I stopped being paralyzed by my fear.

I was alone, and not only did I have my own life to save, but I was also responsible for Syana. She had yelled to protect me, and I was sure she could have slipped away from them when we were being chased, but she hadn't left me.

The worst these bastards could do was kill me, and they'd already made a pretty good stab at that. I let the anger I was beginning to feel sweep over me, driving away the feeling of helplessness.

I reached over and touched Syana. She jerked away from me and looked at me with crazy eyes through the darkness. I wondered if the experience she'd gone through had sent her beyond my reach, or help.

She opened her mouth to scream and I clamped my hands over her. They'd tied my legs, so I held her down with the weight of my body. She bucked and heaved under me, biting my hands.

Finally I knew I'd have to take my hands away and let her scream and bring the outlaws and death. I lifted my hands from her mouth just long enough to raise my arms in the air, and then brought my elbow down into the pit of her stomach. It was awkward, but with my hands tied I couldn't get enough force behind a punch to have any effect.

My blow took the wind out of her. She lay gasping for breath.

"I'm not going to hurt you, damnit. Do you know who I am?"

She got her breath back and whispered, "Animals. You're all animals. But my brother will hunt you down and kill you."

"Syana, listen to me. You remember me. I'm Hank Dell. I came here from earth with you. Remember?"

She shook her head weakly, then stared at me in the darkness. Her wrists and feet were also bound, but she reached out to touch my face.

"Hank? You . . . you were on earth. I remember now."

"That's right, Syana. We met on earth. Do you remember everything now? Did they hurt you, other than . . ."

"I remember everything," she said, shaking her head back and forth wildly. "No," she said, laughing softly, "they didn't hurt me except in that way. What else could they do to me? See, aren't I pretty?"

She held her head up in the moonlight and I saw the mask of blood and bruises.

"I fought them," she whispered. "I fought and kicked and tried to bite, but they were too strong. They tore my clothes off and grabbed and . . ."

I reached out to hold her face in my hands. She looked at me and for a moment I thought she was all right. Then she laughed that crazy laugh again, pulled away from me, and tore off the covering.

She pulled her pants down as far as she could with bound hands before I could stop her and spread her legs as much as the ropes around her ankles would permit.

"Don't you want to, Hank? Why not? It's the only thing I'll be good for any more. They taught me that. They made me as dirty as they are."

I slapped her face with the back of one hand. Her head fell heavily to the ground.

"Shut up and start acting like the Princess I first met. What they did hasn't changed that. They hurt you, and I'm sorry, but when we get out of here you'll get over that. Someday it'll just be a memory."

She was crying now, the tears running down the cheeks silver in the moonlight.

"No, I won't be the same, not ever again."

She looked at me with that same wild expression in her eyes.

"Please, Hank, kill me. Use your hands right now, please."

"You're talking crazy again. Look, what happened to you was bad, but it's happened before. On my world and yours. A lot of women have been raped in worse ways, and by more men, than you. And they lived and had families afterward."

Playing Pollyanna was a tough job. I wondered how many of those women had ever been good for anything in bed again.

She shook her head.

"I don't want to live any more. I feel dirty, and I know I'll never feel clean again."

Her soiled feelings were going to get us both killed, so I lost my temper. I grabbed her face and made her look at me, ignoring her wince of pain as my fingers clutched her sore flesh.

"Look, Princess, maybe you forgot, but we're not the only two people involved in this. There's a world out there that has your brother and Iverson and your friends waiting for the Hann.

"What happened to you was a tea party compared to what they're going to get if the Hann take over. Maybe we can't do anything about that and maybe we can. We at least know where the barrier can be broken. Maybe somebody can still get through and take Krell. But if you crack here, we'll never know if we could have done something."

"But . . ." she said weakly. I had the momentum and I didn't intend to give her time for any second thoughts.

"No buts. If you still feel dirty, you can always kill yourself afterward. But give your brother and your friends a chance. Do you want to know that you've killed them too?"

That was playing very dirty pool, but there was no time to look around for a gentlemanly alternative. Death might walk out of the darkness at any moment.

"What can we do?"

That, of course, was the million dollar question. I lay back and thought about it. Of course, if I had a trusty cannon concealed on my person there'd be no problem. Or if the U.S. Cavalry was to come galloping through the woods.

But neither of those two options was open to me. Finally the only thing I could think of was to hope that only one man was sent to get me, or Syana. That was likely. After all, they weren't too worried about us, leaving us tied by ourselves.

I told Syana to rip part of her tunic off.

"Why?"

I explained why, then had to help her because you just don't tear cloth when you can't move your hands freely. I grabbed hold of a section of her tunic and she pulled with both hands until the fabric tore.

Waiting was the hardest part of it. Once I made up my mind the feeling of helplessness vanished. I knew what I was going to be doing. But nobody came.

The longer I waited, the more I hurt. There was no longer a general over-all ache. Instead, I could feel the soreness of my ribs, the cut over my eye, the ache from my teeth.

There was the soft touch of fingers on both sides of my face. As I turned toward her, she gave a funny kind of shudder I didn't understand until later. Then she began to sing that strange wordless tune again, very softly.

And as it had in my room, the pain began to vanish. It was like feeling a cramp ease, a soft flowing away of the pain rather than the oblivion that drugs would bring.

The rustle of underbrush was the only warning I got. My stomach tightened into a knot and I could see Syana's body freeze.

"Remember, this is our only chance," I whispered.

My first fear vanished as one man stepped out of the darkness. He wasn't that big, but broad across the shoulders. He looked tough and carried a knife in his belt.

I closed my eyes, as Syana had already done. I could hear him walking up to me. I breathed naturally, then gasped as he kicked me in the side. I shot my eyes open and looked up at him.

He gestured for me to get up and drew back his foot to kick again.

I moaned and made motions like I was trying to get up, but couldn't. He kicked me again. I fell back against the ground and moaned, this time for real.

I heard Syana speak softly. I peeked and saw he'd turned toward her. She held out her hands to him, and spread her legs, smiling as widely as her swollen lips would allow her.

I don't know what she was saying, but it must have been hot as hell. He grinned, turned away from me and dropped his pants.

I got my knees under me. Then, bracing myself on my hands, I pushed backward and rocked onto my feet. I swayed for a moment, but managed to stay upright. That was the first step. Two short hops and I tapped him on the shoulder. He was bending over with his knife in one hand, undoubtedly to cut the bonds around Syana's ankles for more freedom to get at her.

He turned and straightened. I ducked under him, butting his chin with my head as hard as I could. It took him off his feet, grunting as he fell back. I was falling forward so I converted my momentum into a leap atop him.

I landed on his groin, which was in a state of some excitement, with both knees as hard as I could and with the full force of my 170 pounds behind them.

He would have screamed then, if my fists hadn't been in his mouth. Even as he'd opened his mouth I was falling on top of him and jamming my hands, clasped as if in prayer, as far down his throat as I could.

If I hadn't hit him as hard as I did, and hurt him as badly as I did, he would have used the knife and I wouldn't have been able to stop him. With my hands tied I could only shut him up, or grab for the knife, but not both. In seconds, though, Syana had slipped her arms around his head from behind as if to hug him.

What she did instead was pull her hands back until the strip of tunic between them was jammed tightly into his mouth. As I grabbed for his knife she kept pulling on the cloth, exerting more pressure on the make-shift gag.

He struck out frantically, trying to pull the gag out with one hand and drive his knife into me with the other. I had his wrist with my hands, but even with only one hand he was too strong for me.

I bit his wrist as hard as I could, then pulled the knife away from him and rammed it into his chest.

He grunted and heaved upward against the knife as if wanting more, so I obliged. I jammed the knife in down to the handle. Then I pulled it out and stuck it in again.

He was fighting at first, so I stabbed him as many times as I could. A little while later I realized I was stabbing a dead man. I left the knife in his body.

My hands, and my clothes, were soaked with his blood. Syana hobbled to my side and looked down at the man's bloody chest. She smiled and grabbed the knife.

"No time for that," I said, taking it away from her. I cut her hands and legs free and then cut my own bonds. As I cut myself free I glanced at the darkness-shrouded body lying near us, and for a second I really couldn't believe I had done that.

It just didn't fit in with the image I had of myself. But then again, the two men lying with bullets in them didn't exactly fit my old image either. I was going to have to do a little renovating sometime soon.

The other bandits, who undoubtedly were waiting for the sport to begin with me, would be coming after the dead man any second, I knew. If Syana and I ran, they would undoubtedly be able to overtake us.

I didn't like it, and I had the uncomfortable feeling that if I'd had the time I could come up with a much better idea, but there seemed to be only one way of getting Syana out of there in one piece. And that meant a good chance they'd get me back.

I gave Syana the knife and said, "You should be able to make it out of here now. Try to get back to your brother and tell him what's happened. Maybe it's not too late."

"What about you?"

"Both of us can't get out of here. I'll try to lead them off away from you."

"I wish I had not said some of the things I said to you, Hank Dell."

"And I wish this was someplace else and some other time, Princess. Most of all I wish somebody else was standing here. Get out of here."

In a second she was lost into the night. I had the time to curse myself for a hopelessly heroic idiot. But it wouldn't do any good for both of us to be killed.

Besides, I had an idea that just might work.

The worst it could get me was killed.

CHAPTER EIGHT

There was no fire where the majority of the outlaws were gathered. The Hann was speaking to them in the language I recognized as that of Ellendon, though in his own growling accent. In the faint light I could see him gesture as he spoke. I had the feeling that if I understood Ellendonian, I'd be listening in on a strategy meeting.

I had crept as close to them as I dared. They must have had lookouts about their camp, but they probably weren't looking for any trouble inside. At least I hadn't been spotted as far as I knew.

I waited for someone to discover the man I'd killed. The longer it took, the farther away Syana could get. But the waiting was killing me.

A shout rang out from the trees where we'd been tied. Suldurus began to shout orders as men shot to their feet and moved out. I huddled close to the ground, hoping no one would look in my direction.

Some of the men came toward me. I shrank back against a tree trunk and willed myself to become invisible. There was thick shrubbery all around me and in the darkness I must have made a pretty small target because no one gave me a second look. One man passed me running, only ten feet away.

When I dared to poke my head up again, several minutes later, the clearing was empty. I looked around carefully, but couldn't see anybody. I was pretty sure they had all been sent out after us. They couldn't guess that a nut with a sensational death wish would walk into the lion's den.

Making as little noise as I could, with sheer terror a pretty good incentive, I made my way toward the tent I thought to be Suldurus'.

Along the way I had to cross the stream. I still had my shoes on, but the sheer coolness of the water not only didn't bother me, it felt better than anything I'd yet run into in Ellendon. I had to stop and run the water, in cupped hands, over my face and chest.

I made a mental note to say a prayer for water every night from then on. I kept going and finally found myself in back of what I thought was the right tent. I crept into it.

Burrowing inside, I started feverishly tearing through the items.

I just had to hope that Suldurus hadn't taken it with him. My hands closed on cold metal and I said another prayer of thanks.

I felt like a man in the desert dying of thirst who falls into an oasis. The touch of that .38 was better than any pep pill.

A gun, as any amateur psychiatrist can tell you, is power. Any Western fan could tell you the same thing.

When I was a kid spending vacations at my grandfather's house in Florida, we'd lived in a house near the river. I'd lie in my bed, with the bellowing of frogs and the roar of crickets and other night creatures turning the darkness into a jungle, afraid to move. I knew if I had a gun in my hands, I'd be safe. I felt the same way now. The only difference was that I was in a real jungle.

I was backing out of the tent when I heard a shout and looked up. An outlaw was coming across the clearing, whipping out an arrow to put in his bow.

I fired the gun after sighting hastily. Luck rode with me, because I know it wasn't my marksmanship. He clutched at his shoulder as he fell, then tried to get up. I took off into the forest without looking back.

That shot would save Syana. I was sure they hadn't reached her yet and it would bring all of them running. Which meant I was going to have to do some too.

I ran as quickly as I could without ramming my head into branches or trees. If I once stopped, I was pretty sure they'd have me. It was rougher in the night than I'd remembered it. Nettles and thorns whipped across my face and hands. If I hadn't kept one hand up in front of my eyes, I'd have been quickly blinded.

I tried to keep my cursing down to a low monotone as I stepped into thorns and poison ivy. Nothing, absolutely nothing, had gone right since I'd met Syana. From the time I'd gotten us hurled into Ellendon it had been a continuous catastrophe.

After what must have been a half hour I stopped, leaning against a tree while I gasped for breath, trying to keep my head from splitting wide open with pain that had come back since I'd left Syana.

I could hear nothing behind me but the normal sounds of the forest. There was the sound of insects, and a few bird calls, and a far-off howling. That stopped me for a moment. I wondered if they had wolves anywhere around. There was nothing, though, to indicate that the human wolves were still on my track.

Just as I got ready to start again I heard a shout from behind me.

I dropped to the ground. There was another shout, and then a scream. It was faint, but I could make the sounds out clearly.

For a moment I thought they must have caught Syana. I toyed with the idea of going back, but there was nothing I could do for her now, except get myself killed. Then, as the shouting continued, I realized it couldn't have been her.

The sounds were those of fear and anger. I could also make out the faint sounds of metal on metal. That was no girl with a knife, that was somebody with a sword whacking on somebody else with a sword. Syana had said there were army patrols in the area.

Besides, I realized, when Syana had vanished her brother must have sent special patrols into this area on the chance she might be in just the kind of trouble she was in.

I thought again about going back, but there was no assurance the soldiers would win, or even that they would be there when I showed up.

Innocent bystanders have a nasty habit of becoming deceased bystanders whenever bullets or arrows start flying. There was a chance that I might reach the soldiers, but if the outlaws caught me again I knew damn well I'd never get a second chance to escape. Better to keep running.

Which I did, but with a whole lot more hope. There was a chance that there wouldn't be any outlaws left to pursue me, and even if there were they would probably have a lot more on their minds than me.

I stumbled through the forest for another couple of hours until I couldn't put one foot down in front of the other without falling on my face.

I nestled at the foot of a tree, my gun held tightly in my hand, and tried to pretend that the rough bark was a soft bed and a fat, billowy pillow.

In a couple of hours I was able to convince myself and I fell asleep.

I awoke to a dream. Not a nightmare like I'd inhabited during my last sleep. The branches of the trees were lace through which early morning sunlight filtered. The dew on the leaves glittered like diamonds as the rays of the sun sparkled off them.

The air was cool and it even smelled green. A good green. If anything could have cured me of my ills, that would have been it.

Unfortunately, even that wasn't quite strong enough magic. Even

on a soft bed and let nature take its course, I realized I had dropped the pistol to the ground.

I thought about picking it up, then decided there was plenty of time for that. There was plenty of time for everything now. I'd be safe here. The outlaws would never be able to find me, nor the Hann when they came. And in the cool, lightless reaches of the lake I'd have the woman in front of me for all time.

I looked down and saw I'd stepped into the water. I thought about rolling up my pants, but that was foolish. What harm would a little water do?

I went in deeper as she drew away from me. I knew she was playing, pretending to flee to add spice to the game. But when I entered the lake completely and left the killing ground behind me, she would be there—soft and yielding and all woman.

The water was up around my waist and the mirror reflected my face but nothing more. There was only the silver surface that cut me in half. The cool water soothed the lower part of me and excited at the same time, almost as if her hands were already on me.

I stumbled on something hard in the soft muck of the lake bottom. It snapped under my feet as I put my weight down on it. For a moment I thought it felt unpleasantly like bone, but then I forgot about it.

She was almost within my reach as the water rose around my neck. I reached out, her shoulders, arms, breasts so tantalizingly close. Almost . . .

The sound of another voice broke the spell. The mermaid's face left mine and turned to someone standing to one side and behind me. I looked at her and the dark water up to my chin, seeing in one split second what had happened.

She looked back at me and the expression on her face would have brought life back to a corpse, but all I could think of was the snap of bones under my feet and the dark water surrounding me. What other things were hidden underneath it?

Without looking back at her, I waded frantically back toward shore. I didn't really have to hurry. When I got back to the shore she was in the same place I'd left her, an expression of great sadness on her face.

She smiled at me again and even as she did I could hardly believe my eyes. The tears she shed fell slowly down over her cheeks and down across the now unsmiling mouth. In that moment I almost threw away all my fears and the memory of the bones, and went back to her.

But it was too late. With one fluid motion, she dived down into the depths of the lake. The last I saw of her was a green movement underneath the silver mirror, and then she was gone.

I didn't know whether to be very sorry or very glad.

My rescuer was an anticlimax. She could have been every man's mother. She was a tall woman, nearly my height, with silver hair and apple checks. She was dressed in a gray, shapeless smock that indicated only that she was a sturdy late-middle-aged woman. She smiled and said something in Ellendonian.

I shook my head, unable to feel happy at my "rescue."

"I'm sorry, but I don't speak your language."

"You speak English?"

Now it was my turn to gawk.

"How? I mean . . ."

"Later. Now, we go to my cottage. You look terrible. What happened?"

I started to explain, then stopped as we were walking out of the grotto.

"What about her?"

"What about her?"

"I mean, what is she? Why did she try to get me in that lake?"

"She is the dweller in the lake, and she has been there as long as my people have lived in the forest. And attracting you to the lake, well . . ." she merely glanced down at my groin but I got the message and blushed. Somehow it didn't seem right for a motherly type to be acting like that.

"There are not many lone travelers who enter this forest. She is a woman, with a woman's hungers. Her problem," she said, with a hint of sympathy in her voice, "is that she is selfish. She cannot make love on land, and any man who attempts to make love to her in her lake invariably drowns. A man is good for only one time with her. You would have died very happy, but you would have died."

I shuddered. The terrible thing was, even now, I wasn't sure if I was glad I'd been rescued.

A twenty-minute walk led us through the trees to a cottage that looked like something out of a Grimms' Fairy Tales woodcut. The timbers that made it up were rough-hewn, and green creepers entwined themselves in and out of the small cracks between the timbers.

There was a gurgling stream a few yards from the cottage and I could see a small garden in the rear.

"This is my home," she said.

I had to stoop to enter the doorway. It was moderately well lighted inside, clean and tidy. There was a cot over to one side.

Along the way I'd given her my sad story and she had listened intently. I remembered now the old "witch" that Syana said she had been seeking, the friend of Iverson. She said she was the "witch." She hadn't known things were so bad, being isolated from the outside world.

"Lie down," she said. With a bit of trepidation, I did. I clutched the .38 in one hand and she must have noticed.

She laughed and said, "You do not trust me, either? You think I have sinister designs on you? Or do you think I lust after your body?"

That made me feel about seven years old. All I could do was shake my head contritely and lay the gun down beside me.

She opened several beakers on a high shelf and mixed the contents together in a bowl. Then she took what appeared to be leaves and a couple of roots and crushed them, adding them to the mixture.

She carried the bowl over to me and told me to drink it down. It smelled like turpentine and I told her so. She told me to drink it. I did, and it tasted worse than it smelled.

When I decided her potion wasn't going to kill me, I began to feel sleepy. I stared up at her face, beginning to waver in front of me.

"What did you put . . ."

"Just something to help you sleep," she said softly, taking my gun off the cot. She placed her hand, remarkably soft and smooth for an old woman, on my forehead and said, "Go to sleep now. You'll feel better when you wake."

My sleep had no nightmares. I could never remember exactly what I dreamed of, but I know part of it was my walking down a starlit beach holding the hand of a girl who looked remarkably like the mermaid.

Only this girl had two good legs, and she used them to skip and then run along the beach away from me. Racing, my chest heaving and burning with effort, I finally tackled her and brought her down in the fine, moist sand.

The next part of the dream is censored, but just as I was approaching the high point, I woke up.

The door to the cottage was open and the sunlight was streaming through. The beams of light illuminated my body, my head lying just outside the light. The sun was warm and I felt good.

It hit me as quickly as that. I reached up with a right hand that didn't hurt and ran my fingers over a set of healthy teeth. No pain. My chest didn't hurt. I took in deep breaths for the sheer pleasure of breathing without pain.

The strange thing was it didn't seem strange. It was the most natural thing in the world that in this place, this one small place, there would be no pain, no sorrow.

How could I have ever thought she was old? What kind of spell had she placed on herself? She looked tall standing in the doorway, that was true. But the smock had been thrown away, not to reveal a sturdy body but a slender, curved, hour-glass figure. Her long, ash-blond hair hung down around her shoulders.

"The mermaid isn't the only hungry woman around here, is she?"

She shook her head, walking slowly toward me.

"No, and I'm selfish too, in my own way. I am charging you for the service I rendered in healing your wounds."

"Well, then," I said, "come on and collect."

She did, with interest.

I woke up again when the sun was still high. I was alone on the cot. I ran a hand over my body, half fearing that it had all been a dream. But I was whole again, and the girl who'd shared the cot with me was no dream either.

I slipped my pants back on and went out to look for . . . I didn't even know her name. She was outside, tending the garden I'd seen when I entered the cabin.

She looked up as I approached her and a lot of beautiful dreams went up in smoke. The old woman I'd first seen, actually only middle-aged but that's old enough, looked back at me. She saw the expression on my face and smiled gently.

"Was the price too high?"

I shook my head uneasily, feeling like a creep for no reason.

"No, of course not, but how . . ."

"It was in the potion I gave you. Part of the effect is a strengthening of the will to live, and the will to love. If it makes you feel any better, what happened is—it's hard to put into words—a part of the healing. But I enjoy that part of my work."

After a moment she added, "It was not completely a dream, if that makes it any easier. I was that girl, twenty years ago."

I felt very disoriented under the familiar sky.

"I get the feeling sometimes that I walked into an acid trip and I haven't come down."

"I know this must be strange to you. Iverson said he couldn't really believe it, even after he'd been here for years."

I leaned back against the cottage wall and said, "Syana mentioned . . ." and then remembered the little lost Princess.

"Syana, she's lost out there. You're supposed to know this forest. Do you think we could find her?"

The old woman shook her head.

"No, and I'm sorry. I knew her when she was but a child. If I could, I'd help you find her, but the forest swallows up any who enter. We might find her, and we might not. From what you say, I think you should try to reach Iverson or the young King, and tell them of what's happened."

I felt obscurely guilty at being fairly safe and in good health while Syana was alone in the forest, or maybe, by this time, dead.

"How long has it been? I mean, how long was I out?"

I remembered what Syana had said about the Hann coming through in two or three days. Maybe they were already here.

"Just a few hours. It is still the same day."

I got my nose rubbed in what I couldn't believe again. Every time I thought I could halfway believe this was really happening, I ran into something I knew couldn't be true.

"A few hours? How? What did you do?"

"You wouldn't understand. It was partially the ingredients I gave you, and partially the words and the ceremony. Some of it is the power I have in me, and some is the power that resides in the Lords of Ellendon."

"It sounds like witchcraft, magic, to me. And there ain't no such thing."

"It is magic," she said, smiling gently, "and you are a strange one to be saying there is no such thing, standing there strong and healthy."

When you're right, you're right, and she had me. Still, I could swallow dimensional barriers, and creatures like the Hann and the

Cyclops and the Chorbal. They could all have some logical explanation. I could fit them into the things I knew. But, magic?

I tried to forget about it, although it wasn't easy. What was it the Queen in *Alice in Wonderland* had said about believing one impossible thing before lunch every day? The way things were going, I'd be up on her in no time at all.

"You said I should try to reach Iverson and the King. How do I find them? I'd have a hard enough time just finding my way out of the forest."

"You shouldn't have any problem. There is a trail, cut through the forest sometime in the past. Maybe it was a road at one time. It will take you out of the forest. Once onto the plain, just head east and you will meet some of the King's men."

"What good will that do me? I don't speak the language."

"Just mention the name of Iverson, or King Dalien, and you will be brought to them. There is a fortress less than half a day's ride across the plains. Legend says it is where the first King Dorian drove the Hann out of Ellendon.

"The King and Iverson will be mustering the army, because it is near the fortress that the Hann must always attack. They will be there."

It sounded risky, but what choice did I have? Not only was it the decent thing to do, because, in a way, all the current problems were my fault, but it was my only chance too. If I hadn't interfered with Syana there was a good bet the King would have the Sword and Ring right now. And, unless somebody got the Ring and the Sword, I was gonna be struck here for a long, long time. Until I died, anyway.

"Let me get the rest of my clothes," I said, going back into the cottage. I dressed and picked up the .38 and went back outside.

When I came out her face was white. I looked around, but I couldn't see anything to account for it.

"What is it?"

She pointed to her left and said, "Through there. You will have no trouble finding the trail. Hurry."

"What's the matter?"

"Someone is coming," she said in a low voice. "I know they are close by. Leave now, and good luck."

Suddenly the spell of the cottage was broken and I was back in the real world. I remembered what had happened to Syana.

"Come with me. If we hurry we should be able to outdistance anyone behind us."

She shook her head again quickly.

"No, they would find us. I may be able to stop them from coming after you. I am known to many in the forest. They will not harm me, they never have."

"You're being stupid. I know what these guys can do. Come with me. I'm not leaving you here alone."

"I will not go with you. Now go, or they will catch you here too."

I should have slugged her and carried her, but I remembered what had happened before and my guts had turned to water. There was no time to argue with her.

As I ran the way she had pointed I thought I heard her say, "Remember me to Iverson," but I couldn't be sure.

I found the path she had talked about. It wasn't much of a path by my standards, but it was a little bit better than the rest of the forest, and it should prove easy to follow. And to be followed by others, I realized. I stopped at the edge of the path, got behind a tree, and looked back toward the cottage.

Like figures out of a bad dream, Suldurus and his men appeared out of the forest, surrounding the woman. I saw them talking to her, and she was gesturing, but I couldn't hear what she was saying.

With no warning, and for no reason I could see, Suldurus moved. When I saw the steel gleam in the sunlight I had the .38 out and pointed at him.

But before I could fire, before I could even really grasp what was happening, the heavy sword came down. I'd give all the money I'll never have to have had my eyes closed then, but they were open.

The blade vanished into the woman's body. I couldn't see anything but the hilt and the short part of the blade, which the Hann held. I still couldn't believe what I was seeing. The woman was standing up, but she seemed to slump a little.

Then I heard a sound like someone gagging, and I wanted to tear my ears off. It seemed to go on and on and on, and there was part of a scream and part of a moan in the sound too.

There was red all over her face and shoulders and dress. The Hann put out one foot and casually pulled the blade out of her. When she fell back I could see she'd been cut almost in half, down to the waist. I didn't really know there was that much blood in a human body, because it was splashed all over, all over the ground, and all over Suldurus.

She lay twitching on the ground as Suldurus walked over her and gestured to his men. Two flaming arrows were fired into the cottage, and in a few seconds the flames were roaring up toward the trees.

I know I was crying, because I felt the wetness on my face, and trying to throw up. I felt like my hand was welded to the .38. I was standing up, taking those few short steps that would take me back to the cottage and Suldurus.

The hardest thing I've ever done in my life was forcing myself to stop and not pull the trigger. I knew I couldn't hit him from that distance and I'd get myself killed before I reached him, but I couldn't live and know he lived. There was no way the two of us could coexist in the world, or the universe. Not now.

The thought that I'd get killed and be unable to take him with me was what stopped, and saved, me. At the moment I would have traded my life for his. But I wouldn't throw my life away, not now that I had a reason for saving it.

Trembling, I made myself turn and run down the path. They would discover it shortly and be after me. God knows why they had followed me. I promised myself that no matter what else happened, Suldurus would pay someday for what he'd done, and before he died, he'd know why.

CHAPTER NINE

Whatever had been in the old woman's brew, it had made a new man out of me, literally. I found I was stronger and faster than I'd been before I was worked over by Suldurus and his boys.

I expected I'd be heaving and gasping for breath in a couple of miles, since long-distance running was never my style, but about five miles later I was jogging along. I hadn't had this much exercise since I'd dropped out of PE in the junior college where I'd gotten my associate of arts degree. And that was a long four years ago.

The trail led me through deep twilight glades, open meadows, across streams and one small river that I was able to wade. Compared to the dash Syana and I had made, it was like taking a stroll through the park.

I was thinking about Syana, and running at the same time, which is a bad practice if you want to avoid sudden, unexpected contact with the ground on the part of your nose. I hit a tree root and fell very gracefully flat on my face.

I heard a solid thunk and looked up to see an arrow still quivering, lodged deep in the tree whose root had tripped me. It would have been a dead shot between my shoulder blades if I hadn't fallen. That was twice that my clumsiness had saved my life.

At the bend of the trail I could see an archer slipping back into the trees. I aimed the .38 at him and he made a dive for cover.

Whatever else they thought of me, my .38 had given the bandits a healthy and unwarranted respect for my marksmanship. There was no way my luck could have saved me again and I probably would have missed. There are times when having a ferocious reputation can be very handy.

I rolled behind the tree and started thinking very hard. If I tried to run for it, I was sure they would have me cold. If I stayed, ditto. There was no way I could hold them off with only two bullets left.

I ran like the fastest rabbit that's ever scrambled for its life from a hungry wolf. My ducking and dodging, bobbing and weaving were so fantastic that the most hardened high school football coach would have wept.

Another arrow whistled by my ear and my heart stopped beating for several seconds. I could have turned and fired and gained myself an extra few seconds, but seconds didn't count. And I'd become fantastically attached to the .38. Once those two bullets were gone, I might as well roll over and let them spear me.

I dived into the underbrush, took a deep breath that didn't seem to bring in any oxygen and made another rolling dive that gained me a couple of yards. Only there wasn't any goal line here and they wouldn't stop coming after me.

I rolled to the side of a tree. Bushes growing to the right formed a natural hedge. If a man squatted down he might not be seen by somebody hurrying by.

I tried once again to make myself invisible. I counted the beats of my heart, wondering on what number the game would stop. I could hear men moving nearby. For old pros at this game, they were making a lot of noise.

The hairs on the back of my neck were standing straight up. It felt like somebody had thrown ice water down my back. It's like one of those dreams where you know you've got to turn around and face whatever is behind you, but you can't.

It couldn't have been more than a second before I jerked my head around. Across a space of no more than twelve feet he stared at me. The arrow was held in his right hand, pulling the bowstring taut.

Even knowing I was dead, I couldn't believe it. I couldn't die. Not shot with an arrow by some bearded savage who had probably never even learned to read or write his own name.

He jerked slightly as a bolt of brown lightning hit the side of his head. The arrow came out the other side, spattering a good deal of his brains on the ground beside him. The arrow in his bow was tipped toward the ground and he let it fly. It sank into the ground an inch from my leg.

He stood there for a crazy moment, still looking at me with eyes open wide. Then he must have realized he was really dead and he crumpled to the ground.

It was so unbelievably weird that I burst out laughing. Except for the blood and gore it could have been a comic skit. The expression on his face had been the thing. He'd known he had me, and when the arrow hit him the expression on his face had been that of a man saying "Why me?"

I felt like telling him to stop fooling and get up off the ground.

Then the reaction hit me and I was shivering like I'd been dropped into a bucket of ice-cold water. My teeth were chattering so hard they hurt.

Even as I was trying to keep myself from cracking wide open down the middle, I glanced around to see who'd given me a new lease on life. As I did, the shouting and the dying began.

I heard a man groan. A bandit staggered toward the tree I was hiding behind. Holding his stomach, he tried to keep the blood and intestines in where somebody had messily opened him up.

He stiffened and fell on his face, an arrow protruding from his back. I could hear the sounds of metal on metal now, and they could only be swords meeting swords.

When I turned back to the man who had nearly killed me, I found myself facing another sword. This one was held by a man dressed as Syana and her captain had been dressed. The sword he carried also resembled theirs.

He had been on the point of rushing me, his body prepared to carry him forward, when he noticed the clothes I was wearing and the gun I held in my hand. He hesitated, rocking back and forth on the balls of his feet as he looked me up and down.

He snapped something at me in the fluid language of Ellendon. I could only raise my hands in a helpless shrug and say, "Don't I ever wish I spoke your language, friend. Easy with the cutlery."

He said something else and again all I could do was look stupid. What I needed was what the heroes in the science-fiction stories always have—universal all-purpose translators. But no such luck. That would make it too easy.

He seemed to make up his mind and motioned for me to follow him. He took off running, lightly for a man in armor. I shook off the shock of the last few moments and went after him.

He moved warily through the trees. Along the way I had to be careful to step over two more bodies. One was another of the Hann's men. The other wore the light mail of the government troops.

It hadn't done him much good. An arrow was jutting out of the unprotected area just below his adam's apple. He had died hard, his hands still around the arrow, trying to pull it out to the last. He, too, undoubtedly, hadn't believed he could die.

I found the time to wonder, as we slipped through more trees, heading around the sounds of battle, how I would have reacted to the sight of a man with an arrow sticking out of his throat only two days before.

Would I as casually have stepped over him? I hadn't had a chance to look at myself in a mirror since I'd gotten to Ellendon, but I knew I had a good two days' stubble and my pants would have been passed up by any self-respecting bum. Would the old Hank Dell even recognize me?

I nearly ran over my guide. He had dropped to one knee and was peering out through more underbrush. The shouting and sounds of battle had stopped. He shouted something in his language and someone called back. He straightened and walked out into the open, motioning for me to follow.

Other men in the armor of government soldiers were in the clearing. Besides these, there were more men dressed in green trousers and shirts and carrying bows. I became the center of attention.

The man who'd found me was talking to another, bigger man, pointing to me and the gun I held.

I didn't much feel like taking center stage and I didn't like the way the men were staring at me. Being a stranger in a war zone can get pretty hairy.

The second soldier, who acted like brass, came over to me and we went through the same routine all over again. He got the idea after a while. Then he looked down at the .38 and reached out for it.

I backed away, holding the gun behind me. The men around me stiffened and I tried not to notice all the swords and bows in the clearing.

He motioned for me to hand over the gun and I motioned back that there was no way, no way at all, that that was going to happen.

For the nth time I felt an itch up and down my spine that meant arrows were being centered on it. I was beginning to get tired of all this. What kind of a world was it where the good guys saved you from the bad guys, and then took you on themselves. This wasn't the way it was supposed to go.

An order that carried the weight of a lot of authority broke the stiff silence. Another man came into the clearing, accompanied by a half dozen more soldiers and archers. He gave me the once over, looked at me hard, and then spoke quickly to the man standing behind me.

As I turned, the man who'd brought me into the clearing brought his armored forearm down on my wrist, hard. The gun dropped and he caught me below the chin with a short, hard right.

I staggered back and managed to make a swing at him, but I was knocked down from behind, and grabbed by two very strong sets of arms. They jerked me roughly to my feet in time with another string of orders.

I had just gotten to my feet when the soldier who'd ordered me knocked down backhanded me. I tasted blood and squirmed, but I wasn't going anywhere. There was something strangely familiar about the man.

He slapped me again, yelling at me in Ellendonian. I told him what he could do to himself in English and he proceeded to backhand me for a while until he, too, realized I didn't speak the language.

I could taste blood, some of it running down from my nose, some where my teeth had cut into my gums. He stepped away from me, gave another order and my hands were tied behind my back.

He picked up the .38 where I'd dropped it, handling it carefully, and pointed the barrel at my head. He pulled the hammer back and looked me in the eye.

It was the soldier who'd appeared on earth with Syana. I wondered why I hadn't recognized him before, although I'd seen him in armor only in the darkness. There was no mistaking him this close up, though.

Fate moves in very mysterious, and underhanded, ways. Laughing boy undoubtedly believed I was working for Krell and that I had kidnapped his Princess. For all he knew, she was dead. As I would be in a few seconds.

There comes a point when you don't feel like fighting any more. I wasn't that tired, or hurt, or afraid. I was just certain in my own mind that my luck had run out. I only hoped that it would be quick —and that the Sunday-school teachers hadn't lied.

He hesitated for what seemed like a long time, with his thumb pulling back the hammer. Then he let off on the hammer and dropped the gun to his side.

He turned away and the men with him moved me, not too gently, after him. As we began to trot through the forest we passed bodies. Most of them were bandits, but not all. I counted twelve, and I knew there must have been more.

I hadn't yet come to the stage of believing in miracles, so the only thing I could think of to explain my rescue was that the government troops must have been waiting for the bandits. Or maybe they had been trailing the bandits, who must have been trailing me. Whichever way you look at it, it spells luck.

The potion I'd been given was getting a real workout, because I proceeded to run, stumble and hobble for three solid hours, which seemed more like three years. At the end of it I couldn't feel my feet hitting the ground, I was that far out of it.

The guys that were running with me, in armor and all, were something else. They moved like their legs were attached to something other than their hips.

At the end of the three hours I ran into the back of the man ahead of me as we suddenly stopped. We had left the heaviest portion of the forest. Now we were in light scrub country, a lot like north Florida.

As I gasped for breath and tried to get feeling back in my legs, I looked up and spotted a dozen men standing beside a whole lot of horses.

There was no discussion. The men who'd been jogging with me went to their horses, hoisting me onto the back of a saddled horse. He made a nervous sound as I slid on, but he wasn't half as nervous as I was.

The closest I'd ever come to a horse before that afternoon was when I was seventeen and a friend who owned one invited me to try my luck. The experience was so traumatic it left me with no desire ever to emulate the plains heroes.

But there was no time to worry about my lack of experience. With one man holding the reins so I couldn't take any side trips, the whole party galloped away. I kind of jounced and slid and clawed for a hold, and another minor miracle occurred. I managed to stay on.

The next six hours are, fortunately, dim in my memory. The major impression I have is of a searing pain in the area where I met my mount.

There were a lot of trees, looking like pines, and brush that looked a lot like what you'd find in some of the still wild areas of north Florida, where I went to school. As we traveled further east, though, it got flatter, the trees almost vanished and there were miles and miles of open, rolling plains.

We began to pass more and more small cottages. The inhabitants, in the few that still seemed to be occupied, were shy, peeking at us from behind half-closed doors as we passed. Then again, living that close to the mountain wild country, they had a right to be shy.

We rode nonstop. These guys acted like they were racing the end of the world, and in a way they were. The only thing that gave me hope was that the horses couldn't stand this pace for long, not burdened as they were with men in armor. Sooner or later we'd have to stop to rest.

About an hour after we'd mounted, according to my lying wristwatch, we pounded into another camp where more horses waited. The soldier who headed my little group leapt to the ground, exchanged a few words with another man and got a nod. I found myself being pulled off my horse and about two seconds later I was on the back of another one.

We did this six times in six hours until the entire world dwindled to the immediate area of my rear end and the only sound in the world was the thunder of horses' hoofs hitting dry brush and leaves.

We crossed a river, the water rising up around the horses' shoulders as they fought the slow-moving current. Because I hadn't looked up in a half hour, the castle seemed to appear out of nowhere.

It was out of the *Wizard of Oz*, with a moat, high towers on four sides, and guards along the tops of the walls.

We came to a halt at the edge of the moat and while I prayed thanks for the end of my ordeal, my captor shouted to the guards on the wall. A few minutes later, with a ponderous creaking, the drawbridge began to settle slowly toward the moat.

It hit the ground with a loud thud, the timbers quivering with the impact. I looked down and saw that the moat, instead of being filled with water, was filled with sharp stakes. The thought of what those stakes would do to a body that fell on them was enough to turn my stomach.

We rode through under the high gates, three abreast. I rode between two burly types, which showed just exactly how little they trusted me. As if I was going to be going anywhere.

In the center of the castle, dwarfing everything else and drawing my eyes away from the clusters of men and boys running toward us, was a twenty-foot-high statue of a man holding a sword out high above his head.

On his left hand was a ring in the form of a figure eight. It had to be old King Dorian the first, and that meant, unless like Stalin he'd gotten his statues plastered all over the place, this must be close to where the big battle had taken place long ago.

It stood to reason. From what little I'd learned, it seemed that the area of the mountainside and nearby plains was ripe for people and things popping back and forth between the dimensions. It wouldn't be too unlikely that the weak link between Ellendon and the Hann would be close-by.

And that meant I would be standing hip deep in the middle of a horde of angry, gray-skinned giants in a few days, unless my hosts finished me off first.

I was pulled down off my horse and hustled into a passageway. The interior was dimly lit by smoking torches. The stones in the wall, I noted, were covered with a green mold, and they just plain looked old.

We went up a row of stairs and then up another, down another hallway, up another row of stairs, and finally into a room where the sun shone through open windows.

The two men who'd brought me all this way fell to one knee in front of a young man sitting at the head of a long wooden table. One spoke quickly and quietly to him and the red-haired, middle-aged man sitting next to him.

Five'll get you ten, I thought, that these must be old Iverson and Dalien.

It was a sucker bet, because after hearing the speech, the young man got up from behind the table and came over to me.

"If my sister is dead, I will have my archers use you for target practice," he said in clear, clean English prose.

"I don't know—"

He slapped me, and after the ride I'd had and my legs feeling like they were made of Silly Putty, I nearly fell over.

"Don't lie, you scum. What did Krell do with her?"

Before I could think of what a stupid thing I was doing, I delivered a beautiful, short, right-handed upper cut to the young King's chin, and found out he had a glass jaw. It was probably the best punch I ever threw, more's the pity.

He crumpled like a scarecrow someone's taken the straw out of. Something hit me in the back of the head and things went black for a moment.

My head was splitting when I came to, lying on the floor with the two bully boys who'd brought me up looking down at me. As I slowly got to my knees I saw that Iverson had helped Dalien up and had given him a glass of something red to drink.

While Dalien swallowed, Iverson said, "For what you've done, friend, the men in the courtyard would gladly pull you apart, slowly. You realize that, don't you?"

I rubbed the back of my neck and didn't worry about getting up again.

"From what I've seen of this place, nothing would surprise me."

He grabbed me by my shirt and pulled me to my feet without trying. His muscles, I noticed, had muscles.

"I don't know what you've seen of Ellendon, but I can tell you from experience that these people can be a lot more innovative in making men die slowly than you could imagine. No matter what Krell is paying you, it isn't worth going through that. I would advise you to answer all our questions very honestly and you just might live to see the sun rise tomorrow."

"You're scaring me to death. Your offer doesn't really do anything for me. I never get up before noon."

I could hardly believe it was me talking and acting. Outside of the fact that I was putting my neck into a noose and pulling it tight, I was prouder of myself than I could ever remember being before. I was finally beginning to act like a hero. Maybe it's something that just has to grow on you.

"You talk a good game," Iverson said, letting go of my shirt, "but I wonder how brave you'll talk when they start lighting up the stakes they've pounded through your hands and feet. That's after they've stripped the skin from your stomach and done some interesting things with knives to your back."

"You've read your De Sade, anyway, haven't you?"

As quickly as it hit me, the feeling of elation vanished. The witty conversation turned me off. It sounded better on the movie screen or on pages of a book. I kept remembering this was real and real people's lives were at stake. And there was real red blood being spattered all over the landscape, not ketchup.

"Look—Iverson, if that's your name—I don't know what your man told you, but I didn't kidnap Syana, and I don't work for Krell."

He shook his head and said, "You're a bad liar."

I shivered, thinking of the last time somebody had said that, and wondered where Syana was, since she hadn't made it back.

"Look, let me sit down—on a pillow—and get something to eat and I'll tell you the whole story. If you don't believe it, you can still toss me to the animals outside. But I'm tired and I'm starving and I'll talk better with food in me."

Dalien had recovered from my punch and he came back into the conversation.

"You have the nerve to ask for food, while Syana is . . ."

He acted like he was going to swing on me, but Iverson put his hand out and stopped him.

"No, Dalien. We can talk to him while he's eating. The few minutes we lose won't make that much difference to Syana now, no matter what's happened to her. And if he's lying, we'll have a couple of days before the Hann get here to make him pay."

Five minutes later I was sitting, very carefully, on a soft pillow at the table, tearing into what tasted like venison. It tasted like heaven, too.

In between gulps I told my story, from the first moment when I'd heard Helen dispatch the unicorn report to when I'd met the government troops in the forest.

I left out what happened to Syana, however, telling her brother and Iverson that she'd managed to escape while I held off the bandits when we first met them.

Even if they believed my story, which I wasn't at all sure about, I would have found myself stretched out over a fire if the King learned his sister had been gangbanged because I'd butted in on earth.

I hadn't thought about that angle before, but if it had been my sister and some clod had gotten her into that situation, I wouldn't be at all satisfied to know he'd done it with the best of intentions.

When I finished I looked from one face to the other to see how much, if any of it, they believed. I could see that Dalien hadn't bought it. He was measuring me for the rack. Iverson, on the other hand, looked like he half believed me.

"It's just screwy enough that it might be true," he said to himself.

Dalien looked at him in amazement.

"You think he's telling the truth? One of the fairy tales you used to tell us would be more believable than that story he just gave us."

"I guess I'm just getting old," Iverson said, pacing back and forth, "but he doesn't sound like he's lying."

I began to think that maybe, just maybe, I had a chance.

I treaded very carefully, knowing that the conversation of the next few minutes was going to be the most important of my life.

"Look, in the first place, why would I come to Ellendon? From what Syana told me, I know that Krell isn't ever going to find this place healthy again. If you guys don't finish him off, the Hann will. What reason could he have to send me into a world where both sides are looking to skewer him? And why in the hell would I be stupid enough to come?"

Iverson ran his fingers through his thick red hair. For a man who must be in his late forties, he was pretty well preserved, and strong as an ox. Maybe it had something to do with the air. If you didn't get a sword or arrow in the stomach, you'd probably stay pretty healthy.

"I can't answer for your stupidity, Dell. I've got to admit that it doesn't make much sense, unless . . ."

He stared at me as if he was trying to read my mind.

"Unless Krell was crazy enough to think he could still work out some sort of deal with the Hann. He does have the Sword and the Ring. Maybe he thought that the Hann would still be willing to work with him in exchange for his keeping them out of circulation until after the big battle."

Dalien entered the conversation, saying, "And the Hann didn't buy it. When the deal blew up in your face, you had to make a run for it with the Hann and his men on your trail."

"Have you guys considered one small fact? Namely, that I make one hell of a poor ambassador. I don't speak your language and I don't speak the language of the Hann. I'd need Syana to translate. And what if she were to escape? Do you think Krell would be stupid enough to take a chance on something like that screwing up his deal?

"Besides, you guys are outsmarting yourselves. Why wouldn't Krell just come here himself. With the Ring and the Sword he wouldn't be in any trouble. He could always skip out if things got hot. That way he'd be sure of what was happening."

"He has a good point," Iverson said to Dalien.

I sat back for the next few minutes and let them argue about it. The King was for stringing me up on general principles, if only because my meddling had gotten his sister lost in bandit country. I was very glad I hadn't given him the full story because now more than ever I was sure that would have been the signature on my death warrant.

Iverson took a deep swig of the red stuff that smelled like cheap wine and said, "Dalien's right about one thing. Even if everything you say is gospel, your meddling has caused us a lot of trouble. It just might get us all killed. If you hadn't been there when Syana and Captain Rellim arrived on earth, they might have gotten the Ring and the Sword."

"Sue me. How the hell was I to know what was involved? What would you have said before you popped up here if somebody had come up to you with a story about another world and unicorns and monsters and mermaids. You would have called for the men in white, wouldn't you?"

"I probably would have done that," he agreed. His voice suddenly grew cold enough to send a few shivers down my back as he said, "That doesn't change what did happen. I love Syana as if she were my own daughter. If your meddling gets her killed, or causes this world to go under to the Hann, the last thing I'll do is put one of your own bullets in your brain."

There was no snappy comeback to that one because he meant it, and I sensed he could do it without a second thought if it came to it.

"So?" I said finally.

"I don't know," Iverson said. "Dalien, suppose we put him on ice for a while, tonight anyway, and decide what to do with him after we've had a little time to think about it."

"I applaud your decision, gentlemen," I said when Dalien gave a nod. He said something to the guards and I took another little trip down through the castle corridors.

They weren't taking any chances. We came to a barred door. One of the guards produced a set of rusty keys and opened the door. There was a sound like somebody running their fingernails down a blackboard, and I was gently propelled inward. I landed on my face in dirty straw, stubbing my foot on something hard along the way.

I got to my feet and walked back toward the door, stumbling on a loose brick again. There were no windows and only the small, two-by-two-foot window in the door, through which the dim light of the torch cast an even dimmer radiance. It was almost as dark as night in the cell.

I could just barely grip the bars with my hands without standing on tiptoe. I listened to the tread of the guards as they walked back through the dim corridors, and then I was alone.

I don't know how long I stood there that way. I couldn't remember when I started or when I found myself sitting in the darkness next to the door.

It was a situation where Norman Vincent Peale would have thrown in the towel, and I was never an optimist to begin with.

It was a situation someone is going to have to invent a new word for, because despair, hopelessness and defeat don't even come close. I found myself wondering if there was any way things could get worse.

With my luck I'd probably find out.

CHAPTER TEN

The creak of the cell door opening brought me to my feet awkwardly, stiff from the position I'd been lying in.

In the light of the open door my watch showed that four hours had passed in the darkness. It could have been four days, or four minutes.

Iverson stepped in, holding the keys in his hand. I looked beyond him and couldn't see any guards.

"Let's get something straight right off. I didn't bring any guards along because I want this to be a private conversation, but the day'll never come when you can take me. So save yourself some pain and forget about getting out of here."

"Why would I want to? I don't have anything waiting for me out there."

"If you're who you say you are. If you're lying, and you can see there's no way for me to be sure, your friends might be waiting for you out there."

Despite myself I could see his point.

"Who's President now?"

"Connally."

There was no sign of recognition of the name.

"How long have you been here, anyway?"

"Twenty-two years. I came here in 1957. But I never heard of anyone named Connally."

"I don't know if he was even governor of Texas then. He was riding with President Kennedy when Kennedy was killed."

"Kennedy? John Kennedy?"

"That's the one. He must have been a senator when you came here."

He shook his head slowly.

"Kennedy, of all people. I used to live in Massachusetts, for a while. I never thought he'd make President. And you say he was killed?"

"A guy by the name of Lee Oswald shot him as he was driving in an open car through Dallas. They got Oswald, but Jack Ruby shot him before they could get him to trial."

He looked at me as if I was telling him some strange and wondrous fairy tale.

"Take it slow, Dell. I want to hear it all."

"Why?" I asked, although I didn't want to antagonize him. There was always the chance I could still swing him over to my side.

He propped his back up against the open door.

"I may be dead in a few days. You may be. Maybe everybody in this castle. Before I die I want to find out what's happened to my home.

"It's funny to call it that. I've never regretted coming to Ellendon. There's no way to compare it to what I left. Here I'm alive. You can't know what it's like, Dell, to live without movies and cars and every inch of green covered by cement.

"You can't know what it's like to live without worrying about the Bomb dropping on your head, or income taxes, or being run over by some drunk idiot."

I just had to say something. He was getting too idyllic for me to stomach.

"Yeah. All you have to worry about here is getting stabbed or knifed or shot with an arrow. And do you have any coffee here, or books? What do you do if you get a bad tooth, or appendicitis?"

He smiled at that.

"I know what you mean. I felt the same way when I first got here. All I wanted to do was go home, any way I could. They wouldn't let me go though, because they were afraid I'd talk about what I'd seen. And after I was here for a while, I didn't want to go back.

"They've got something, I guess you'd call it magic for want of a better word, that works as well as any high-priced doctor you could get on earth. Sure, you can get knifed, or stabbed, but there was always the chance of getting killed back on earth. Here, if it comes, it'll be clean and open and you at least have a chance to fight back."

He shook his head again, saying, "No, Ellendon is primitive all right, but it's got earth beat any way you look at it. Life is rough and simple, but at least you feel alive every morning. Can you say the same thing about your life back there?"

It was like a dentist missing with the Novocaine and when he puts the drill down it cuts right to the core of the nerve. In a few words Iverson had told me why my life was worth nothing, not even to myself.

"But, with all that, seeing you brought back memories. I guess you can't ever get away from what you are, what you were. I wouldn't go back to earth now, even if I could, even if it meant I could save my skin. But I don't want to die without knowing what it's like now, what's happened since I left."

He was silent again for a moment, then said, "It's strange to say this, and I don't think I knew it until right now, but I'm a little homesick."

So for an hour I spun a tapestry of magic tales about a weird and dangerous world called earth. Along the way I mentioned Kennedy and Johnson and Vietnam, Whitman, Speck, Manson and Cleaver, The Black Panthers, Women's Lib, Gay Lib, Yellow Power and the Down with Rome Backlash.

There was Moonday and James Bond, L.S.D. and the brain ticklers who used electric currents fed into the brain for their kicks. Also the pollution fighters and their May 27 Day of Vengeance when three leading industrialists were executed in '78.

There were the riots in the cities, the prisons, the colleges, Berkeley, Kent State and the U of F, Watts and Woodstock and Attica.

As I was speaking a strange sense of unreality came over me. What was I doing in a stone cell in Ellendon spinning tales of a bloody, terrible, glorious fantasy world called earth. I couldn't expect Iverson to believe the myths when I didn't believe them myself.

Iverson didn't say a word throughout. When I stopped I wondered what he was thinking, if he felt any loss for a world that he had known, which was now as dead as if it had never been.

"I don't know whether to envy the hell out of you, Dell, or feel very sorry for you, growing up in that kind of a world."

"Right now I'd take it over what I've got, no contest."

"I don't blame you."

He hefted the keys up and down in his hand and I constructed a momentary fantasy of myself escaping from the castle and Ellendon. But, as with most fantasies, it foundered on a cold, cruel fact. In this case, Iverson's fists, and arms and shoulders and . . .

"For your sake, and ours, I'm sorry you got into this, Dell. I believe you're telling the truth, and you're not really to blame for all this. But, Syana was closer to me than my own daughter would have been, if I'd had one. When I think of her out there alone, surrounded by those animals . . ."

I decided I'd better take his mind off that.

"I may never have another chance to ask you, so I'd better take the opportunity. It's been bugging the hell out of me. What is all this around us? Do you know what's going on around here, and how did you get here, anyway?"

That seemed to do the trick.

"I wish I could tell you. I wish I knew. I was in the Army when I came through. I enlisted in '56, as a thirty-two-year-old private.

I'd been to college, worked as a rising young businessman, got married and divorced. After that I must have worked in a hundred jobs around the country, ranging from gas-pump jockey to an oil-field worker in Oklahoma.

"I joined the Army mostly for the hell of it. I wasn't going anywhere in particular and the Army was as good and secure a way to kill time as I knew. On a furlough I fled to Chicago, picked up a girl and got a motel room. The next morning, when I stepped out the door to pick up a paper, I stumbled through into Ellendon."

He grinned at me.

"If you think you had a hard time adjusting to Ellendon, brother, you should have seen me those first few hours. I was sure I'd gone around the bend, out of my head for good. I was stumbling around and pinching myself. I must have been black and blue. I couldn't figure out what had happened. I didn't believe in heaven, or hell, but even if I had, this didn't look like either one.

"Then I ran into Frisa."

I thought I had seen his dark side, but I hadn't until that moment. It frightened me because I knew I could never have, or stand a chance against, that kind of deadly anger.

"She was the woman you ran into in the forest, the one Suldurus killed. God, I wish I'd been there. Or that I could have talked her into leaving her cottage and coming into the civilized part of Ellendon. But she wouldn't have come, I know.

"She was real, and all woman. I knew I wasn't crazy then. She took me in and fed me and taught me her language. When I'd learned it she took me down to a village and left me there. From the village I eventually made it to the court of Dalien's father, Bytus."

I asked him a question that bothered me, because it tore even the fragile logic of this place to shreds.

"I don't understand how you got here from Chicago, landing on the mountainside, whereas I got here from Sarasota. Why should we start from different places and wind up in the same one?"

He shrugged.

"I wasn't a scientist to start with, and I don't think they go by our rules here, anyway. I thought at first when you mentioned coming from Sarasota that it might have something to do with the fact that the earth, and I guess Ellendon, is revolving in space, and moving through space. Or maybe distance isn't the same here as there. Who knows?"

"I don't know about you, but I'm curious about what we're into. How can there be unicorns and giants and mermaids? And that magic that Frisa used, or Syana back on earth. How can you believe in that?"

Iverson shook his head as I paced.

"That I've never been able to figure out, and I quit trying a long time ago. I didn't believe in magic before I got here, but I've seen things I can't explain any other way. I've seen some things I know you wouldn't believe if I told you. They've got something here they call the Lords of Ellendon, and what they can do I still can't believe.

"All I know is that this world is real, Dell. You bleed when you're cut, and you can taste the food and the wine. Your ass gets just as sore on top of a horse, and a woman feels just as good. So I take the magic along with everything else."

"And some of that blood may be Syana's. Why won't you let me take some of your troops out to where Syana and I were together last. We might be able to find her. Or the barrier between earth and here might break again, and you'd have a chance to get to Krell. Why are you just sitting around here?"

"You know better than that. I believe what you've told me, but I can't trust you. You might lead the men into an ambush."

"So you're just going to write this world off by not even trying for Krell?"

"It's not that simple. I'd go after Syana myself, if I could. But the thing is, we don't know exactly when the Hann are going to come through. It could be five minutes from now, or five days. And when they do, we're going to need every man we've got here.

"Sure, we might be able to use what they call the Talented Ones, but it would be a gamble on finding Krell even if they went into the mountains. And since he's wearing the Ring, he could always run to another world, and we'd have to search for him again.

"We stand a better chance of gathering all our men here. The Hann have the equivalent of our Talented Ones. The old legends say that it's not only the natural process of both worlds coming together again, but the work of the Hann that opens the Gates.

"We think if we can kill these Talented Ones, we'll be able to close the Gates without the Ring and the Sword. Or, the Gates will close by themselves. It's not certain, but there's a chance. We're going to lose a lot of men, but there doesn't seem to be any other way."

The unfairness of it hit me once again. It was a juvenile reaction, I knew, but I couldn't help feeling that nobody had the right to do this to me.

"And I'm in for the duration, right? You won't trust me to fight, so if you lose they'll just come down here and slaughter me like an animal. And even if you win, I've got a funny feeling you're not going to let me go."

"You're right. We can't let you go. If you're with Krell, we don't want you going back to tell him the invasion failed. He might start getting ideas again. If you're not, we still don't want anyone on earth who knows about Ellendon.

"It's not that bad, really. If we can find Syana afterward, and she confirms what you've told us, you'll be given your freedom. This wouldn't be a bad place to spend the rest of your life. Ellendon would be enough for any man, but there's a lot more of this world I'd take a look at if I were your age. There's got to be a way around the mountains and volcanoes that surround Ellendon. There's a whole unknown world out there."

Somehow the rhetoric didn't start my blood singing through my veins. If Syana died before she could confirm my story, I'd be a prisoner the rest of my life. If she lived, she'd tell her brother she'd been raped. I knew I'd never leave Ellendon alive then, no matter what Iverson or Syana said.

He turned toward the door. The brick in my hand weighed a ton as I took the two steps that brought me to his back. He heard me and was turning when the brick caught him in the side of the head.

As simple as that. Muscles and all, he slumped to the floor. He lay with one arm under his head.

Brick in hand, I dropped to his side and tried to figure out why I'd just assaulted the only man in Ellendon who'd been halfway decent to me. Not to mention being the only other man from earth.

The answer was the keys he held in his hand, and the half-opened door. Once he shut it behind him, it would be all over for me. Only the hand that held the sword might be different. Either the Hann, or the King.

I reached down and felt for a heartbeat, and then a pulse. I couldn't feel anything. That didn't mean much. I never could find my own pulse and there have been times I couldn't find my own heartbeat. But here it meant Iverson might be dead. I couldn't stay around to find out.

I took the dagger he wore on his belt, which I hadn't seen, and the keys. I would like to have seen that he got medical attention, but I couldn't afford to have him discovered. So I closed the cell door, after moving him where he couldn't be seen from the outside, and locked it.

Once outside the cell and into the narrow corridor, I tried to figure out what my next move was. It was obvious I couldn't get all the way out of the castle without being spotted, and there was no way I could avoid being recaptured.

Unless I had a hostage. And the only hostage around valuable enough to make my life absolutely secure was the King. The only problem, of course, was how to get to him. I didn't even know if I could find my way out, much less find him. But I had nothing to lose by looking.

I followed the crumbling steps as they wound ever upward. They hadn't been kidding when they called it a dungeon. It must have been a couple of stories below ground.

When I got to the first crossing of passages I hugged the wall and took a quick peek around the corner. There was no one around. Thinking back, it seemed I had come straight down, so I went straight up.

I kept going without seeing anyone. The time of night, it must have been around 2 A.M., was a big help. I might be able to get to the top of the castle without running into any of the kitchen help. Or being run through.

That situation changed suddenly. I nearly walked into an old woman carrying a plate of cold food. As I came up behind her she heard my steps and turned. As she caught sight of me she dropped the tray and started to scream.

I was at her side in one step, pressing the knife to her throat. She fought to swallow the scream, her skin like leather where I had my hands on her throat. She gulped, trembled and then, with no advance warning, fell against me.

I lowered her to the floor, keeping the knife against her throat in case she was putting on an act. It was no act. I pushed an eyelid up and saw white. She had fainted on me.

Dell the mugger! I was becoming a really ripe character, slugging old men in the head with bricks and attacking old ladies. If this little jaunt through Ellendon didn't kill me, it would do ineradicable harm to my moral fiber.

I gently slapped the old lady's face a couple of times until she made gasping noises and opened her eyes. She took one look at me and I thought she was going to faint again. She opened her mouth and I touched the dagger to her throat again.

"Sssshh," I said, with my finger to my lips. She got the message.

"Where's the King? Dalien?"

A gleam of recognition shown in her eyes when I mentioned Dalien's name, but she continued to shake her head in puzzlement. I pressed the dagger a little deeper into her throat. It changed her mind. She pointed down the corridor she had just come through.

"That's better. Now, take me there."

I got the message across with gestures again. She didn't act too happy, but she led me. I took the tray, minus the hunks of cold meat, along with us. Made of solid, heavy iron, it would be a good club if I needed one.

I did. We walked through the corridors for five agonizing minutes until we suddenly came to a large open area. A man slept sitting near the doorway of a small room. He was snoring hard, and loud, but I couldn't take the chance that he might wake up during the coming excitement.

I sssshh'ed the old lady again and drew the dagger lightly across her throat to show what would happen to her if she made any trouble for me. Not that I would have, even at that point, but by then she probably would easily have believed me capable of molesting infants, or worse.

Still holding the woman with one hand, we crept up to the guard. I stood to one side, holding my breath, as he moved against the hard wooden bench he sat on. I grabbed the tray securely in my right hand, letting the old woman go, and brought it down on the back of his head.

He fell heavily to the floor, but he had a hard head. Groaning loudly, he managed to get to his knees. He was looking around as if he couldn't see anything. I didn't want to think about the possibility that maybe he couldn't see—now. I hit him again, harder.

The old woman had stepped away from me, but when I turned back to her, she froze. I beckoned to her and she came back without trouble.

I heard a noise from inside the doorway and grabbed her, pulling her back with me to the wall. A second later the King, dressed only in a woolly nightgown, stepped through the doorway rubbing his eyes.

When he saw what lay on the floor his eyes opened wide and he opened his mouth to call for help. I let the woman go and got him in a hammerlock. I held the knife in my right hand to his throat as he twisted.

"One word and you're dead," I managed to get out while grappling with him.

"You!" he gasped furiously as I spun him around and slammed his back into the wall. I held the knife to his throat. His hands were stretched out to grab my arm, but he held them still as I dug in with the dagger.

"Me, in the flesh. We're going on a little trip."

The old woman had backed away again and was on the point of running. I shook my head and showed her the dagger against her King's throat. Nonverbal communication can be marvelously effective sometimes.

"Do what you will, but my men will kill you."

"Don't be stupid. I know how important you are right now. You can't afford to get yourself killed. There are too many people depending on you."

I could sense he was almost on the verge of committing suicide. Then, as he thought about it, the tension in his body eased.

"You're bluffing. Kill me and my men will cut you to pieces. You will have no one to protect you then."

"Maybe, Your Majesty, but what do I have to lose? I'm pretty sure you'd kill me sooner or later."

"What are you going to do?" he said finally, apparently resigning himself to whatever was going to happen. I didn't loosen my grip on him or the dagger. He could be trying to lull me off guard.

"I'm going to ride out of this castle with you. I'm sure if you tell your men you're going out for a night ride with a friend, they won't stop you. And in the darkness I doubt there'll be anyone who was close enough to me this morning to recognize me."

"And then what? Where can you go? Are your Hann friends waiting?"

That stopped me. I hadn't gone any further in my thoughts than wanting out. Where could I go? There was no one I could turn to. Only Syana would have helped me, and the odds were good she needed a lot of helping herself right about now.

It was then the big idea hit me, but I would have gotten it by a process of elimination sooner or later. The only safe haven was earth. And the only chance of getting back, although a long shot, was to go back to the mountains where I'd first arrived. There was a chance, just a chance, that lightning might strike twice.

"Don't worry about it."

"Am I going to go like this?" he asked suddenly.

I saw it would be unusual for the King to go riding in his nightgown.

"All right. You can dress in your room. Where is Iverson's room?"

"We were sleeping in the same room. Where is he?"

"How should I know? Go on in," I said, guiding him with the knife in his back. I motioned and the old lady followed us in.

"Which is Iverson's bed?"

The King pointed to one near a window overlooking the courtyard. I dragged the King along with me. He realized what I was looking for and jerked away. I couldn't stab him though.

I felt a hard form at the foot of the bed and pulled the blanket away. I had the .38 aimed at the King's back as he reached for a sword hanging in a scabbard near his bed.

"Don't. I can kill you before you turn around."

He stiffened, not moving away from the sword, but not moving any closer.

"You know I've got the gun, and Iverson must have told you what one of them can do."

"You win. What now?"

"Get dressed."

The old woman had stood like she was rooted to the floor during the excitement. I told her to come over and turned her around. She trembled as if she expected that would be it right there. I pulled her hands behind her and tied them with a strip of heavy cloth that looked like a scarf.

After I'd gagged her, I brought the guard in and did the same with him. Then I motioned to the door with the gun.

"Let's go. And don't make any mistakes. I'll have the gun in my pocket, but I can kill you a lot quicker than any of your men can pick me off, and I'll be at your side every second."

He smiled a very grim smile.

"This won't do you any good, Dell. One way or the other, you will die in my land. Your bones will be scattered to the wind and there will be no one to remember you, or mourn you."

His words struck home, but what was the difference really? I didn't want to die, but would there be any mourners if I'd been run down by a car on earth? I didn't really think so.

I followed him down the stairway out into the courtyard. There were men on guard, but Dalien merely glanced at them. They stared at us, but made no move to stop us. I walked behind and to the left of him, the hand holding the .38 sweating badly.

We walked into the early morning darkness and the smell of horses and burning wood. It was chillier than I remembered from the night before. Men were gathered around a fire near what I thought were stables. We walked toward them, the castle battlements looming up in the moonlight like cliffs.

Some of the men stood up when we got close enough for them to recognize Dalien. One of them threw a hasty question at him, to which the King replied sharply. The man who'd spoken looked puzzled and said something else.

I didn't have to speak the language to know that Dalien reminded him he was a nobody and Dalien was the King, and if he wanted to keep his head on his shoulders, he'd better follow orders and mind his own damn business.

Two horses were brought out and bridled. I let the King mount first. He stared down at me and I knew the few seconds I was mounting would be the most dangerous of all. My hands would be occupied and he might be foolish enough to take the opportunity to call for help. Or, glimpsing his character a little better, go for me himself.

The King sat quietly, never taking his eyes off me. When I was up I motioned to the gate and the King nodded.

We rode toward it and even as we did the drawbridge began its creaking journey toward the opposite bank. When we'd passed out of earshot of the men in the courtyard, I said, "Where did you tell them you were going?"

"I just told them I felt like taking a ride. I've done it before. Our patrols are out scouting around this area."

We rode over the drawbridge in almost total silence. Except for the sound of insects in the night and a distant howling there was only the ring of the horses' hoofs against the wood and iron of the drawbridge.

When we'd gotten about a hundred yards from the castle, I reined in my horse. Already I was beginning to wish they'd invented cars on Ellendon. Anything but another six hours in the saddle.

"What now?" the King asked.

I was pretty sure of the way to the river, but beyond that it would be all guesswork. I'd never find my way to the mountains by myself.

"Dalien, you're going to be riding with me, so for your sake how do we get to the mountains the quickest way? As soon as we get there, I'll let you go. The quicker we reach them, the sooner you'll be free."

Of course, I had no intention of letting him go. If we ran into bandits again he would be on my side for the duration. If we ran into government troops, he would be a hostage. I expected he would be smart enough to see that.

Instead, he said, "The less time I spend with you the better I'll feel. There is a shorter, though rougher, way to the mountains."

It was hard to believe he was that desperate to get rid of me but I wasn't in any position to refuse his help.

"Which way?"

"After me," he said.

The next few hours gave me the time to think, which was bad. I started to think of what the odds were against having lightning strike twice in the same spot. The barrier between the worlds might break a hundred yards away from me in the forest and I'd never know it. I might wander back to earth in five minutes, or maybe not in fifty years.

I forced myself to stop thinking along those lines. I would find a break in the veil and I would reach earth again. I'd be back in my green bug and drive back to my tiny apartment. I'd be getting drunk and happy on Saturday nights.

And when I picked up a paperback on the newsstand with a mighty-thewed hero slaying dragons on distant worlds on the front cover, I would sneer with the age-old arrogance of those who've been through the real thing.

When I got back!

Dalien picked his way through the moonlit land as though he were very familiar with the area. When I asked him he said he and his father had often hunted wild beasts in the forests near the mountains.

As we rode I kept my eyes open for a trap but there was nothing to disturb the stillness of the night except the sounds of the hunters and the hunted.

"I'm sorry we had to meet like this, Your Highness."

He said nothing as he continued to stare at me.

"What I mean is, whether you believe it or not, I am not in this with Krell. Coming here under other circumstances would have been the biggest adventure of my life. It could have been the best thing in my life. Except it just didn't work out."

"I'm your prisoner, Dell. Why protest your innocence to me? It doesn't matter what I think of you now, does it?"

"To hell with you, Your Highness."

I had been telling the truth. What wouldn't I have given to have come to Ellendon, to have traveled across the dimensions, under different circumstances. If Syana had come to me then and given me the chance to visit a strange new world I wouldn't have hesitated to leave the prison of my days.

Only things are never the way they should be, and circumstances are never right. Ellendon had become hell and adventure a dirty word.

It was still dark when the horses began to snort and fight us, trying to avoid going the way we wanted. I was using the reins on mine as hard as I could, and even so I could barely keep him headed in the same direction as the King.

I could see the King was having the same trouble, but he was making his way easier because he was a horseman.

"What's the matter? Why are they fighting us so hard?"

The King shook his head without looking back. The whinnying of the horses grew louder and, try as I might, I found it almost impossible to follow the King.

"Hold it," I said finally, just barely keeping my mount from bolting to the rear. The King pulled his horse to a halt and said, "We must keep going if you wish to reach the mountains."

Paranoia was easy to slip into in Ellendon. I began to wonder why the King had so easily consented to show me the way to the mountains when he could have gone in circles to give his men time to catch up with us. Also, why the horses were whinnying as if they smelled or sensed something very unfriendly ahead of us.

"There's no reason for the horses to be so skittish unless they know something of what's out there. I've got the feeling you know too."

"It could be they sense a traga, an animal that resembles a large mountain lion on your earth. Or maybe a pack of wild dogs is out. But we cannot turn back."

Fighting to keep my mount from throwing me, no easy task as he began to rear into the air and claw at it with his hoofs, I tried to think clearly. What the King had said sounded logical enough, and who was I to argue with him about anything on Ellendon.

On the other hand, I got the very strange feeling that something was watching us. Trees loomed up in the darkness, spidery branches reaching out like clutching hands. It was a weird scene.

But not weird enough to cause the feelings running through me. I'd been through a lot in the past couple of days and my nerves weren't too steady at the best of times. I do have a vivid imagination, but not that vivid.

I was nearly strangling the horse with the reins, enough to calm him down to the point I could stay on him.

"What is it? Are your men out there? If there's an ambush, you'll be the first down."

I had the .38 out now and aimed at the King.

"As far as I know," he said in a strange tone indicating he was feeling the same things I was, "no one is out there. Do you want to go the long way about to the mountains? It will take extra hours."

I was tempted to tell him yes, but the thought of what might be waiting behind me was all too real compared with a mere feeling I now had.

"After you."

This time I stayed with him. The horses continued to fight wildly, their struggles growing more frenzied. Then my horse was bucking wildly and I couldn't stay on.

I hit the ground on my back. The wind was knocked out of me for a second. When I got to one elbow I saw the King was fighting to hold his horse steady. My own horse was gone, his hoof beats fading rapidly.

"It looks like we ride two on one."

He shook his head.

"No, this is as far as I go."

The jaws of the trap had sprung. Whatever he had been planning from the time he so easily agreed to guide me was now ready.

I pointed the .38 at his head, saying, "What I said before still goes. Don't make me prove it."

He let his horse carry him a few yards away.

"You won't shoot me now."

"I've got all the reason in the world to. Get off the horse."

"I can't go any farther with you. The only way you'll get me down is by shooting me."

"Don't make me. I'll shoot you here just as easily as I would back in the castle. A lot easier, in fact, because here I still have a chance of getting away before your men catch up to me."

"Do you know where you are?"

I had risen and I risked a quick look behind me. The moon had come out, a crescent shape giving just enough light to create the illusion of mist rising out of the ground, circling and twirling amid the branches of the trees.

When I didn't answer, he said, "This is the Land Where No Man Goes."

When they start using that tone of voice I get uneasy.

"This is the land of the Lords of Ellendon. It is sacred to them and no man or animal may cross over it and live."

I tried to throw off the suffocating feeling of being watched.

"We're doing pretty good so far. I haven't noticed any bolts of lightning being tossed around."

His horse began to buck, but Dalien held it steady.

"They are real and they need no lightning to do their bidding."

"I don't know what you're trying to pull, but I don't buy it. I won't tell you again. Get down so I can mount."

"It would do no good. The horse cannot be forced to go more than a few yards. Then nothing you could do would stop him from fleeing. You know the feeling this place gives you, think how it affects an animal."

He had a point.

"All right. We'll both ride him out of this place and then we'll find a way around it."

He shook his head again.

"I fear not. Your path leads you there," he said, pointing in the direction we had been traveling.

"You really want to commit suicide, don't you?"

For the first time he smiled.

"You won't shoot me. You see, if you go this way you will find a shortcut that will lead you to the mountains in a few hours, even on foot."

"That doesn't change one thing. You're going with me, even if you have to walk."

He shook his head again. His calm air of certainty was annoying. "I fear death less than I fear the Lords."

"Come off it, Dalien. You're not superstitious. You're just trying to pull a fast one, and it won't work."

"I'm not superstitious, Dell, but I will not anger the Lords. And you will not shoot me."

"Just what makes you so damned certain?"

"Because if you shoot me there would never be a hiding place that would spare you from my men. Even if the Hann overcome my world, some of my men will survive and they will come looking for you. You don't want that kind of threat always behind you."

He had me, at least in the terms in which he saw me. I wasn't going to shoot him anyway, but I'd been hoping I could bluff him if he really thought I was a bloodthirsty murderer.

"All right," I said, lowering the gun. "But if you're not lying, what does this get you? I'll make the shortcut and get to the mountains before your men. Why'd you show me the shortcut?"

"Because you don't believe in the Lords, and you will never reach the shortcut. You don't believe, and that is what will kill you."

He gave his horse a dig in the ribs and it took off like a bullet.

The sound of the horse's hoofs retreating in the distance made the night lonelier than it had been. I rubbed my shoulder where I'd hit the ground and looked around.

Which didn't help matters any. There really was mist rising out of the ground, although I hadn't seen any when we first rode through. Fog is an eerie thing at best, but I felt like taking off after Dalien now.

It was more than nerves. It felt like someone was running ice-cold water down my back. No matter how fast I turned I couldn't seem to shake the feeling that there was someone, or something, just behind me.

I couldn't stay there. No matter how bad it was, it couldn't get so bad I wouldn't try to make it back to the mountainside and earth. So I walked into the darkness, the world spinning wildly beneath my feet.

There was something in the trees. I couldn't see anything. I stepped closer to one tree, looked into the ink-blot pattern of its branches. I stood in a pool of shadow that hid even the faint radiance of the moon. There was nothing to be seen, but I knew with everything in me that something was close-by.

There was only a twittering like frightened birds and they came at me. I screamed and fell back and the night became hell.

When I was a kid my cousins and I used to play in an old orchard that had been abandoned years before. One day, when it was close to dark in the half twilight, I was running from one of my cousins in some game and I dived under a gnarled old tree that had once borne green oranges.

I felt a soft stickiness across my face and ears and shoulders. And then scurrying, many-legged creatures crawling across me. I'd rolled clear, trying to pull the cobwebs off me and brush the spiders off, unable even to scream.

It must have been only seconds before my cousins and I got the spiders off, but I kept brushing my face and back and hair for hours. When I got home I washed and washed and I dreamed that night of falling through yards of soft cobwebs while spiders big as cats ran across my body.

I'd never forgotten the feeling of those furry little legs crawling across me. Now they really were the size of cats.

I hit the ground rolling, knocking the first of the furry bodies off me. I came up swinging the gun butt in front of me and knocked another of the furry monstrosities to the side.

As the gun hit its body, it gave in squishily and the thing chirped like a goddamned parakeet as it cartwheeled through the air.

I back-pedaled in fourth gear seeing the light of tiny eyes sparkling like a miniature field of stars as they came leaping at me.

A white blur lunged between me and leaping monsters. It was higher than the trees, or so it seemed to me, looking up at the gleaming horn that must have been five feet long.

The unicorn brought its hoofs down on the squirming mass of hairy flesh. The sound was like someone smashing a soft-boiled egg with a hammer. There was gore on the knife-sharp hoofs as it brought them high into the moonlight and then down again.

One of the spiders hurled itself through the air at the unicorn's mighty head, as silver as a dime in the moonlight. With a motion so quick you saw only the afterimage, the unicorn skewered the mewling body on the gleaming, corkscrew horn.

With a flick of its head, the unicorn sent the dead body flying. I was still scrambling backward, the memory of those shapes hurtling out of the darkness at me too vivid.

The spiders were turning back now. Though there seemed to have been a living carpet of them coming across the grass at me, they were running now, covering a yard with each hop, heading for their trees again. The unicorn didn't follow. It snorted and stomped some of the already crushed bodies a little farther into the dirt. Then it turned its horn on me.

I could understand why Mrs. Carr had seemed a little drunk when she'd described the unicorn. It was the kind of sight that would have intoxicated the strictest teetotaler.

This was the magic I hadn't found in Ellendon, or on earth. It was every dream men have ever had of something better than themselves. I could understand why the unicorn had captivated men throughout history.

To call it a horse with a horn on its head was like calling man an ape who had come out of the trees. Both were true, but neither came close to describing all the things that both were.

I knew, without knowing how, that there was intelligence behind the eyes of the unicorn. I couldn't read the luminous gaze it directed at me, but it was not the mute stare of an animal.

I shook my head and forcibly fought away the sense of wonder and magic the sight of the unicorn sent over me. The horn, while beautiful, was covered with blood and it could just as easily make a very big, and messy, hole in me.

It lowered its head, pointing the horn precisely at my stomach and took a thunderous, yet strangely delicate, step toward me. I let my gun hang at my side. I didn't want to make a decision yet on whether my life was worth killing something like the unicorn.

I backed up and it followed me. I took a step to my left and it snorted, taking a quick step closer. I froze, then moved cautiously to my right. That was the way.

A few more moves established the pattern. The unicorn wanted me to go with it (him?). I wasn't in any position to argue and I was curious to see where it was headed, not to mention the fact that the dark trees seemed infinitely safer with the huge bulk near me.

We walked for a hundred yards through the trees until we came to a small clearing. In the center was what looked like a Persian ziggurat and near it a stunted tree.

There was nothing else in the clearing and I looked around curiously. What was there here that could have drawn the unicorn? It kept prodding me to move, heading me toward the structure.

There were strange symbols carved into the stones. Men and animals and things I couldn't even come close to identifying. There was a darkened opening at the base of the structure, which must have been twelve feet high, but I couldn't see inside.

I was peering into the opening when I heard a muttered whisper. When I looked up there was no one there. I looked back at the unicorn but it couldn't have been him. It had been a human sound. Then I heard it again.

I looked the tree over, stepping closer. There was no one on it, or in the branches. Where else could the voice be coming from? There was simply no other place anyone could hide in this open field.

The voice was coming from the tree.

The whisper brought my eyes up and into contact with two gleaming eyes set in a human face, growing out of the tree.

CHAPTER ELEVEN

I'm really very credulous. Unicorns, mermaids, Cyclopes, flying monsters, giant spiders in trees, the Hann and magic Rings are acceptable. Faces growing out of trees are not.

The face, its wrinkled lips moving slowly, spoke again. It sounded like it was speaking in the language of Ellendon.

"Oh, Jesus, I must be flying. But what am I flying on?"

When the face heard me speaking to myself it first frowned, then looked puzzled. I started to move away from the tree but the unicorn was poised as if to suggest it wouldn't like that. So I took a step closer to the tree and took a better look at the nightmare.

"Are you for real?" I asked, knowing how stupid the question was and that the face probably wouldn't understand me. On the other hand, what do you say to a face growing out of a tree that you've just met? Nothing in my upbringing had prepared me for this delicate social situation.

A closer look didn't make it any more believable. The face, complete with ears, was distinct, the flesh growing into the grayish bark without a clear dividing line. The head was like a bas-relief carved into the wood, using human flesh as clay.

It looked like the face of an old man, the wrinkles in the leathery skin almost making it blend in with the bark around it. Only the eyes were young, abnormally large for the face, glowing a deep golden hue in the moonlight.

"Earth?" the voice whispered.

"What?"

"From earth?" the voice said again. Despite the slurred, low tone, I could understand it without difficulty.

I could only nod silently.

"How?"

"It's . . . it's a long story. Are you for real, or am I dreaming?"

"Real. Go . . . transporter."

The unicorn snorted and pointed with its horn to the doorway into the ziggurat.

"You want me to go in there?"

"Yes."

It was all too far out. It didn't frighten me because it seemed like an esoteric shaggy dog story. I wondered what the punch line was going to be.

"What's down there?"

"Go."

The unicorn snorted again, pawing the grass, and gave me the general impression any more dawdling on my part was going to make it unhappy. So I went.

I could see a stairway leading down into the ground. It took a sharp turn and I could see a dim light where it did. I went down toward the light.

When I turned the corner I thought I'd wandered into a transplanted discotheque. I couldn't tell how big the room was. There was a strobe centered somewhere in the ceiling. The room was caught in the eternal frozen glare, the strobe running so rapidly it was almost impossible to see anything.

On the back wall, twenty feet or two hundred yards away, green and blue squares played tag with each other, forming kaleidoscopic tapestries that might have been fifty by fifty feet, or fifty by fifty miles. It was like standing at the narrow end of a telescope staring out into an open-ended infinity. The illusion was so strong for a moment I almost tried to grab something to stop my slide down into the abyss.

I turned to find my way out. Even the unicorn was better than this. I'd take my chances with that wicked horn. But there was nothing behind me. I mean nothing. I almost threw up.

It's like the old analogy. Try to imagine what the area you can't see in the back of your head looks like. Not darkness, but nothingness. You can't do it. I can't do it any more. But I did then.

I closed my eyes and the darkness was a blessed relief. Suddenly there was nothing anywhere in the universe but me. I could feel my feet but I couldn't feel the floor I was standing on.

A moment later I fell on my head. I opened my eyes and found that, wonder of wonders, the walls had come back. Only, not the walls I had entered. No kaleidoscopic screens here. Bright metallic walls, unseamed, with no openings at all and no light source, although a harsh white light lit every corner of the room.

I got rather shakily to my feet and inspected my cell, because it had that distinct air of being a cell. They all share a certain something that you can almost smell after a while. In some of the worst cases you really can smell it, but even the brightest, best-cleaned cell acquires a scent of its own. It's the scent that trapped animals give off, soaking into the walls, compounded of fear and despair and rage.

It's a good thing that my claustrophobia is of a mild, unadvanced type, because the cell was tight. There was nothing, not even the slightest crack in the shiny metal to indicate there was a world outside.

It was beginning to look like my friend the unicorn and the Face had suckered me. And that Dalien had made a very smart move when he showed me his "shortcut."

Since there was little else I could do till my jailers turned up, I just kinda stood around and scratched the stubble on my chin. It had been three days since I'd last shaved, and my whiskers were beginning to itch bad. Not that that was the only part that itched. In all the excitement, bathing had fallen by the wayside. In addition to everything else, I smelled.

A whirling spot of blackness appeared in the wall directly in front of me. I stepped back as it grew larger, spinning in ever wider circles. A gargoyle stepped through the hole. An instant after he did the circle disappeared, leaving the wall as unflawed as ever.

I didn't even notice. My attention was riveted on my visitor. Standing about four feet high, it had a face that could have come off a thirteenth-century French cathedral. High, pointed ears topped a bare bowl head the uniform color of brick. Two saucer-shaped eyes were set almost on opposite sides of the head. Beneath the snub nose was a mouth stretching from one side of the face to the other. Two large fangs drooped over the lower lip.

The body was barrel shaped, neuter, hairless and also the color of brick.

The pistol was in my hand before I was aware I was reaching for it. Something told me that this kid and I were not compatible, any way at all.

I noted it was carrying rags in one taloned hand. It glanced at the gun, then opened its mouth. The last thing in the world I expected was the voice that came out.

"You don't need that, son," it said in a tone reeking of magnolias and mint juleps. It could have been Colonel Sanders.

I shook my head, then pounded my ear to see if maybe I'd gotten some cotton stuck in there.

"What's the matter with you, boy?"

"You," I said, pointing. "Are you, or are you not, a native of the lower Mason-Dixon region?"

The gargoyle grinned, a blood-chilling expression with those fangs fully revealed, and said, "No, I just passed through there once, a century ago. Had a good time too."

I rubbed my forehead wearily and wondered why I hadn't become a TV repairman. That way the worst I'd have to worry about would be fighting off the IRS as they kept trying to raise my tax bracket.

"Am I going completely crazy, or what? You aren't, no offense, the kind of old Southerner I'm familiar with."

"I didn't look the way I do now," and looking down at its body again, grinned, adding, "and a good thing too. Don't know what Charleston would have made of something like this. But we don't have time for talk. Get moving."

"Moving where? And where am I? And who are you? And what was the face growing out of the tree and . . ."

He tossed the rags at me.

"I'll tell you while you're changing. Get into those."

"Why?"

He frowned in what I guess was irritation. On him it was impressive, especially with muscles running under the swarthy skin like snakes as he changed position nervously.

"Because if you want to live to see earth again, you'll have to trust me."

It was good enough answer. I stripped.

"To answer them one by one. You're on a world called Aeia by its inhabitants. You're in the home of one of the Lords of Aeia, which is perched right on top of the highest mountain range in this world."

The clothes he'd brought were a rough pair of trousers and a tunic, similar to what the Hann and his men had worn.

"I'm that face in the tree you saw."

When I looked at him he said, "Don't try to understand it. Just accept it. I'm that face, but I've been able to keep control of this body."

"All right, I can swallow that, I guess. But why'd you sucker me into that lightshow that dumped me in here?"

"The transporter. It's a long story, like you said, but I'll make it short. The Lord of Aeia, who rules here, by the name of Gaell, made a surprise visit to Ellendon about six months ago. Because he had the jump on me he overpowered me.

"Then he imprisoned my mind, and body, in that tree, which isn't really a tree by the way. He left me powerless to control my own roost, or any of my servants. Only the unicorn stayed at my side. I was able, though, to capture control of this body, and a few others. The others have all been discovered and destroyed."

He fixed his saucer eyes on me and said simply, "You're my last hope. If you don't make it, this body will be discovered and destroyed. I'll be condemned to imprisonment, or death when Gaell gets back from . . . where he is now. What's worse, there are people depending on me out there, and I can't help them stuck here."

It sounded like a big fight, or maybe just a little war between the gods.

"You mean you dragged me into the middle of a civil war between super spooks?"

He grinned.

"You could look at it that way. But if you help me, you'll be rewarded. You can ask anything. The Lords of Ellendon can do much. And I hope you can see I had to get you here."

If what he was saying was true, I could. If I'd been in a bind like that, I'd have grabbed the nearest help around, whether or not my patsy wanted to come to my aid. Another thought occurred to me.

"Could you send me back to earth?"

"Easiest thing in the world. Could send you back with an armload of gold or perfect tens, twenties, fifties, one hundreds, or even ones. Say a basketful of one hundreds?"

The sun was rising inside me and somewhere nightingales sang and people's hearts were bright, etc., etc. Instead of being a bad break, entering the land of Lords was the best thing that'd happened since Krell put on his magic act. I made a mental note to look up that gentleman when I got back, but this time I'd be a little more careful about it.

"You've got a deal. What can I do for you?"

"There's an area these bodies cannot enter, the control room. Gaell wasn't stupid enough to give these servants, loyal as they are, a chance to betray him. I can't explain it to you but there is a barrier that would kill them. Because he never expected any humans to get here, there are no barriers to men. You can get into the control room and free me from the imprisonment that holds me."

"Just like that?"

"Not quite. We'll have to get past the guards and the lasers and the electrified floor. But we have a chance, a better chance with you than any of the rest. The others didn't make it because they couldn't really help thinking of all this as magic, and fear made them careless."

"The others?"

"The dimensional transporter you fell into was only one of seven scattered throughout Ellendon. Eleven others have come through from there before you, and all have been killed or captured."

"Great."

It was good to know the odds were with me, at any rate.

"Why so unhappy? From what I picked out of your mind while you were in the transporter, you were up to your eyeballs in trouble before you ran into me, and at least this way you'll have a chance of making it home."

"Right," I echoed, but with very little feeling. I had the funny sensation that throughout the entire Ellendon episode I'd been marching bravely forward into a bog of quicksand and that I'd still think things were improving when I was in it up to my hairline.

However, never look a gift god in the mouth.

"So, how do I get through the lasers and electrified floors and such? You know a secret way in?"

"No, but I think I can get you to the inner room. Beyond you'll be on your own. The barrier that would kill this body you can just walk through. It's a system of radiation that blanks out these nervous systems."

When I'd finished dressing, the gargoyle stared at me for a moment, said, "One last precaution," and the inside of my head exploded. I was still blinking and trying to find my head when I came to. I was standing up and the gargoyle looked as if he hadn't moved.

"What," I said, trying to shake the swirling feeling out of me, "what'd you do?"

"I just made sure you would be able to do your job without me. It's time for us to go. We won't have long before the guards show up."

"What did you do to me?" I said slowly, pointing the gun at him once again.

"You technicals do have your charm, but you can also be irritating. The Ellendonians obey much better. If it'll make you feel any better, I implanted a posthypnotic suggestion. When you get to the inner room you'll know exactly what to do to free me. I couldn't just tell you. It would take too long and you might forget, or make a mistake."

He had a good point. It would be ironic, although that didn't really come close, if I made it into the control room and forgot what I was supposed to do.

The gargoyle, who I decided to dub "Garg" for short, flashed his hand across a featureless portion of the wall. Whatever the source, the whirling appeared in the wall, growing rapidly until it was large enough for Garg to step through. He looked back at me and said, "Come along. We must go through together, or not at all."

He jumped, and I dived through, the hole being too small to walk through unless I squatted down. Entering that featureless darkness I felt more like diving than walking anyway.

I landed on my hands. We were in a larger area, which I saw was a hallway leading off a long, long way in both directions. It made me wonder just how big the building itself was.

"Don't let the size of this place slow you down," my guide said. "Gaell does it for effect. I could have had a place as big but there's really no reason for it. And it wastes power to maintain it."

As I trotted behind him, I saw we were coming to another hallway meeting at right angles the one we were in. I heard footsteps coming toward us that way.

"Guards," Garg said. "Quick, get out there."

He pointed beyond the corner from which the footsteps were coming.

"Why?"

"Don't ask questions, damnit. Just do as I say. Get out there and don't use your gun."

Reminding myself he was my ticket home, I didn't stop to think about what the guards might do but dashed out into the corridor. Coming toward me at a run were two fellas who might have been twins of my guide.

When they saw me they broke into something that sounded like the gobbling of turkeys and drew three-foot-long rapiers that looked needle-sharp. From the way they were brandishing them, I got the idea they were hostile.

Instinct sent me stumbling backward away from them as they came at me on their stubby little legs. The temptation to draw the .38 and use it was overwhelming.

I was reaching for the gun beneath my tunic when they passed the corridor opening where Garg was waiting.

He was on one of them with the motion of a snake striking. He drew a small dagger, maybe twelve inches long, at the side of one of the guards, and sunk it deep into the guard's chest. In and out so quickly I had a hard time following the motion with my eyes.

Still, the guard had strength enough to pull the dagger, with Garg gripping it tightly, out of his chest and throw him off. The guard whirled, bringing his sword around and trying to skewer Garg with it.

Garg used the dagger to deflect the sword, then got in close and stabbed the guard again, grabbing his sword with his other hand.

As they struggled for possession of the sword, all of this happening in less than a few seconds, the second guard turned and saw what was happening and went to help his comrade. I jumped him from the back and grabbed his sword hand, also trying to grab his dagger the way I'd seen it done.

Unfortunately, it didn't work out the same way. The guard peeled my hands off the dagger without effort, reached around and grabbed me by the scruff of my neck and threw me. The little four-foot-tall humanoid bounced me off the wall so hard I could only lie gasping for breath when I hit the floor.

He could have finished me then, but he went for his partner. By this time Garg had managed with another quick motion to get his dagger free again and slice at the guard's throat. Sliced so deep from ear to ear that the head almost fell off. The guard let go of the sword then.

If I'd had the time and energy I would have thrown up, an activity I was getting used to what with the rather gory and violent pastimes I'd been indulging in the last couple of days. But I didn't so I just said a short concise prayer that my gargoyle could handle their gargoyle.

The second guard went for Garg's heart, the rapier boring straight in, but Garg parried the thrust and I sat back to watch the fanciest display of swordsmanship I'd ever seen outside an Errol Flynn movie.

Garg ended the match a few seconds later by ramming his blade through the guard's chest, right about where a man's heart would be. Or at least that would have been the end of any duel I'd ever heard of before. But not on this turf. The skewered guard, unable to get to Garg around the sword stuck in him, swung his own sword in, trying to slash at Garg's neck.

Garg ducked and grabbed his sword hand, forcing the guard back against the wall. Then he proceeded slowly to strangle the guard with his own sword. This I didn't watch, only listening to the gurgling noises.

"We don't have the time," Garg said a little later. He tossed one of two swords to me. I caught it by the curved handle. It was so small I could barely get my fingers into the handle guard.

Without another word he took off down the corridors. I followed fast on his heels. While we were running I panted out the question, "Why are we running?"

"When we left the cell it set off an automatic alarm. Those two were only the closest. The others will be here soon and there may already be guards at the entrance to the control room."

I had gotten over my first idea of these beings as supernatural. Now I knew there must be some logical, scientific explanation for everything that had happened to me. But little things jarred with the picture of super science.

"Why swords? Why didn't the guards use guns?"

Without slowing his pace the gargoyle answered, "You won't find any guns around here, or anywhere on Ellendon. People who have guns have other machinery, or it sets their mind thinking in those directions. And they also start wondering if Lords can be killed. Besides, when nobody else has them, they're not needed."

As we came to another turn we found ourselves in a hallway lined with doors on one side and large crystalline windows set in the other wall about stomach height. Through the doors I could see machinery that looked like nothing so much as row upon row of computer consoles.

When I glanced through one of the windows, I was caught. I slowed to a trot, then stopped, forgetting about my guide for a second. A golden globe danced on feather-light stanchions sunk deep into purple mountains. The sky beyond and between the splinter-sharp peaks was so deep a blue it was almost black.

The world slowly tilted and fell into the abyss as I stepped closer. Endless vistas of air swam in front of me as I made a mental journey down the frozen peaks, mile after mile into the lower cloud regions. The ground below was invisible. I wondered what I'd see if I could step outside this building and look straight down.

"No time for sightseeing, boy. In case you've forgotten, there's a lot riding on you."

I hadn't forgotten, or at least only momentarily. I didn't like the way he seemed to regard me as a useful tool, but I held my comments.

We made two more turns without running into opposition. Then we came out into a large square. Garg put his hand out to stop me as I almost ran past him into the hall. The floor was set in what looked like red and white blocks of marble, each about six feet wide.

"What's the matter?"

He didn't answer, but took the dagger out of his belt and threw it a couple of feet in front of him onto a white square. Sparks glittered along the length of the blade as the floor seemed to growl.

"You would have been fried to a crisp before you'd taken your second step."

My throat seemed awfully dry as I remembered how easy it would have been to have kept going. And how hard it would have been to come back.

"How do we get across that? Fly?"

He grinned. Even knowing he was on my side, I'd never quite get used to that.

"Don't I wish I could. No, we'll have to wait for some more

guards. The screens will show that something has entered the electrified area. Someone will come to investigate."

"And we're going to wait for them? Okay, okay, I know. You're the boss."

We didn't have to wait long. Within a minute we heard more steps. Garg motioned me to flatten myself against the wall of the passageway that met the main corridor leading to the electrified square.

On schedule three guards, swords drawn, came trotting past us to the foot of the hallway. They saw the dagger lying on the floor and nothing else.

Without a word Garg launched himself across the distance between us and the guards. Even as they turned their heads slightly and saw us he hit one of them in the breastbone with a good old stiff-arm.

The guard was hurtled a half-dozen feet backward onto the white square. He didn't even have time to scream. I tore my eyes away from him as his skin began to turn black and smolder. I caught a second guard in the midsection, leaping feet first. The kick sent him staggering a few fatal steps backward. He too died silently.

The third guard had his sword out, but Garg did too, and they lunged back and forth. I had my own sword out, feeling rather ridiculous. I got as close as I could and made a tentative stab in the air at the back of the guard. The point touched his skin, but didn't go in. Before I could exert any pressure, the guard turned toward me.

Sword out, he came straight at me. I stumbled back and fell, by pure luck managing to parry his sword. Before he could come back at me Garg sent his sword through the guard's back. The guard wiggled like a fish on a hook until the sword was pulled out, but before he could complete the turn back he was stabbed again.

He was still turning when I landed on his back and grabbed for his sword hand. The guard shook himself and I went tumbling off. I was beginning to get an inferiority complex. These shrimp, no matter how sturdily they were built, had no business throwing me around like an undernourished three-year-old.

With no help from me, Garg finished the guard off, skewering him two or three more times before he finally got the idea and died.

"What do we do now?"

"Simple," he said, taking the guard by the feet and dragging him over to the corner where we had waited.

"We do some more waiting."

"Explain that one again."

"Simple. The screens will register that two bodies have died out on the field. They'll send somebody out there with special gear to retrieve the bodies, assuming they're us. We kill the ones with the gear and use it to cross the field. Understand?"

It sounded good except I kept remembering how hard these ugly little fellows were to kill. I said as much.

"The Troich are hardy in their natural state, but these were designed especially for guard duty."

"That answers a lot of questions I've had about this whole deal —the unicorn and the mermaid and the Chorbal. You've been using genetic engineering, haven't you?"

"You know I'm not going to answer that, don't you?"

And even that was a good enough answer. For whatever reason, my host wanted all us lesser beings to go on thinking magic was real, when it was only a science so advanced we couldn't begin to understand it. Anyway, I'm more comfortable with super science than magic.

It sounded like the Charge of the Light Brigade being re-enacted. And it was coming our way.

Garg said, "When you get the protective belt, strap it on and take off, no matter what happens. Keep going straight and you'll reach the control room."

As the first of the guards came around the corner I saw he was wearing an unusual belt around his middle. It was studded with metal squares raised above the surface of the belt. As soon as Garg saw it he launched himself like a human missile at the guard and three companions.

He hit the group like a bowling ball, knocking the guards around like tenpins. He rolled into the wall with the guard wearing the strange belt. He did something to it and it came loose. As he took the belt off four more guards came around the corner.

He tossed the belt over the heads of some of the guards he'd knocked down and I caught it in midair. I whipped it around my waist and thanked whatever deities were in charge around here that, although these guards were little, they were big around. When I sucked in my stomach to the point that my ribs hurt, I could barely make both ends meet.

I dived for the red and white squares and in midair realized I had no way of knowing if this belt would protect me against electricity, or if it would work for humans, or . . . One of the guards tackled me and brought me down just short of the squares. He drew his dagger and prepared to use it on me. Beyond him I could see two guards thrusting their swords into Garg, who hurled himself onto their swords and forced them back away from me.

I kicked the guard off me, got to one knee and jumped toward the squares. The guard was on me again but we fell in the square. He opened his mouth in a silent scream while his body jerked and trembled spasmodically.

I pulled loose from him. His skin gave off a smell like old tires burning. A dozen swords were being thrust into Garg as he fell in the center of as many guards. A couple of them drew their daggers and threw them at me. The hilt of one hit me in the shoulder and nearly knocked me over. I ran for the other end of the hall and another doorway.

When I looked back I couldn't see Garg's body any more. I momentarily mourned the death of a guy who'd saved my life, but reminded myself he'd said he wasn't really there. He was only sacrificing an expendable tool.

Some of the guards were standing near the open hall but no one was trying to come in. Apparently they'd only had one belt. There must be more around, but it would take them a little while to get another one here.

The second room was smaller than the first, leading to a pitch-black doorway. But I had only a second to notice that because in the next instant pencil-lead thin beams of light bathed my body.

It puzzled me for a second until I took the dagger I was carrying in my belt out and tossed it onto the floor. Where the light hit it the metal turned cherry red, then white. The dagger melted in a half-dozen places.

The studs on my belt were glowing a dull red. Somehow it was soaking up the energy the lasers were throwing at me. I'd never heard of any kind of defense against lasers, but anybody that could travel across dimensional barriers wouldn't worry about simple problems like that.

I peered into the pitch-black passage, wondering if the belt could handle whatever was in here. It was blacker than it should have been, even if there was no light at the other end.

The light from this room should have shown me something of the interior, but it was as if the darkness were tangible, filling the tunnel like a solid substance.

I'd thought the featureless nothingness I'd encountered in the transporter was the worst thing I'd ever seen, but this frightened me in a different way. Think about the darkest night you've ever fought nightmares in and you'll have some idea what I faced.

I got up enough nerve to stick my hand in, and it was as if my arm were cut off at the elbow. I jerked it out like it was on fire.

I tried to think what to do while I knew the gargoyles were coming. The gargoyle had said to keep going straight, but he hadn't mentioned this.

Maybe the belt I was wearing wouldn't protect me against the next trap. On the other hand, it was a sure bet it wouldn't protect me against the gargoyles. Damning the gargoyle for getting me in this fix, I entered the darkness.

I went in running, hoping that if I got some momentum up it would be harder to turn around. I took five or six running steps, hands extended out into the darkness. I wanted to stop to feel my face, my hands, my body and remind myself I was real.

Something was in the darkness with me. Even though I could see and hear nothing, I knew something squatted in front of me. Something huge and hairy and tentacled, with jaws a yard wide, mandibles clicking. Drooping from the ceiling were tendrils of light, airy webs, but I knew that when they caught me they'd bind me like steel.

The ground below me oozed and bubbled as I sank in to my heels and then to my knees, the ooze penetrating up through my pants, along my bare skin. I could feel the squishy things beneath the ooze running their tendrils up and down my legs.

Something buzzed angrily behind my ear. I couldn't turn, my neck was frozen. I could feel the air fanned by those huge gossamer wings, the sting a sharp needle a yard long projecting out from the striped, barrel body, poised to be driven like a spike at my face.

There was a dry rustling, a sound like autumn leaves brushing the ground, as the many legs carried the long, dagger-shaped body toward me. I could sense the spiny carapace tensing as the long, curved stinger, wider across than my hand, was whipped back.

A rattling like a thousand maracas filled the inside of my head. From all sides, below and above me, the sound came. I felt the dry, scaly, somehow slimy bodies rubbing up against me, the rattling increasing as they drew back their fanged heads.

For a timeless instant I was frozen. My neck muscles wouldn't allow me to scream. I was aware of every square inch of my body, could feel the hair rising on the back of my head, feel my lungs straining to hold air and not move even a millionth of an inch. My heart stood still, waiting.

I blacked out. I don't remember how I got out of there, but I found myself lying on the floor outside the passage.

For what seemed like a long time, but must have been only seconds, I lay trembling on the floor as the lasers bathed me in a warm, cheerful glow. My face was wet, though I could never remember crying or why I would cry.

I couldn't bear to look at the passageway. I got away from there as fast as I could, scrambling on my hands and knees. The things in there might come out after me at any moment.

I heard shouting from the other room. What they were saying I didn't know or care. It probably meant one or more of them with belts like mine were coming after me. That meant I had only seconds to live.

I got to my feet somehow, wiping the tears out of my eyes. I drew my pistol and waited for the little runts. They'd take me, but I'd get at least one or two of them.

When I realized I was playing Davy Crockett at the Alamo, I snapped out of it. There wouldn't be anybody around after my last stand to make up any popular ditties. Remembering the silent and messy way the gargoyle had got his knocked the last remnants of lingering romanticism out of my head.

The black interior of the passageway was as forbidding as ever. But I noticed something I should have seen immediately, and which I would have if I hadn't been frightened out of my mind.

There was no way I could have gotten out of that tunnel if all the horrors I'd felt had been in there. And how had I known they were there? I hadn't seen them, or felt or even heard them. Everything I'd "felt" had been within me.

I remembered a professor I'd had in college, in a psychology class. He set up a piece of fancy machinery and turned a switch. The class literally went up the walls. Afterward I couldn't remember what I was so frightened of, but there was no one there that hadn't been terrified.

It could just be something that simple, I thought. And it might pay to emulate old Odysseus. I ripped away some of the fabric where my pants were torn at the knee, and wadded the material into my ears.

As I walked into the darkness I saw a band of the gargoyles entering the laser room. They broke into a sprint in my direction.

I didn't have the time to worry about it. The darkness stole my body again. I held my breath for a moment, waiting for the creatures to come out of my subconscious again.

Every frightening thing I'd ever come in contact with, or seen anywhere. Scorpions, like the one that nearly stung me in the face when I was twelve, or the hornet that had stung me when I was nine and nearly killed me because of an allergic reaction I had to its toxin.

Spiders and rattlesnakes like the ones I'd seen in a movie once and dreamed about afterward. Dreamed of a dark, dry cave full of writhing, squirming reptile bodies and myself trapped in their midst, unable to move without letting them know I was there.

But there was nothing now in the corridor other than an air of being watched, of movement out of the corner of my eye. I was afraid, sure, but nothing like before.

I trotted forward trying to feel my way along. As I ran the feeling of being watched grew stronger and I could definitely feel something behind me. There was the clicking of something dragging itself across the floor at me.

As I ran—faster now—I felt the floor begin to soften beneath my feet, bubbling as I stepped into patches of ooze. Even with the cloth in my ears, the unheard sonics, which could drive a man out of his mind or change his emotional state when handled by an expert, were getting to me. If the cloth hadn't been there I would have been curled into an embryo and locked deep inside my own mind already.

But I couldn't go much farther. I could feel the creatures stirring, like figures slowly forming on a screen. In moments I knew they would be real. Maybe they would have no bodies a biologist could get his scalpels into, but they would be real enough to me. And my death would be real enough too.

I had gone too far. I couldn't turn back, I couldn't see any end to the tunnel and time was running out.

The monstrous crawler with fangs and tentacles, a spider-octopus, heaved its bulk into my path. In a few seconds I would run into its gaping jaws. I almost tried to stop myself, to somehow turn back.

The thought of what must have happened to the other poor bastards that made it through the lasers and electrified floor when they reached this last, subtle trap made me mad enough to run into the jaws of death.

I fell into the light, landing on my face and skidding along the burnished metal floor. I began to laugh so hard I cried. I would like to see Gaell's face when he got back to his pad and found whatever his former prisoner had cooked up for him.

I got to my feet and examined the gleaming console panel like something out of a NASA blockhouse. Gargoyle, do your stuff.

With no conscious thought or guidance, I reached out to a row of blinking lights in front of me, passing my hand across them. They winked out. My hand froze before I could drop it to my side. I was going to glance down when I realized I couldn't move, period.

"So you made it this far. I'm surprised."

The speaker had a dry, deep voice. He sounded amused.

"You'd think he'd realize his situation is hopeless," he said bemusedly, as if talking to himself about his godlike prisoner. "I have to give him credit for trying, at any rate."

Then, his tone changing, "I don't know what to do with *you*, though. My cells are filling up. Should I give you to the Troich? They haven't had any fresh meat for some time. I wonder, do you have any preference? A quick death, or a fight for your life with another prisoner?"

It took no mental effort on my part to figure out that entering the control room must have triggered an alarm. Funny that my gargoyle hadn't thought about that in advance.

What was giving me a headache was the fact that Gaell was speaking the language of Ellendon, and I understood him.

CHAPTER TWELVE

Suddenly I could move. I turned to face the voice.

He looked like a god. Six and a half feet tall at least with shoulders a yard wide and a face like Hollywood's last six prettiest boys rolled into one. He wore a simple white toga. He smiled and I had a hard time not liking him. I supposed he was using sonics now to play with my emotions.

He looked into my eyes and the world exploded into white again. When I opened my eyes he was looking at me thoughtfully.

"You are a brave man, Handell. For a savage to make it through my traps into my control room, even with his help, is amazing. For that I will give you a quick and merciful death."

"Don't do me any favors," I said in the language of Ellendon.

He laughed and said, "I almost wish I could keep you around. You're a funny fellow."

While I was trying to keep up my end of the conversation my mind was whirling as I tried to figure out what was happening. The only possible answer was that the gargoyle had somehow given me the language of Ellendon by hypnosis, or something like it.

But why? And then I remembered what Gaell had called me. And it clicked. With my new name, it suddenly all made sense. I decided to test my idea.

"Why not send me back to my home in Ellendon? I cannot harm you there."

"I'm afraid not. I don't trust my neighbor, even in the prison I placed him in. An enterprising fellow such as yourself might just come back and cause me more trouble. I'm afraid I'll have to eliminate you right now."

I was right. Now the only thing that stood in my way was the fact that he might be able to move swiftly enough to protect himself. I had to throw him off guard.

"I guess I should have expected that," I said, as he pointed his hand at me in a final way.

"What?"

"When they made you gods they forgot to give you testicles."

His face clouded over and I thought he was going to toss a thunderbolt my way.

"How would you like to die for a thousand years or so?"

"Not particularly, but I can't blame you for ducking a real fight. On man-to-man terms you know a human could whip you without working up a sweat. You've been sitting around so long throwing thunderbolts and letting your pets run your errands you haven't got what it takes any more."

His thunderbolt-throwing hand trembled as he clenched his fist, then relaxed. He smiled again, a little weaker this time.

"You know, I'm tempted to let you go anyway. Anybody with courage like yours is rare enough without killing them off. But, I still can't let you go. Since you want it this way, I'll kill you with my bare hands."

He flexed his muscles and said, "Come, little man, you may use your knife if you wish."

That confirmed my guess. I shook my head and grinned at him. "I won't need it."

He laughed at that and I found myself genuinely sorry I'd have to kill him, even remembering the dark tunnel and the sonics. He was the perfect example of the likable bastard.

I moved toward him slowly, trying to look dangerous. Right now I felt about as dangerous as a wet noodle planning to whip a tiger to death. I got to within a few feet of him, feinted with my left and swung at his chin with my right.

I don't know how he did it, but he got behind me and kicked me hard. I went down, my behind aching from the force of his kick. He was busting a gut laughing.

"Enjoy it while you can," I growled and got up and went for him again. This time when I got close enough I tried to kick him where it would do the most good. He caught my foot, upended me and threw me across the room. I hit the far wall and lay in the corner.

He approached me slowly as I started breathing again.

"Time to end the game. I've enjoyed it and I thank you for the exercise."

"Don't thank me yet," I gasped and pulled the .38 out from under my tunic, pointing the barrel at his chest.

I didn't aim exactly, but the bullet hit him in the upper left chest. Assuming he was built like me, it must have gone through his heart. The impact of the bullet jerked him backward and away from me.

I aimed the second time, in the split second I had left as he managed to turn and look at me with surprise written in his eyes. The second bullet tore the top of his forehead off and sent him reeling backward.

I couldn't get up. I sat there feeling numb and good at the same time. Unless he really was a god, the last shot had killed him for sure. I had won and the gargoyle would send me back to earth. I found it hard to believe it could all happen as easily as this. After everything that'd happened.

I stared at the .38 for a while, wondering what Ellendon would have been like if I hadn't had it. Funny how important a $90 hunk of metal can be.

I made myself look at the corpse. It proved he was real enough. Blood and brains lay on the floor around his body. I stared at it, feeling nothing. No guilt, no horror, none of the things I would have imagined feeling.

His lips moved. In that ruin of a face his lips moved, the blood running down the side of his mouth onto the bright metal floor.

"Very smart," he said faintly, the words sounding as though he were speaking from under water, very far away. "Tell him I'll remember . . . the next time."

His head fell to one side. His skin turned a pale, milky white and I could see the organs that made up his insides traced in blood red beneath the transparent skin. It was like a chart out of an anatomy book. The red lines began to glow brighter against the transparent skin.

Pulsing like a neon sign, his body grew brighter and brighter and I could hear a hum like electricity in the wires coming from his body. The red lines ran together in a blue that faded, leaving an after-image on my eyes. When I'd rubbed them there was nothing where his body had been.

I touched the floor where the body had been. It wasn't even warm. Whatever else these Lords were, they weren't human.

I turned back to the instrument panel and let my body take over. For five minutes I pulled levers, pushed buttons and made passes in front of the panels. Then I just stood there while nothing happened. I hoped I'd done everything I had to.

The panel blurred and I wiped my eyes with the back of my hand. The blur was still there and the floor started to ripple beneath me. When the ceiling started revolving faster and faster and my feet floated out from under me, I realized what that tricky bastard of a gargoyle had done.

I had the time to think of a lot of curses on the way down to the floor.

"Hank."

Someone was shouting at me from the end of a long, long tunnel. I wondered what they were doing down at the other end of what must be a very narrow stretch. And what I was doing listening to somebody stupid enough to get themselves trapped in a tunnel.

"Come out of there," I mumbled, trying to twist free of the hands that were grasping at me. I just wanted to go back to sleep again.

"Wake up, Hank, please."

I managed to pry my eyelids open. A girl with long blond hair was standing over me. She would have been pretty except for ugly bruises about one eye and the swollen and cut lips. Somebody had really let her have it.

"What'cha want, sugar?" I mumbled, still not too sure I wanted to wake up.

She touched my shoulder in a prim way with the tips of her fingers and said, "Hank, He wants to speak to you."

"Sleepy," I said, rolling onto my side to get away from her.

"Hank, He wants to speak to you. You did it, you freed Him."

I said something that even here is unprintable. If it fazed her she didn't let it stop her shaking me. I finally decided she was never going to stop shaking me and it'd be easier to wake up and get rid of her so I could get back to sleep.

Along the way back to the real world I remembered who I was and where. Syana backed away when I reached out to touch her.

"What're you doing here, Syana?"

Unmistakably it had been fear I'd seen in her eyes when I went to touch her. I knew then that the scars they'd left inside her were uglier than anything Suldurus and his men had done to the outside of her.

She wouldn't look me straight in the eye.

"I fell into the same kind of trap you did, Hank, one in the mountains. He told me what had happened and I tried to get to the heart of His enemy's hold, but I was captured before I got halfway there."

"I'm glad you made it, sugar. I was afraid Suldurus and his men . . ."

I stopped as something crossed her face that I couldn't put a name to, and didn't even want to try. I changed the subject.

"So Himself wants to talk to me, huh? Where?"

"Follow me."

As she walked ahead of me she told me how she had been running from Suldurus and his men when she accidentally entered one of the spots of ground sacred to the Lords. Before she could withdraw, horrified at what she'd done, that dimensional transporter had "cast a spell" on her. More sonics, probably.

Once here she'd been contacted by another gargoyle servant of the Face. Only she hadn't been as lucky as I, never even making it as far as the electrified room. Now He had taken over this hold and sent all the prisoners except the two of us home.

My turn and I told her what had happened to me since I'd last seen her in the forest. She breathed a sigh of relief when she heard that her brother and Iverson were still alive and that the invasion hadn't begun yet.

For a second she came to life again, shedding the tense, frightened shell she'd hidden behind since her rape.

"Do you know what you've done, Hank? Now He is free and will recover the Sword and the Ring and we can defeat the Hann. We've won."

I couldn't help smiling. It was strictly out of Hans Christian Andersen, with the young hero ringing in some miracle at the end to save the day.

Unfortunately, since nothing that had happened to me since I'd landed in Ellendon had been by the book, I had the funny feeling there was going to be a kicker somewhere along the line.

The room we arrived at was the first conventionally sized enclosure I'd seen on this world. There was a large window set in one wall and outside I could see the sun dipping below the high mountains.

The view caught my eye so I didn't notice Him until He stepped toward me. He was a little more life-sized than His counterpart, but not much.

Picture a James Bond standing about six foot three in a white toga, which must be the businessman's special around here. He smiled and I got that "old friends" feeling that meant more sonics.

"Glad to see you back," He drawled.

"Thanks for the nap."

"This is how I looked in 1875, except for the toga," he said, motioning along the length of his body.

"You carry your age well."

Syana gave me a look like I'd just thrown a rock through a cathedral window. One is not flippant with one's deities. She looked like she'd bolt if He said boo. Very different vibrations from the girl I'd first met.

"How did you pull that trick in the control room?"

He smiled at the memory. Revenge is sweet, no matter what they say.

"I simply gave you a false set of memories that would be triggered if Gaell showed up. It was a very superficial job, but Gaell had no reason to probe deeper."

"But why didn't he spot the gun?"

"For the same reason he didn't discover your real identity. He had no reason to suspect you weren't just an ignorant Ellendonian. And when his sensors showed you were carrying a metallic object, he naturally assumed it was a knife."

"Neat. But why didn't you tell me about the sonics? You nearly got me killed."

"I didn't know they were there. None of the gargoyles knew what was in that corridor. It's just a good thing you were the one who made it that far. None of the others would have had any idea of what was happening, or how to fight it. I owe you a great deal, Dell, more than you'll ever know. So, how do I repay you?"

"Well, for starters you can send me back to earth. Then you can give the Ring and the Sword back to Syana's people and chase the Hann off and . . ."

I almost asked for a few baskets of legitimate tens or twenties, but my mind kept getting in the way of my daydreams.

I didn't doubt this guy could whip up gold or silver or paper money, but even if he could, it wouldn't do me much good. Any money he gave me I wouldn't be able to spend. Not without explaining it to the friendly neighborhood tax examiner. When a reporter who draws $9,000 a year starts spending more than $9,000 a year, his income tax form becomes a minefield.

So when the income tax man asked me, "Mr. Dell, where did you get the $10,000 you purchased the new car and clothes with?" I'd innocently tell him a friendly supernatural being had whipped them up in return for my freeing him from a tree in which he was imprisoned.

Within a few hours I'd be telling my adventures to a guy who was really Napoleon in disguise and a man who was being persecuted by Martians nobody else could see, and other people like me.

The same problems, only worse, applied to anything else he could produce. Gold I couldn't keep and how would I explain where I got it? I couldn't think of anything I could cash in for wealth that wouldn't create more headaches than it was worth.

I felt like the man who'd won the sweepstakes and lost the winning ticket.

He broke into my thoughts, looking a little embarrassed.

"I'm afraid there are going to be some problems, Dell."

"I'd like to speak to him alone, honey," he said to Syana, and she vanished faster than light.

He coughed and said, "I'm afraid I'm going to have to acquaint you with the facts of life, and they're not too pleasant."

The sinking feeling in my stomach told me the kicker was about to arrive.

"I'm not going to be able to do anything of what you asked."

"Nothing? What about sending me home?"

"I can't even do that. I'm sorry."

"You're sorry? What the hell are you talking about? You said if I helped you you'd send me back to earth."

"I know that's what I said. But think back. Would you have risked your life if I hadn't promised to help you?"

"No, and if I'd been smart I wouldn't have helped you anyway. Not now that I know you're a damned liar."

"That's what I thought your reaction would be. The Ellendonians I can count on. Being from earth and a scientific culture, you needed a different approach."

I pressed my head against a wall and wondered why I wasn't screaming.

"You mean you lied just to get me to risk my neck? Knowing all the time that you couldn't help me?"

"That's exactly right, I did what I had to do, although I can't expect you to understand that."

"You can't."

"I guess not. And I can't explain exactly why I can't help you."

"How about starting with little words. If you make it real simple, you might get the message across."

He walked over to the window with the majestic view and said, "Let's just say there is something very, very important going on a long way from here. I've been kept out of it, on purpose, because I am not one of the least powerful of the Lords. I have to go there now, and I'll need every ounce of energy, every tool at my command, when I do."

"How much energy would it take to send one man back to earth?"

"More than I can spare."

"What about Syana and her people? I thought you said they were 'your' people? They risked their lives to help you, some of them died. So now you just kiss them off and let the Hann butcher them?"

"You're making me feel like a real villain. If I could, I would help them. They have been faithful to me and the other Lords of Ellendon, and I don't like to leave them in trouble. But, for all that I care for them, Ellendon is only one world. The fate of many worlds depends on, in some small way, my leaving now."

"You're a wonderful fellow, you know that?"

"I detect sarcasm," He said. "I shouldn't even be sending you and the others back to Ellendon, at least not with your memories intact. The Ellendonians don't really understand what's going on, but you do.

"I thought seriously of completely removing your memory of what happened here while you were unconscious. That's why I primed you to blank out after freeing me. But I couldn't forget that you did rescue me. I owe you something for that, if only refraining from tampering with your mind."

"Your goodness is beyond understanding."

At this point I didn't care if I made Him mad or not. I had thought I was out of it and I was going to be up to my neck again—back to Ellendon, crawling with bandits and Hann and the King, all of whom would like to see me come to a messy end.

"I'll send you and Syana back now."

"Where?"

"Back into the King's presence. I can do that much for you."

I thought again of what would happen as soon as the King found out what had happened to his sister. On the other hand, I couldn't really think of any other place on Ellendon I was crazy to visit.

It was like being given the choice of death by hanging, firing squad or sleeping pills. You were equally dead in any case.

He called Syana in. She kept her eyes on the floor as she asked, "Lord, I thank you for coming to our aid. Without you—"

"I cannot help you, girl. This is a battle in which the men of Ellendon must prove themselves. You must fight without the aid of the Ring and the Sword."

"But . . ." she objected, finally raising her eyes to Him. The expression on His face killed the sudden rebellion and she said, "Yes, Lord."

He raised His hand and a section of the wall slid back to reveal a checkerboard of twirling lights, like the display I'd seen when I first fell into the transporter.

"Wait."

I said it not knowing what excuse I was going to use to postpone the inevitable. My mind went into override trying to find something, anything, to head off the inevitable.

I clutched at it like a drowning man grabbing a Mae West. Maybe, just maybe, there was still a way out.

"Syana, let Him send you to your brother now. I have to find out something. I'll be along in a little bit."

I forgot myself and reached out and touched her shoulder. She made herself stand still, but she couldn't help shuddering.

"I'm sorry, Hank. It isn't you."

"I know, sugar, and I'm sorry too."

He did something to the panel and she was gone. I found myself pushing my hand through the space where she'd been standing. I couldn't quite believe it, though I'd seen it happen. Big things like monsters and alien supermen I could believe. It's the little things, like people disappearing, that are hard to swallow.

"I can't waste much more time, Dell. What did you want?"

"Syana said the Ring and the Sword were given to her people by the Lords, and knowing what I know about you, I'm betting that means you made them."

After a moment in which he appeared to be weighing his answers, he said, "Yes."

"Which means they must use the same sort of energy your transporters do. Would you have some way of locating them, of tracking them by the energy they radiate?"

"It could be done. Why?"

"How about seeing if you can locate the Sword?"

"From what I've already learned, Krell has it on earth."

"He told us he didn't have it, that it got misplaced. I'm betting he was telling the truth. He didn't have any reason to lie at the time."

"I can try."

He moved over to another section of the wall, which slid away to reveal a glowing, three-dimensional grid looking like a way-out radar screen.

He did something to the controls and rings of green light began to spiral out from the center of the screen. Suddenly a spark appeared in the top left of the screen.

He played with the controls while the spark continued to pulse as the spirals of light washed over it.

"No doubt about it. That's it."

He returned to the transporter screen and, without looking back at me, said, "Believe it or not, Dell, but I wish you good luck."

He and the room vanished.

I closed my eyes as the featureless blankness swallowed me and then I was treading air. The old flip-flop feeling in my stomach told me I was taking another elevator ride.

I fell on my behind a few seconds later. It's a good thing I didn't have an audience, because it's a most undignified way to pop up out of thin air.

Especially on a clump of rocks. I opened my eyes and found myself on a rock-strewn hillside.

It was early morning. Assuming that the time scale on Aeia ran the same as Ellendon, it had been only a few hours, if that, since I'd run into the unicorn.

I got up and rubbed my bruised backside. A second later I heard a thud. Lying on the rocks beside me was the .38. I picked it up and put it back in my trousers. It was useless now with no bullets, but I'd developed a sentimental attachment to it.

The only thing I could see was empty hillside. Far below I could see trees growing in what looked like a valley. Below the valley there was more hillside. It was quite a view. I had thought He—I didn't even know His name—would send me directly to where the Sword was, but He'd sent me only to the general location. Which might mean a lot of rock-turning-over before I hit the right one.

I started wandering in circles away from the spot where I'd landed, examining the ground carefully. There was nothing that even looked like a sword. I hoped he hadn't pulled another swift one on me, just to make extra-sure I didn't get back to earth.

I went down the hillside. Before I reached the trees I saw a ledge jutting out into the air. It was a cover for a cave that must have been about ten feet wide and high. The interior was dark enough to give me second thoughts about entering, but it would be a good place for a sword to get lost where it couldn't be found again.

I started to walk into the cave. The inside had a funny smell that I couldn't quite place. I thought I'd smelled it before.

The cave widened as I went in. I kept to one wall, feeling my way along carefully. I'd gotten about thirty feet in when I heard something at the entrance.

A big, manlike shape blotted the little light that came in. I kicked myself for not remembering that caves are popular as hideaways for all kinds of big, unfriendly things.

I moved back as fast as it moved toward me. It didn't make any sounds except a loud, harsh breathing. That was also familiar, but I couldn't fit the pieces together.

Suddenly there was a wall where there hadn't been one before. Now there was nowhere to go but forward. The occupant of the cave was still advancing in its unhurried way.

It was still only a dim shape. I figured the cave must be about twenty feet wide here. There was a chance I could get out if I could fake it to one side.

I slid over to the far right. As I'd hoped, the shape also moved to the right. It was about ten feet away from me. I touched the metal of the .38 and spent a hopeless few seconds wishing I had just one bullet left.

I made a dash to the left, aiming to go around the shape. I was running when I remembered where I'd heard that breathing before and where I'd smelled that odor. It was then that something hit me in the side of the head.

I shook my head, reaching around to rub my neck. It felt like somebody had operated on my scalp with a dull knife and neglected to sew me up.

Rubbing the back of my neck and head took some of the pain and soreness away. I rotated my head back and forth, which made it even better.

Where was I?

I looked into the dimly lit features of a face that Frankenstein's monster's mother couldn't have loved.

The Cyclops saw I was awake and grinned, or gave what it thought was a grin. It was even bigger, and uglier, than I remembered. Considering what I remembered, that was something.

I was seated in the bottom of a wooden cage, or, rather, something like bamboo. The bars were held together by rope. The whole affair was only about five feet high. When I stood up I had to stoop over.

There was a torch now set into the far wall and its guttering flame plus the light from the sun outside enabled me to get a good look at the interior of the cave.

I grasped the bars in my hands while I looked at the bones and residue of countless fires. The Cyclops produced a stick about an inch thick and four feet long. Before I could move he whipped it across my knuckles.

I jerked my hands back, the knuckles burning where he'd hit them like somebody had poured gasoline over them and lit it. I moaned while I got as far back in the cage as possible.

The Cyclops moved closer, bending over to look into the cage. It poked the stick in through the bars, jabbing at me. I squeezed as close to the rear of the cage, set against the cave wall, as was humanly possible, but I couldn't get away from the prod.

He jabbed the stick in my side. I batted it away and moved to the other side, which is pretty hard to do when you're hunched over. He followed me to the other side and jabbed me in the stomach. Each time he'd put his full power behind the stick. If that end had been sharpened he could have used it for a spit, with me as the main course of the barbecue.

As it was the blow to the stomach took my breath away and I knew I'd have a nasty bruise there. When I rubbed my side and stomach the Cyclops made a sound like laughter.

I knew then it couldn't be anyone but the character I'd kicked in the groin. He hadn't forgotten apparently. He'd just decided that a quick death would be too merciful. I wondered what he had in mind when the torture was over.

He flicked the stick rapidly at the side of my head. It struck across the temple, hard enough to break the skin. The blow rocked me against the side of the cage. I fell, holding the side of my head while great bells pealed inside my skull.

I got back to my knees, wiping the tears out of my eyes. I hoped he could understand every English word I was using, then I remembered he couldn't speak English so I switched to the language of Ellendon. He continued to laugh and jabbed at my face.

I fell over backward as I tried to brush the stick away. It scraped the edge of my cheek, burning it but not drawing blood. I grabbed the end of the stick before he could pull it back.

I had the stick with two hands, he had it with one. He gave it a tug and it felt like some of my skin went with it as he jerked it free.

He laughed a little bit more as he made a few tentative jabs at me, then threw the stick down. He lumbered over to a pile of furs spread out in one corner and lay down. He turned away from me toward the wall. In a few minutes he was snoring.

While I assessed the damages I thanked whatever deities were looking out for me that he'd had enough fun for the day. There was no serious damage, although my ears were still ringing.

Trying to think of some way out, I looked around at my new home. Whatever else he was, the Cyclops was also a slob. Beyond the area where he was lying was a charred mass of soot and half-burned wood. Around that was a treasure trove of bones.

An archaeologist would have been in eighth heaven, except that most of the bones had been cracked open or splintered, undoubtedly by the giant's very tough teeth.

Toward the rear of the cave were more bones and a lot of garbage, including wood and old helmets and armor, a painting in what looked like an ornate frame, candlesticks and a lot of other things indicating I'd fallen into the hands of an overgrown pack rat.

I nearly shoved my head right through the top of the cage when I caught sight of it. Lying almost hidden beneath the bones and a helmet that had grown reddish with rust was the hilt of a sword. I had no way of telling for sure, but the way it gleamed in the dim light of the torch made me think it might be the Sword of the Gates.

The more I looked at it, the more I thought it could be nothing other than what I'd been dreaming of. Light played on the hilt like water, rippling smoothly instead of gleaming off it. I hadn't ever seen anything like it, except the Wanderer's Ring.

I gripped the bars of the cage and pulled but I couldn't feel them give at all. I hit the bars with my fists and winced. I was so close to getting home, and yet so far. The only thing in this whole world that could stop me from going home was this wooden cage and the Cyclops.

That was more than enough.

The noise I made hitting the bars should have wakened the Cyclops, but he continued to snore merrily away. What did he have to worry about anyway? He'd probably been up all night pulling the wings off owls, having graduated from flies a long time ago. That was about his speed.

I lay back against the cage, staring at the Sword, which might have been a thousand miles away. The Lord I'd helped had really paid me back for my service. There he was, jetting off to God knows where, and here I was.

After a while I got tired of feeling sorry for myself. It was pleasant, but it wasn't getting me anywhere, literally. What I had to do was think myself out of this cage over to the Sword.

I tried the easy way first. I closed my eyes and visualized the Sword lying among the bones and junk. Then I tried to teleport myself.

The image came through perfectly, so clear I could almost touch it if I stretched out my hand. Unfortunately, when I did I felt the bars of the cage.

I would have scored low on any TP test, I could see. After the experts at Duke University had conclusively proved that telepathy existed in 1975 they'd moved on to the other wild talents, including teleportation.

They'd run tests on thousands of volunteers under a wide range of conditions and collected a great deal of data. The only hang-up was that everyone who'd ever taken the test got a zero. Meaning they didn't go anywhere.

Some experts had theorized that teleportation, if it did exist, might be closely linked to survival, might be some sort of pain reaction. In the same way that the nervous system carries a message of pain when a man sticks his finger into a flame, causing him to jerk it out, maybe a man would have to be facing extreme pain or death before the teleportation instinct would switch on.

Of course, there was no legal way they could run such a test, but I had a suspicion they nursed the secret hope that one of their volunteers would find himself in such a situation. I'd never taken the test but I was certainly in the right situation. Science flunks out again.

The easy way being eliminated, that left only the hard way out. I tested all the bars but they were solid. The only thing that would develop if I tried to pull a Tarzan would be a hernia on my part.

The stick the Cyclops had dropped caught my eye. Remembering the way he jabbed at my face brought the old story of Odysseus and his Cyclops to mind. It was a good thing that this Cyclops wasn't a classics lover or he never would have dropped the stick so close to my cage.

It was risky, I told myself. If it didn't work I'd be dead in the short run instead of the long run. But I didn't much like the idea of living through what the Cyclops would do to me anyway.

I dropped to the foot of the cage and reached out through the bars to the floor and the stick. No luck. It was about six inches farther than I could reach without dislocating my shoulder.

That stymied me for a while. But when you're that desperate, you think of things. I took the tunic off, ripped it and tied one end of the torn cloth through the trigger guard of the .38. Then I threw the pistol out past the stick.

When I pulled it back toward me it slipped over the stick. A second toss didn't do much better. The third time out I got the stick maybe an inch closer. A couple of minutes later the stick was in my hand and the .38 back in my pants.

Now all I had to do was gather the courage to throw my life away.

They say a dying man sees his past life flash before him, but what I saw were all the things I hadn't seen. All the women I hadn't had, the places I'd never been, the things I'd never done and never would unless I was very, very lucky in the next few moments.

I took off my shoes and let fly with one. It hit the Cyclops in the back of the head. He shook himself and turned toward me. He picked up the shoe and headed for me. That's when I let him have the other one right in the face.

He roared and came at the cage like an express train. I was afraid he was going to trample it and me in the rush. He stuck in one big paw, swiping at me.

I took the stick out from behind me and, dodging under his hand, snapped it in his eye. The roar deafened me. He jerked back, putting both hands over his eye. I was wondering why I hadn't put the eye out by sticking the end of the prod in deeply, as I'd planned.

The only reason I could think of was that putting out anybody's only eye was somehow much worse than murder. I couldn't explain that one even to myself.

His eye was out of commission for a while, anyway, because he kept one hand over it when he came back at the cage. He grasped the bars of the cage and tore them out with one motion.

I leapt through the opening and bounced off him, falling onto my side. He felt me hit him and wheeled around, groping for me.

I rolled away from him as he stumbled toward me, hands spread wide to each side to stop me from getting around him. I dived for one side of the cave and got past him. He heard me and followed.

I yelped as I came down in my stockinged feet on sharp bones, but somehow I hopped across them to the Sword, gripped the hilt and pulled it free of the mess hiding it.

hoped somebody wouldn't go and call the cops. It would be embarrassing explaining how I'd gotten into the shape I was in.

Finally a battered Datsun pulled over to the side. A bushy head of hair was stuck out the window and from somewhere in the middle the owner of the hair said, "Looks like you could use a ride."

"Powers of observation are tremendous. You're absolutely correct."

I got in the passenger side, propping the Sword up in the center between the driver's seat and me. My chauffeur tried not to, but his eyes kept swiveling back toward the Sword and me.

"Don't ask. You'd never believe it."

He laughed and said, "I've got a feeling it'd either be illegal, immoral or both."

"No, just impossible."

We rode along in silence for a while. I wondered what my good samaritan would make of me if I'd told him I had, within the last few days, killed a god, battled a Cyclops, made love to a witch, rescued a princess and kidnapped a king, among other things.

Putting it that way in my own mind made it seem more fantastic. I knew in a short time the memories would become dreams. It was better to think of it that way than to remember the blood and gore, the men and women who'd died, the girl who'd had her womb and head messed up, maybe for good.

We pulled up outside my motel. I got out and closed the door of the Datsun. Before I could thank him my hairy friend said, "You know, man, you're going to be a vexation to my spirit. I'm not going to be able to rest for wondering if you were real or some kind of spook."

Throwing away all my carefully made plans and vows to keep my mouth shut, I said, "Do you really want to know the story?"

He nodded.

"All right. I ran into this Cyclops first, and then I captured this princess from another world. She led me to an Evil Regent who hexed us into her world and once we got there we were captured by bandits. I managed to fight my way clear and finally get this magic sword, which brought me back to earth."

He looked at me funny for a moment, then laughed weakly.

"I really wish you hadn't answered. I get the weird feeling you really mean it."

I just grinned. He shook his head wordlessly and started the car, then drove away. I could see him staring back at me as he drove away. It was worth the risk to see the look on his face.

I knocked on the manager's door. When Mrs. Kelly opened the door and saw me I thought her lower dentures were going to drop out of her mouth. I resisted the temptation to gently close said orifice.

"Mrs. Kelly, I've lost my keys. I wonder if I could borrow the duplicates until I can have some more made up?"

She closed her mouth, went inside and came back a moment later with the duplicate keys. She never said a word. Her husband would never believe it.

I had already walked past my car before I realized it was my car. I looked inside and saw my keys were in the ignition. The doors weren't locked.

I'd left my car at Krell's place, I knew that. So who had driven it back to my apartment? The only person who came to mind was Krell, which was crazy. Or only seemed crazy for a moment. Then it began to make sense.

When Krell sent me to Ellendon he wasn't planning on my coming back, ever. He naturally assumed I'd either get myself killed or, with the Ring and Sword missing, be stuck there. He must have known enough of how the cops here operated to realize that would lead to an investigation.

There wouldn't be any body around to prove foul play if my car was found near his house, but a lot of snoopers around his home and digging into his past would be the last thing a dimensional exile would welcome.

So he'd gotten it back to my place, somehow. He'd probably driven it himself. There was little risk he'd be seen if he just casually left it in the motel parking lot and walked off. Who notices a man driving a green bug?

Thinking about Krell was unpleasant, so I stopped thinking about him. Just like that.

The first thing I did inside was go to the scotch. Then I remembered that Syana and I had finished it. The second thing was to shed the debris of the last two days, throw them in the trash and turn on the water in the bathtub.

I'm usually a shower man, but this time I wanted to luxuriate, to submerge my body in the sybaritic, sinfully sensuous pleasures of hot water and soap. It would be a novel experience not to stink any more.

I glanced at the clock on the kitchen wall. It was 8:30 A.M. I got out of the tub and slipped on some shorts and opened my front door. The Saturday paper was on my front step. Besides, as I began to readjust to the sane world I could see that it looked like an early Saturday morning, which is a different thing than, say, an early Sunday morning.

I had first seen Syana and the captain in the wee hours of Thursday morning. We'd gotten to Krell's house before daylight. I scratched my head trying to figure out what had happened to the week I'd lost in translation. At least a week. I knew all the running, sweating, killing and ulcer-making hadn't happened in just two days.

The more I thought about it, though, the more it appeared at least possible. As the details came back more clearly the incredible pace at which I'd been moving the last couple of days hit me. What had made it all seem longer was the shift from darkness here to morning there.

Even so, it didn't seem possible that it had been only two days ago that I hesitated to shoot a man because I didn't like to see living things punctured by fast-moving objects. Two days since I had stepped out of the civilized world into that of the hunter and the hunted.

That had been a different person, I knew, as I glanced at the pistol I'd laid on the dresser. I had killed two men with it, and shot up something that looked like a man but definitely wasn't. The changes didn't show in the mirror.

I lay back in the hot water, closed my eyes and started enjoying. I didn't feel like I had enough energy to scrub myself.

For no good reason I thought of Syana. I tried to put her out of my mind the way I'd handled Krell, but it didn't work. I saw her as she'd been just before she'd been zapped back to her brother's castle, a frightened girl who'd been hurt deep inside. What chance would she have of ever regaining a normal life in that feudal nightmare she called home.

What chance would she have for any kind of life at all, with the Hann swarming over Ellendon, maybe in hours, maybe right now as I sat with my fat ass in a tub of hot water.

That did it. That was the thought I'd been bending my whole

mind to stay away from, because I knew deep down what I was going to do, what I was going to have to do.

I put up a good fight against my better instincts though.

"What are you," I asked myself, "some kind of martyr, or nut, or both?"

I had gotten out of Ellendon the first time in one piece only by the skin of my teeth. I had bent all the reasonable odds for survival out of shape my last time around. That kind of luck couldn't hold out.

I'm no coward, or at least not one to the point of embarrassment, but there are risks that any sane, halfway smart guy won't take. Like stepping into an empty elevator shaft, for example, and that would be a lot safer than going back to Ellendon.

There was a good chance the Hann had already established their beachhead. It was probably too late to help the Ellendonians anyway.

I didn't owe them anything. I had stuck my neck out far enough in the first place trying to help Syana. It wasn't my fault things hadn't worked out. I'd already earned first place in the Hall of Schnooks for my hero-ing. I didn't need to set any new records.

They were only a bunch of savages anyway. Playing around with their bows and arrows. They probably blew their noses on their fingers, for God's sake. They weren't noble savages, they were primitives who went around cutting each other up for the hell of it.

Not to mention the fact that even if they were able to drive the Hann off with my help, the King would still come after me for what had happened to his sister. Besides, I didn't even know if I'd killed Iverson.

The list of reasons for staying out of it was pretty lopsided. On the other side of the argument . . . there wasn't a single reason I could find. It was an open and shut, nailed-tight, lead-pipe cinch of a one-sided argument.

When I got dry I put on some clean clothes, put six bullets in the .38, dropped another two dozen in my pocket, in view of past events, and grabbed the Sword. I gave the room a last look, probably the last one I'd ever give it.

I waited a few more seconds for the phone to ring and hear my aunt in Jacksonville tell me she'd suffered a heart attack and needed me, giving me a good excuse for chickening out, but the damned unco-operative phone just sat there in surly silence.

I remembered I was supposed to be at work that afternoon. If everything went well I'd be back before then, and if they didn't work out I wouldn't have anything at all to worry about—ever again.

On the other hand, if I went back and got delayed, my superiors were definitely going to wonder where I'd gone. Explaining might be a little difficult.

I called Dan Lee at home. Three rings and he answered.

"Dan, this is Hank. I hate to do this to you on short notice, but I'm not going to be coming in today."

"I hate to have you do it to me too. Why not?"

"Personal emergency, Dan. I'm going to have to leave town for a couple of days."

"This personal emergency couldn't be a broad in another town, could it?"

"I'm serious. Something's come up and I've got to go. I don't know how long I'll be gone, but you can send the troops out to search for me if I'm not back by Monday."

"And you still can't tell me what the deal is? Okay, you wouldn't pull a stunt like this without a reason. I'll get somebody to fill in for you, and if I don't hear from you tomorrow morning I'll do it again. But you'd better be back by Monday, or have a damn good excuse, or there'll be somebody else sitting in your chair."

"I understand. Thanks."

I put the phone down with a curious feeling of finality, as if the whole deal was already over. In a way it was. I was committed now, I couldn't turn back.

The winding two-lane road leading to Krell's place could have been a Chamber of Commerce invitation to come on down and see Florida. There was no one else on the road so I pulled off.

I was only a couple of hundred yards from the dirt road that led to Krell's home. I didn't want to drive up and warn him I was coming. More than that, I had a feeling that either Krell or I might be dead in a short time. If it was him I didn't want any of his neighbors, or any motorists passing by, to tell the cops they'd seen a green VW parked near his house a short time before he was murdered.

There were no houses and no motorists nearby so I gripped the Sword of the Gates and started thinking hard of the spot where Syana and I had come out in Ellendon. It wasn't particularly easy to think of Ellendon with any longing, but I gave it the old college try.

I was concentrating so hard on the Sword and my mental imagery that I didn't notice the transition. When I looked up the car was sitting in an open meadow that could only be the Spot.

Outside of some scratches along its side from the branches of small shrubs, the bug had taken the trip pretty well. There were too many trees around, though, for me to do any driving, so I left the car and started off on foot in the direction of Krell's house on earth.

A hundred yards later I decided I'd better pop back to earth to see where I was. I did the eye-closing and wishing bit again and when I opened them I was standing in the middle of the two-lane road.

Luckily it was still deserted. If the injuries sustained by being struck by a car hadn't done me in, the ignominy of being run down after all I'd been through would have. There are some insults to the dignity that just can't be survived.

I approached the house through the woods, making a dash through the open space to the side of the house. I couldn't hear anything from inside. I stood against the wall feeling very conspicuous while I thought about how to get in. I didn't want to smash in a window, not in broad daylight.

I knew I wasn't good enough to jimmy open a lock, and even if he was asleep the sounds I'd make forcing the door open would wake him up.

The minutes agonized by while I stood going nowhere. Now that I was actually here there wasn't any smooth plan of action in my mind. So . . .

When the solution hit me I knocked myself in the head with my palm a couple of times as I comprehended the full depth of my stupidity, then walked around to the front door.

I pulled the pistol from my pocket and, holding the Sword in my left hand, rapped on the door with my knuckles. There was no answer at first. I rapped again, wondering if this idea was just simple enough to work or if I'd been batted around one time too many in the last couple of days.

"Who's there?"

I knocked again and Krell repeated the question. When I didn't answer I heard him approach the door. He opened it slightly and looked out.

I kicked the door hard, knocking him backward. Before he could grab the door again I had the pistol aimed squarely at his chest.

"Don't even blink. This time I'll blow your head off if you even give me a little excuse."

He wasn't about to try anything, not right away. For a moment he looked at me as if I had two heads, then as if he was sure he knew me but couldn't remember where he'd seen me. Then he started to believe his eyes and his jaw dropped.

"The others—are they here?"

I opened my big mouth, as usual without thinking about what was going to come out, and said, "No, this is a solo trip, but I don't think you're going to give me any trouble. Actually, I kinda hope you try something tricky."

He raised the hand on which he wore the Ring and then saw the Sword I held in my hand. That shook him for a second, then he seemed to regain the old self-confidence. Apparently he didn't have too high an opinion of me, not that I could blame him, judging from our last encounter.

"I see I underestimated you. Not only did you survive, but you found the Sword. Where was it?"

"That's not important now."

"It's amazing. When we were attacked by bandits I lost the Sword and almost lost my head. It was all very confused."

"I didn't come to chat with you, Krell. I want the Ring."

He walked over to an easy chair and sat down. For a man with a gun pointed at his navel, he was acting very cool and calm.

"Why do you want the Ring?"

"That's not really important, either. The only thing you need to know is that I'm going to have it. You'll either give it to me or I'll take it off your body. And I think that as long as I hold the Sword you can't play the same kind of game you did the last time."

The funny thing was I didn't feel like an actor in a bad movie when I said that. It was all very matter-of-fact because I discovered I meant exactly what I said.

"I still don't understand it, though. The least you can do is tell me why you want to steal my Ring. What possible use could you have for it or the Sword?"

"I don't have the time to argue with you. It's not your Ring or Sword. They both belong to the people of Ellendon, and I intend to see that both get back to them."

"Why? Surely you must know that by this time the Hann have

taken Ellendon. You can't help anyone by going back and getting yourself killed."

When I told myself the same thing it sounded realistic, but coming from him I didn't buy it.

"Are you going to give me the Ring peacefully or not?"

"You've changed. I think you would kill me."

"Very perceptive of you, and I owe you the credit for the change." He stood up and walked toward me.

"What really hurts, Mr. Dell, is that if you'd come a few minutes later, I'd be gone and you'd never have found me. I've already secured new lodgings. I'm living there now, in fact. I came back here because I had left some money here, and that little greed is my downfall."

When he got within a half-dozen feet of me I waved the pistol at him and said, "No closer. You can toss the Ring to me."

He shook his head and said, "No. So close to the Sword there's no telling what might happen if there were no human contact, even for an instant. It might hurl itself into another world."

It sounded like an excuse for him to get within swinging range, but I had no way of telling that it might not be true, and I didn't want to lose the Ring now.

I propped my right hand on the hilt of the upright Sword and held my left hand out for the Ring. He moved slowly and carefully, his eyes glued to the gun. I had the hammer pulled back to the point that if he blinked it would go off.

He put his right hand out and slowly twisted the Ring off his finger. He held it between his thumb and index finger over my hand.

"Gently. You'll never come closer to dying than right this second."

He let go of the Ring. Instead of dropping it in my hand, he let it fall a half foot away. I instinctively reach out to catch it. As I did he put his right shoulder into me.

I hit on my shoulder and rolled to my feet. I'd relaxed the finger on the trigger of the .38 and it hadn't gone off. I'd been bluffing there. I didn't want to fire a gun in this house. If anyone heard it the cops might be called. The sooner his disappearance was discovered, the more chance I might be tied to it.

I swung to cover him with the gun, but he kicked it out of my hand. It went spinning across the room. I thought I knew what he had in mind when he grinned at a private joke. I leapt in front of him and grabbed the Sword, which had fallen to the floor.

The grin faded and he came at me again. I managed to move far enough so his next kick didn't catch me in the face. It only caught me in the chest, knocking me onto my back. He came down hard with his heel on what would have been my chest if I hadn't rolled out from under.

I caught and blocked the next kick by folding my arms across my chest. He swung at me, the Ring on his hand again, but this one I managed to avoid altogether. As tall as he was, and with me on my knees, he couldn't aim accurately.

Before he could draw back his foot to kick again, I grasped the hilt of the Sword with both hands and brought it back. Then I lashed out, bringing it down in an arc at his chest. If it had connected he would have been split down the middle, but he scrambled backward, tripping over his own feet.

The Sword clattered off the floor as he fell and almost instantly was on his feet again. There was nothing wrong with the man's reflexes. I couldn't believe how fast he was moving.

Only about this time I was no slouch either. I was on my feet and swinging the Sword at him on the dead run. He side-stepped it and caught me good in the pit of the stomach, doubling me over. While I was bent over he hit me in the back of the neck and I went down to one knee.

Before he could hit me again I swung my whole body from the waist, whipping the Sword around as I did. This time he saved himself only by literally throwing himself backward. He landed hard, and not on his feet either.

Before I could raise the Sword to go after him again, the old colored flames blinded me and before I could move to get through them he'd vanished. I just stared at the space he'd occupied a second before. This I hadn't been ready for, though I should have been. Now what?

I could go back to Ellendon with the Sword alone, I thought as I retrieved the gun. It would be some help, but from what Syana had said the only way to be sure of winning was to have both the Ring and the Sword.

I couldn't let him just skip out like that. And yet I couldn't follow him. He might have gone to Ellendon, but on the other hand, there were plenty of other worlds he might have run to. And there was no way to track him across the dimensions.

Or was there? If the Ring and Sword were that closely associated, there might be some sort of link. It couldn't hurt to try and find out.

When I opened my eyes I was back on Ellendon again. The open area where I'd left the car was some ways off. Here the trees grew more thickly together. I tried to grow eyes in the back of my head as I walked into the dappled morning world. I stopped, thinking I'd heard something.

The world exploded as I cartwheeled through space. The curtain of skyrockets and flares lifted for a few seconds and I saw a giant swimming through space toward me. I couldn't seem to move my hands very well, but I pulled the pistol up and fired.

It sounded like a cannon going off next to my ear and it must have taken ten seconds for the vibrations to die away. The giant came on as though nothing had happened. Maybe bullets didn't bother him. Just to find out I worked on the trigger of the gun again for a few hours until I managed to get the hammer pulled back.

The gun jerked and the cannon boomed. The giant kept coming, charging like a wounded elephant. Dimly, from far away, I heard the roaring of some angry beast. Then the giant blotted out the sky as he fell on me.

I couldn't breathe. That's what woke me up. I gasped and fought my way up through the darkness toward light and air. No matter how hard I inhaled there was no air. There was a ringing in my ears and a funny hollowness in my chest.

Something pinned me to the ground. Panic gave me the strength to get my hands, my right hand actually, under me and shove upward. The weight rolled off me and I could breathe again.

For minutes I did just that until the unreasoning fear ebbed away. Then I tried to remember what had happened. Even on my back the world seemed to be spinning slowly around. My left shoulder began to hurt. Actually, that's like saying Vesuvius was one of Pompeii's minor problems. If I'd had the strength I would have screamed. As it was I lay back and moaned a lot.

I opened my eyes after a while and propped myself up on my right elbow. Krell lay face down near me. I inched my way to him and managed to tilt him a little toward me.

Both bullets had hit. One in the lower stomach, the other smashing through the underside of his chin and out through the top rear of his skull.

I should have been used to it, but I turned away and wanted to be sick. A little later I looked back and found the club. It was only a rotten branch but Krell had nearly killed me with it.

I felt the back of my head and my fingers came away sticky with blood. I carefully touched my left shoulder and at that point performed one of the greatest feats of my life. I managed not to lose consciousness again.

It felt as if the blow had broken something, or somethings. I must have been turning and throwing my arm up when he brought the club down. My shoulder had taken the main brunt of the blow. If he had connected I'm pretty sure I would never have awakened.

A real stroke of luck. Here I was getting ready to save a world with a broken shoulder and what felt like a concussion. The paraplegic brigade to the rescue.

But when there's no one else around, even a cripple has to do something. The first step was to make it up to one elbow again. I felt as if I'd climbed a ten-story flight of stairs by the time I got up on my right elbow. Inching along, I crawled over Krell's body.

I tried to move my left hand to take the Ring off him, but I couldn't twitch a finger without the pain hitting me. It felt as if somebody was jabbing a long needle into the muscles of my upper arm and twisting it.

I finally had to lie on my back, freeing my right hand. I groped blindly until I found Krell's hand and pulled the Ring from his finger. I slipped it on my own for safekeeping.

I groped my way to the Sword, lying a half-dozen feet away. I propped myself up on it, having a hard time getting my balance, but finally making it to my knees.

Using the Sword for support again, I got to my feet. I felt about a thousand feet tall, with my head sticking up through the clouds. Now all I had to do was start crossing the land in seven-league strides. I nearly fell over when I took my first step. I saved myself only by using the Sword for a crutch.

Through the trees I saw a squat shape that could only be my bug. I hobbled toward it as fast as I could, feeling stronger the longer I stayed on my feet. Now there was only a persistent ache in my shoulder and a light-headed feeling as if I was half stoned.

Moving very carefully, I made it to the car without aggravating either my concussion or my shoulder. I did some quick wishful thinking and when I opened my eyes the car and I were sitting near the edge of the road.

While the motor idled I tried to decide what to do next. I'd never get to Dalien's court on foot, not now. I had no assurance I'd run into any of the King's soldiers, either. And, come to think of it, if I did I couldn't be sure they hadn't been given orders to kill me on sight.

So, what could I do? It would be nice if I could just drive to the rescue, but the Hero's Code of Ethics prohibited any shoddy tricks like that.

Or did it? It was a weird idea, but why not drive to the King's castle? Once out of the mountains the land would be flat enough for the VW to make it, and even a VW bug could outrun any horse ever born of mare.

We had headed east the entire time traveling to the castle. So if I headed east I'd be almost certain to run over it.

The big question was how to get out of the mountains. If I were on Ellendon I'd just head east, but I couldn't cross the mountains in my bug. On the other hand, why couldn't I drive to a point on earth that would be parallel to the flat country of Ellendon.

That seemed like a good idea, but troublesome questions kept popping up. For example, how could I be sure that Ellendon was oriented in the same way as earth? Maybe going east here would take me west, and farther into the mountains, on Ellendon.

If I didn't hit it right the first time I wouldn't get a second chance. I doubted if I'd be able to make more than one trip, if that.

The more I thought about it, the more confused I got. Even if I hadn't just been hit on the head it would have given me a headache, but as it was, I couldn't concentrate. Ideas seemed to keep slipping away from me. Maybe there was some logical way of telling which direction to go, but I couldn't do it now.

Ellendon's future was going to depend on dumb luck. I decided to head east, toward Arcadia, and hope for the best.

I turned the car around in the road, a tricky maneuver when you can use only one arm effectively and the road is rippling gently up and down, and headed back for Sarasota.

Somewhere, sometime there may have been a more unlikely rescuing hero than a spaced-out, crippled Hank Dell, but I doubt it.

As I was driving out of Sarasota on State Road 70 I thought of Krell for the first time since I'd killed him. I wondered what his neighbors and the cops would think when they discovered he was missing.

I had committed the perfect murder. Krell's body was lying so close to his own living room, and yet so very far away. No one would ever know what his fate was. As no one would ever know mine if I ran out of luck this time.

CHAPTER FOURTEEN

I remember little of what happened on State Road 70. There are vague, jumbled images of a light that seemed to stay red for five minutes, of cars honking behind me when I slumped over the wheel and fell asleep despite my best intentions.

But they're only picture postcard scenes out of a blur, caught when I came out of the warm, comforting fog that cradled me. I almost rammed into the rear of a car twice. One time a guy got out of his car, mouthing something back at me. When it looked like he was coming back at me I almost took aim on him through the window. I caught myself and was frightened for a moment at what I might have done.

But I had to keep going. I'd lost all my hesitation back there somewhere. Nothing mattered now, nothing at all, except where I was going, and it wasn't particularly to aid the Ellendonians.

It wasn't clear, nothing was, but I knew I was trying to reach a place I'd never been before, a place that wasn't on earth or Ellendon or anyplace else. A place where life was real, where I counted.

Nothing I'd ever done before, or probably ever would do, had meant anything. I felt as thin, as immaterial, as any ghost and I had the funny feeling that nobody could see me, that nobody could stop me because nobody even knew I was there.

If I hadn't been born, if I'd never lived, what would it matter? No difference, except that now I was carrying a Ring and a Sword. It wasn't so much that it would save the lives of innocent men and women on Ellendon, although that was part of it.

What I really wanted, more than even going on living, was to know for just a second that I counted for something. That I had for once done something that had made a mark on the world, that no one could erase, that no one could ignore.

It was as if I had been starving for something without knowing it all my life, and now that I knew I couldn't stop until that ravenous hunger was satisfied.

"Try and stop me, you bastards," I muttered, not knowing who I was challenging.

During one of my lucid spells I had crossed the Myakka River about fifteen miles east of Sarasota. That should be far enough. I pulled off the road and lay my head against the wheel to stop the throbbing that was going to tear the top of my head off and jerked awake some time later. I couldn't afford to be stopped by any cops that might notice me slumped over in the car. Without checking to see if anyone was around, I jumped to Ellendon.

The car shuddered and started moving forward. I clutched the emergency brake and the car stopped, throwing me into the windshield. Not hard enough to break anything, but it didn't do my head any good. When it shrank back to about the size of an overripe watermelon I managed to pry open my eyelids and take a look at the outside.

I'd landed in the front yard of some peasant. A head timidly peeked out of the open door of a hut and when it saw me looking quickly popped back inside.

I'd come out onto a slight incline, rolling down to a point just in front of the hut. It was early afternoon I could see. It would be easy to find my way to the east now. I switched on the ignition, tried to shake the cobwebs out of my head and went east.

There were a lot of bumps and gulleys I didn't remember from the horseback trip, but the VW took them faithfully. Of course, the constant bouncing left me a solid mass of pain, but after a while that didn't matter either.

All that was left were eyes looking out the windshield and one hand glued to the wheel.

The gulley opened itself out in front of me so quickly I couldn't even put my foot down on the brake. The front wheels shot over the top and the front nosed down. The front of the bug hit the other side and the car bounced backward. I blacked out and the next thing I knew I was lying across the seat with the motor racing, but I didn't seem to be going anywhere.

The car was tilted toward the sky. I jerked the door open and half slid, half fell to the ground. I had shut the ignition off. I could see where the rear wheels had bogged down in soft sand. While I was out the car must have just dug itself in deeper; it would take a tow truck to free it.

At the same time I saw what had happened, the aftereffects hit me. I lay down against the car to clear my head for a minute.

When I opened my eyes again the sky was dark and stars were out. There was no way of telling how much time had passed. All I could do was count the throbbings in my shoulder and wonder why things always turned out this way. I'd come so close and now a patch of soft sand would make it all meaningless.

No. Not after what I'd gone through. I wasn't going to stop now, even if I had to walk through an army of the Hann. If I had to crawl through an army of the Hann.

I retrieved the Sword and gun from the car and crawled to the top of the gulley. Somehow I got to my feet. I felt like a man trying to walk up the down escalator, because the ground was flowing swiftly past me.

Wrapped in my own fog, I didn't hear anything until I stumbled into the middle of it. I heard a shout, so close I should have been able to see who made it. I jabbed the Sword into the ground to free my right hand and took the .38 out of my belt. I had wandered into one of the light clumps of tree and brush that dotted the open countryside near the castle. All I could see were dark shapes that could have been trees or men or monsters or just about anything.

I heard metal hitting metal and knew I'd found the action. I wanted to move forward to find out what was happening. If the government soldiers won I'd make it. But I couldn't hold the Sword and gun at the same time. I couldn't leave the Sword behind, but I had to have the gun in my hand.

Finally I tucked the Sword under my right arm awkwardly and walked toward the sounds of combat.

I tripped over something and fell onto my left shoulder, the pain of some giant hitting me with his fist blotting out the sound of the scream I must have made. My eyes were wet with tears when I rolled onto my side.

I'd fallen over a body. I turned the man over and found an archer who'd had his throat cut. The blood was still running freely.

I turned and fired at the sound of steps behind me. Before the echo of the shots died away somebody fell into the grass a dozen feet away.

It was another man dressed like the first, except that he carried a sword. I hoped he was a bandit.

I knew the sound of shots would bring men to me so I made tracks for someplace else. I squatted down beside a tree to assess the situation, and stop the whirling in my brain.

A dark shape loomed up out of the trees and then another. They moved silently, the moonlight gleaming off their swords.

"Dalien," I said softly. It was the only word I thought I could use that might tip the government soldiers to the fact I was on their side.

When I spoke the shapes stiffened, then separated, one lunging to the left and the other to the right. I could have fired then and possibly gotten one of them, but I still couldn't be sure they weren't the King's men.

I waddled away from the tree, Sword tucked awkwardly under my arm, afraid to stand because of the target I'd present. I settled down beside another tree a dozen feet away and waited.

I held my breath and strained to hear grass being crushed underfoot or another heart beating and suddenly thought of the old line about ignorant armies clashing by night. If there was ever a situation it applied to, this was it.

There was only the feeling you get a split second before you see a car coming head-on at you. I didn't really see it coming but I fell over onto my right side. Even so, the sword caught my arm.

Lightning lit up the inside of my head as I found the Sword of the Gates in my right hand, all five feet and fifty pounds, and drove it straight up at the night-black shape that blotted out the world in front of me.

It was like punching a door with my fist, but something gave and I drove the Sword deeper into the darkness. Someone was moaning and my right hand was covered with something hot and wet. I pushed at the shape now leaning against me.

As he fell away the sword thrust into my arm drooped. I grabbed and jerked it out and there was no pain, only a tremendous thundering that I realized was my breathing.

I pulled the Sword of the Gates out of his body. Then I tried to hold back the blood that was oozing out of the gash in my left arm by clamping my right hand around it. It didn't work. The damned stuff kept leaking out around my fingers.

I heard another sound and put three bullets, all that remained in the .38, into the night where it came from. He staggered into my sight, sword held high, and I almost thought he'd make it. But his knees gave way before he reached me.

There would be more and more and more. They were as numberless as the grains of sand, as unstoppable as ants or locusts or the wind. I couldn't stop them. I had a magic ring and a magic sword and a gun, but they would keep coming until they pulled me down.

I got to my feet. I couldn't feel myself doing it, but I know I got there because when I looked down I could see my feet against the ground.

Funny. I'd always been afraid of the dark, and now I walked through it without fear. There wasn't anything left to fear. What could they do to me that they hadn't done?

I was a little boy again, looking up and up at a huge shape that was human only in outline. There was no sound in the night now and I knew we—my nightmare and I—weren't on Ellendon any more. We were in that shadow land where steps are taken through molasses and faces are masks and something unspeakable lurks behind closed doors and pushes at shuttered windows.

The eyes were torches beneath horned brows and light shimmered on porcelain fangs. As I raised the Sword of the Gates it brought its own sword smashing down, knocking mine out of my hand. As I fell back and reached for the gun in my belt, a massive fist sent me flying.

The taste of dirt in my mouth was no less bitter than the knowledge that this was how it would all end. The King and Iverson and Syana were done for. Because I'd failed. I had thought I could be a hero, but I couldn't fool reality. Dreams are only dreams.

I was grabbed by the shoulder and jerked to my feet. The fingers of that huge hand clamped into my shoulder like metal prongs. I saw the sword it held poised above its head. That was its way. It could have finished me off as I lay face down, but I would never have known I was dying. It had to make me face the image of that sword slicing down.

I closed my eyes and wanted to be somewhere else, anywhere else. The honking of the horn snapped my eyes open to be blinded by two brilliant flares. In the instant I'd had them open I saw Suldurus twisting to stare into the lights. His hold on my shoulder loosened and I broke free.

When I could see again I was back in darkness, the Sword of the Gates lying near me. Suldurus was nowhere around.

After the world stopped revolving around my head I figured out what had happened. I moved a dozen yards away and went back to earth. It was a deep twilight, almost dark now.

A big trucking rig had pulled off the road a hundred yards away. The driver was getting out of his cab. I found what I was searching for before he reached us.

The force of the truck's impact had hurled Suldurus off the road into a tree. It was a big tree, maybe a foot in diameter. The Hann had snapped it cleanly in his passage.

He was too heavy to turn over, but one arm lay twisted unnaturally far behind his back and one leg was broken, the bone showing where the leg had almost snapped off. When I saw the blood seeping into the grass I didn't really want to turn him over.

"Hey, buddy," I heard behind me, "is he dead? I honked, but it was too late. He came out of nowhere."

I grabbed Suldurus' shoulder and closed my eyes. When I opened them I was in night again. That poor truck driver was going to have a hell of a time explaining the blood on the front of his truck and on the grass, but I couldn't stick around to explain.

I left Suldurus to the darkness behind me because I couldn't stop. I'd lost my gun somewhere along the way but that didn't matter either. It was nearly the end and time was running out. Things had come full circle. Suldurus was dead and I'd evened all the old scores. Now if I could just deliver the Ring and the Sword I could go to sleep. I was very tired.

I missed a step and the next thing I knew I was sprawled on my side. It was like stepping into an elevator shaft—very final. I knew I wasn't going to be getting up again so I relaxed and lay back against the soft ground and shut my eyes. That was very easy.

I was wondering whether they build statues to heroes who almost make it when I fell asleep.

In the middle of a very confusing dream about editors with glowing swords who were chasing me around the newsroom while a big, gray-skinned monster sat behind a typewriter yelling for us to be more quiet, I woke up.

That surprised me. I realized the reason why I was surprised— I expected to be dead. I still couldn't believe it, so I heard myself asking anyone in my vicinity, "Am I dead?"

"If so, you're the loudest corpse I ever saw," a rough voice said. With great effort I peeled my eyelids back and stared at a redhead sitting near my bed.

"I hope you're not a sample of the angels around here," I heard a stranger say with my vocal cords.

"That's a sure sign you're alive. Your surliness is back, although whether that's an improvement I don't know."

Things came back to me pretty quickly.

"So I made it back before the big rumble?"

"Right."

"How long?"

"Things broke wide open three hours after our men found you, and you've been out for three days since then."

"Three days . . ."

"That was an ugly blow on the head Krell gave you. If you were still back on earth I think they would have had to open you up and do a little excavating inside your skull. Here we had some witch women cure your ills."

I suddenly remembered Iverson should be dead.

"I thought I killed you."

He rubbed the back of his head and grinned.

"Don't remind me. I still have a splitting headache. If you'd hit just a little harder you would have killed me. I felt like taking you apart with a dull scalpel when I woke up, but when we learned the truth . . . well, a headache was worth it."

I was slipping back into the grayness, but I asked, "What truth?"

"You've been talking off and on for three days. Some of it the witch women pulled out of you and some you babbled. We know why you did what you did, but I'll tell you about it later. You're still in pretty bad shape. Go back to sleep."

He was a forceful man. I did.

The next time I woke up, Syana, Dalien and Iverson were in the room. There was an open window across the way and I could see blue sky beyond. One of Dalien's arms was in a sling and there was a bandage around his head.

"Looks like you forgot to duck."

He smiled at that and for the first time since I'd met him looked like the young man he was, younger than I. Then he glanced at Syana and the smile faded. I knew he'd never forget what had happened to her and we would never be friends.

"Just some wounds acquired in the battle. I was lucky."

"It was bad," Iverson said. "Be glad you missed it. Even with the

Ring and the Sword enough of them got through to kill a lot of our men. They're bastards, but they're terrible fighters."

"How did you find me?"

"Suldurus and his band were making hit-and-run attacks closer to the castle the last day or so before the battle. That night our men were waiting for them. When you started firing away with that pop gun of yours they came looking to find out what had happened.

"By the way, what did you do to Suldurus? Our men found what was left of him."

"He ran into something bigger than he was," was all I said.

Syana was dressed in a long white gown and bore little resemblance to the girl in green I'd first met. And her eyes weren't the same. She'd been fearless and arrogant and confident. Now there was fear.

"So everyone lives happily ever after, huh?"

"For five hundred years, anyway," Iverson said.

"We owe you a great debt," Dalien said formally. "We know how much you did to aid people you had no reason to want to help. Were I in your place, I might not have dared death for people who imprisoned and threatened me with death."

There was nothing I could say to that, so I didn't even try.

"How can we repay you?"

The $64,000 question. The bed was like silk under me. It was a good ending to the story. They had bound my arm up, but it didn't hurt much and I couldn't even tell I'd been hit on the head.

I had challenged monsters and bandits and traitors and gotten beaten up in the process, but I'd won. Maybe dumb luck had been on my side, but I'd still won. In the fairy tales I'd get the hand of the Princess and half the kingdom, but I didn't really want the Princess and I knew damn well I didn't want even a little bit of the kingdom.

"Build me a statue."

"A statue? Of course, but we would like to repay you, and a statue is too cheap a reward. If you wish to stay here you will be granted the lands and powers of a noble of the court. If you wish to return to earth, we will furnish you with gold and silver or any other treasure you desire."

I almost laughed, but he was sincere and I knew it must have taken an effort for him to make the offer. He would never like me but he was overcoming his personal feelings enough to be fair.

Still, I couldn't take gold or silver back with me. I'd already gone over that route. And to stay here?

"I'm sorry. I can't stay on Ellendon. If you want to reward me, just build me a statue. I'd like to be able to think of that when I get back to earth."

"Why can't you stay, Dell?" Iverson asked. "We know enough about you now to see that you aren't happy on earth. Be honest and admit that. What will you have if you go back? A job as a reporter, living in a small apartment and getting drunk on Friday night. Is that a life?

"Here you'll have a chance to live. You've seen only the bad in Ellendon, the scum and the death. But there are thousands of miles of forest and mountains and good people you haven't seen. A lot of this land is still untouched. You won't find anything like it on earth.

"There are other continents, lands beyond Ellendon. Someday someone will go over the mountains or through the volcano belt to explore them. God only knows what might be out there. You're young and you'd have the chance to see a good bit of this world. Be smart, stay here."

What he'd said was correct. What would I have if I went back? Probably no job and a lot of questions to answer if I wanted it back. And even if I kept the job, so what?

Ellendon was probably the kind of place he'd said it was. I'd seen only one tiny part. I'd probably fall in love with it if I gave myself a chance, but I wasn't going to give myself that chance.

"I'm sorry again, but I can't stay. It's hard to put into words, but I've seen too much killing here. Maybe someday I might want to come back, but not right now. I want to wash the blood off my hands, first. And for some funny reason, I'm kind of homesick for earth."

Syana stepped to the foot of the bed and looked me in the eye for the first time.

"If I'm part of the reason you're going, don't let me drive you away, Hank. I . . . don't blame you."

"I appreciate that, but as long as I'm around you'll always be reminded of what happened. You deserve better than that. If I could, I'd make what happened un-happen, but I can't."

"I wish you'd stay," was all she said in words, but she said a lot more with her eyes.

"I can't, but you'll be all right. Nothing can keep you down for long, Syana, you're not that kind of person."

That'a boy, Dell, I told myself, dish out the pablum. You know that's a lie and she knows it too, but she's got too much pride to beg.

It was another one of those doors that close behind you and you can never reopen them again when she walked out of the room without looking back.

I didn't particularly want to face Iverson and the King any more, so I closed my eyes and said, "I'm tired now. How about giving me a chance to get some sleep?"

There was silence but I knew they were still standing there. Finally, Iverson said, "It looks like there's only one kind of payment you'll accept."

"That's right. The statue . . ."

He was holding the Wanderer's Ring out to me and if there had been anyone around to test me for telepathy, I would have passed. I knew his devious, underhanded plan right down to its cutest wrinkle, and the terrible part was, I knew it was going to work.

"You may change your mind after you've gone back to earth and then it'll be too late, so take the Ring with you."

"You're crazy. That's one of the symbols of your King. I couldn't take it. Besides, what if I lost it, or if someone took it away from me?"

"We would not have it at all were it not for you," Dalien said. "Ellendon itself might not be free were it not for you. You are worthy to hold the Ring. If we need it, the Sword will bring us to you."

"I couldn't—"

"Take it," Iverson said, and he was a forceful man.

It was cool to the touch and I could barely feel the pulsing of the strange energy that powered it. I slipped it on my finger knowing that, as surely as I was lying in bed, the day would come when I was bored on earth. I would remember Ellendon and the mysteries I'd not even scratched.

What kind of magic really works? What lay beyond the mountains and fields of Ellendon I'd already seen? What lay beyond the volcano belt? Who were the Lords of Ellendon? Would the nameless double-crosser I'd run into ever come back? And what about the other worlds? Aeia was only one.

Then there was Syana. I'd always run from the real thing where